KATHA PRIZE STORIES

The best fiction published during 2001-2003 in ten Indian languages, selected by a panel of distinguished writers and scholars.

13

edited by
Geeta Dharmarajan

KATHA

KATHA
A-3 Sarvodaya Enclave
Sri Aurobindo Marg
New Delhi 110 017
Phone: 2652 4350, 2652 4511
Fax: 2651 4373

E-mail: kathavilasam@katha.org
Internet address: www.katha.org

KATHA is a registered nonprofit society
devoted to enhancing the pleasures of reading.
KATHA VILASAM is its story research and resource centre.

Cover design: Geeta Dharmarajan
Logo design: Crowquill

Typeset in 9 on 13pt Bookman by Prakash Acharya at Katha
Printed at Nutech Photolithographer, New Delhi

Distributed by KathaMela, a distributor of quality books.
A-3 Sarvodaya Enclave, Sri Aurobindo Marg, New Delhi 110 017

Katha regularly plants trees to replace the wood used in the making of its books.

ISBN 8187649-81-X (paperback)   ISBN 81-87649-82-8 (hardback)

CONTENTS

KATHA AWARD WINNERS FOR 2003-2004

THE WRITERS

Ashita	Madhuri Mohan Shanbhag
Chezhian	Meena Kakodkar
Jhareswar Chattopadhyay	Neelakshi Singh
Kashi Nath Singh	Santanu Kumar Acharya
Kengba Yengkhom	Sibananda Kakoti
Khoiren Meetei	K Srikanth Reddy

THE TRANSLATORS

Bibhas C Mohanty	Pravabati Chingangbam
J Bhagyalakshmi	Rachna Sethi
Indira Menon	Ramiah Kumar
Pamposh Kumar	Tirna Ray
Parismita Singh	Thingnam Anjulika
Parnal Chirmuley	Vidya Pai

THE JOURNALS

Ajir Asom	Kanaiazhi
Andhra Jyothi	Sambad Pratidin
Bhashaposhini	Kadambini
Chumthang	Tadbhav
Jaag	Naharolgi Thoudang
Vipulshree	

THE KATHA AWARDS

The KATHA AWARDS were instituted in 1990.

Katha requests an eminent writer, scholar or critic in each of the regional languages to choose what she/he feels are the three best stories published in that language, in the previous two years.

Our Nominating Editors sift through numerous journals and magazines that promote short fiction. Many of them consult their friends or other Friends of Katha in the literary world to help them make their nominations. The nominated stories are translated and from these are chosen the Prize Stories.

Each author receives the KATHA AWARD FOR CREATIVE FICTION which includes a citation, Rs 2000, and publication (in translation) in that year's *Katha Prize Stories* volume.

The editor of the regional language journal that first published the award winning story receives the KATHA JOURNAL AWARD.

The translators are handpicked from the list of nearly 5000 names we have at Katha. Each of them gets the KATHA AWARD FOR TRANSLATION which includes a citation, Rs 2000, and the opportunity to translate a prize story.

The A K RAMANUJAN AWARD goes to a translator who can, with felicity, translate between two or more Indian languages, as Ramanujan himself was able to. A K Ramanujan was a Friend of Katha and this award was instituted in 1993.

The KATHAKAARI AWARD goes to a writer who renders the stories from our folklore and oral traditions into the written form, thereby making the stories available to future generations.

The KATHAVACHAK AWARD goes to a storyteller who with creativity and elan recreates folk tales from the oral tradition as stories to live our lives by.

Every year or so, Katha holds a literary festival. The award winning writers, translators and editors are invited to it.

The Undiscovered Country

And once again Katha comes to you with stories from the land of many possibilities and countless surprises, showcasing the many ways writers from across the country read the diversities and identities that is India. *Katha Prize Stories 13* talks of things that are touched by the everydayness of our diurnal lives, of human predicaments that lift us above the mundane, and of questions that come naturally to most of us, the larger quests of life and living, the whys, wheres and the what ifs.

"A love of storytelling is as universal as governance, marriage, religion, jokes, and the incest taboo." Says Denis Dutton stoutly in his "The Pleasures of Fiction," echoing what many others have said: "Why are humans so obsessed with fiction? ... [We] expend staggering amounts of time and resources on creating and experiencing art and entertainment – music, dancing, and static visual arts. Of all the arts, however, it is the category of fictional storytelling that across the globe today is the most intense focus of what amounts to a virtual human addiction ... The origins of this obsession with comic and dramatic fictions, are lost in remote prehistory, as lost as the origins of language itself ..."

In the volume you hold in your hands, are twelve stories that reiterate the story's joy and purpose. Handpicked through a rigorous and eclectic process, as usual for the Katha Awards, this winning collection by emerging and established writers spans the human experience from Buddha's times to the present globalized times we live in. Some of them, their writers and translators would say are untranslatable – and having edited them, I have to but smile wryly. Hopefully, the rhythm and cadences and the power of the original comes through. As also the larger ideas the authors are daring to put down on paper.

We have two Manipuri stories in this volume, each different from the other, each standing witness to the thriving storytelling technique which is singularly theirs. I would like to draw your attention to one of them especially, if only because it is an allegory, steeped in its own metaphor: "A Dream Tale" by Kengba Yengkhom. The writer says his story talks of the clash of the old and the new, nature and nurture; the Nominating Editor told us it was all about India and Manipur and Myanmar. "See?" he asks excitedly over the crackling line from there to here (or our there to their there, what does it matter?) And he tells me about the unique culture that is Manipur and how, with national roads leading directly to the Golden Triangle of Southeast Asia, and Burma producing nearly 84 percent of the opium in the world, drug trade and abuse has become widespread, especially in Manipur. He talks about heroin, locally known as Number 4, and how young people are turning away from India to Myanmar. "Do you not see these in the news?" he asks. "This story talks of just that! Remember the writer says –

And then I heard it. The sweet strains of a woman singing ... Accompanying it was a musical instrument. Then slowly the singing faded ... I got up hastily and walked towards the southern veranda of the music hall ... But there was just a path moving west. At the back, it branched. One went down the hill slope. It was well trodden, lots of footprints. The other climbed up the middle of the hill. Untrammelled. But there was a light far away in that direction. For a moment I paused. Which way should I go? That very instant the terrifying sound of a powerful beast preying upon a lesser beast came from the direction of the path that headed up the hill."

As I understood it, the sweet music was India; this is increasingly turning to be Myanmar. The powerful beast is India, preying on Manipur, the lesser beast, at least that is the way the youth seem to perceive it as ... 4.5 lakh educated youth, increasing unemployment, social tension, what more is needed to fuel insurgency and alienation? Do we see it like this when we read the newspapers, see the news on TV?

Nor do we really know what moves and impels Assam. What the media gives us in India is no more or less than what the international press gives. In "The Last Meal on the Water Fresco," by Sibananda Kakoti, we have the story about Sankardeva, one of the greatest proponents of the Bhakti cult, a living presence in

Assam even today. The most glorious period of Assamese literature was the 15th and 16th centuries, when Sankardeva and Madhava Deva took Asomiya language and literature to unprecedented heights. Without once naming him, Kakoti tells us a story set in 15th century Assam. In 1489, Sankardeva was forced to leave the Ahom country and take refuge in Cooch Behar where Naranarayana held court. This story talks of the troubled last days of Sankardeva. We, as editors, mulled long and deep over the story, asked many a question, before we realized that here was a story that provided a key to an India we didn't know at all. It is a wonderfully imaginative story. We recommend it to you, discerning reader.

As we do the Oriya novella: "Anoma's Daughter," by the veteran writer, Santanu Kumar Acharya. History would have us believe that Siddhartha, who later became Gautama Buddha, was born in Lumbini village, in what is now southern Nepal. But this story questions this premise on the basis of certain archaeological findings, and research tracing back to 1928, from rocks and inscriptions and old sculptures of Asoka in the Kapileswar temple grounds, in Orissa. It is painstaking research that is garbed in a story format. Racy in style, not unlike a mystery well told.

What attracted us to the Tamil story, "The Harmonium," was entirely different. Unlike the piano, tuning a harmonium can be destructive. You need to be absolutely delicate, to say, move the pitch up, or down to flat. As some who know say, the margin for error is small indeed. We thought the story seemed to carry the argument of identity and culture on to yet another interesting path. As did the Malayalam story, gentle and touching and so amazingly short with its aphorisms and pithy phrases. The Marathi story brings up questions of gender and culture, habit, tradition and freedom, the Bangla, the perspective of women as mothers, men as fathers. Each in its own way creates an imagined India, each captures a piece of today's India in ways that individuals can never, without the gift of storytelling. Stories and myths, as has been said, are the building blocks of imagination in the world today – not grammar as Chomsky would have us believe.

The role of myths in our lives has come in for major question in India, and we who live in the metros oftentimes seem to believe that stories created for television – whether it be by the news channels or those that spin the soaps – are enough, that mythmaking should be left to the people who have the voice and the power. So the story has been robbed from the makers of it – the ordinary people, and the folk tales in the making, the epics too, lapse into a culture of silence. We have invested all the power in those who have a voice, voice to those who have power. This leaves the rest of the masses – us – without much of a say in any matter. So the question: Can we give ourselves a counter culture that will bring us another freedom that we need so badly – the freedom to choose the culture we want, not choose a mass culture that is so dictatorial? The Bhakti poets showed us the way many centuries ago.

I think of Kabir and Bhakti if only because I have been working these last few weeks on a story by Kashi Nath Singh. Biting satire, the twists and turns of folk singers out to please a crowd, the native wit that startles and stumps the reader in turn. And then I stumble on something that makes this Katha search for literary excellence a suddenly more meaningful one. "Kaun Thagwa Nagariya Lootal Ho," the title of Kashi Nath Singh's story, is the first line of a Kabir mystical poem which talks of death and dying and that which robs the body of its soul.

Each of the ten languages represented here, proud winners of the Katha Awards for creative fiction, carry a lingering taste of the fantastic. They come in excellent translations by people who are by and large newcomers to the field of translation – for the one rule that we have held on to assiduously in Katha is that each year the people who are awarded for translation will be new to Katha. They bring to us the magical realism of the Hindi and the Telugu stories, the deep questions of the Malayalam story, the troubled spaces of the Tamil and the Manipuri, the reflective nature of the Asomiya and the Oriya, the Bangla and the Marathi, reminding me of the translators whom Andhra and Tamilnadu and Kerala were reading in the 60s. They brought the fictions of Bengal to life in South India. It was a time for diversity, and the celebration quiet and purposeful. But then, times changed and we did too, and translations went out of fashion. What we discover each time we come to *Katha Prize Stories* time is that things do change, except for the passion for language and mother tongue ... *The guru will go according to his will, The disciple according to his.* But each of us perseveres for, as Ashita says, "Life is faith strung together with small beliefs. What purpose does mere commitment serve if it doesn't lead to knowledge?"

Stories as storehouses of knowledge. Leisure time friends, they are also carriers of information about who we were, who we could be. This is true of stories in all and any language. Yet even excellent stories written in the various languages of India could fade within the narrowing walls of regionalism, could well be flowers that bloom to die by the wayside. So the question:

Why do we in our country so love stories which are the other's, what fascination does lands unknown and cultures strange hold for us? A student in Tamilnadu once told me, "Thaghazhi is difficult – we cannot even pronounce his name, how can we understand his stories?" And we had come to Thaghazhi from a vibrant and knowledgeable discussion of Marquez and magic realism. (There was even a journal called *Marquez* in Tamil; probably still is.) Latin America is closer to many of us than the boondocks that is India, the by lanes of Dickens's world still hold familiarity, and the US is maybe as close as our television screen. Our bookshops must be unique in the world. In our cities, they stock only English titles, the others – translations mainly, for the bhasha books are rarely in sight – tucked away from the discerning eye. And our newspapers too – other countries fete their own; we push the foreign boat out, entertain their creations extravagantly.

Part of the debate about diversity and identity in today's India revolves around complex issues of onus and ownership. Within India, a nation whose cultural heritage throws up new elements every 200 metres – we recognize a great many cultures that live and let others live. Diversity and identity. This debate is a crucial one in many cultures throughout the world today. In India, the debate promises to impact the way we educate our future decision makers. As well as to find an answer to the questions: Is there indeed something called *an* Indian culture, and if so who gets to decide what it is made up of? For many of us, what is at stake is the character of our identity.

But then, what is the role of story in all this? Can stories keep us in our culture? In 1950 Octavio Paz said, "Contemporary man has rationalized the myths, but he has not been able to destroy them." Fifty five years later, we can repeat him, but a thought troubles: For more than four hundred years, the British ruled us, yet the country carried its centuries of tradition and heritage accepting change, other cultures gracefully, maturely. Well into I would say the 80s, we still had something we could call our own. Today, when the world flounders, when it questions the route it has taken, when it turns to India for amongst other things pranayama and yoga, we play down what we have. In Austin, a learned professor told me, "We have more Sanskrit scholars in the US than you have in India." Is this important at all? Is our culture so fragile that losing a few Sanskrit scholars is going to spell the end of India as we know it? And if yes, does it matter? Do stories like Acharya's and Kashi Nath Singh's matter?

These stories and the questions they raise inside me, my mind still in edit mode, I sit, watching children running and playing in front of me in the Katha school of ours set in one of Delhi's largest slums, mulling over our collective futures. There are the usual sounds of excitement. In one corner is a child assiduously painting a collage, in another is discussion that spill over from the previous week – the Natyashastra. This trimester and the previous one – our children have been learning through the syllabus that we in Katha call VidDuniya. This trimester's is titled, Khojwalon ki Bharat: the Discoverer's India. We have discussed the idea with most of the 1300 children, cutting across age and abilities: There is an India that all of us see, with its colours and magic, its leaders and heroines, its filth and despair, beauty and hope, its fun and laughter. There is the imagined country we see and don't see through cinema and television, through newspapers and magazines. But there is another that only those who want to, can see ...

Our special curriculum and syllabus has once again got the kids, from 3 years to 16 excited about the many routes we can take in a country like India – from the Ramapithicus and Dinosaur route to the Silk and Frogs' Legs Route, from the Heretic to the Bhakti and Zero Route – 13 routes in all to explore and experience their maths and science, their sociology and language in, in 6 months. And there in Phulwari where the preschoolers are, is this child drawing a dinosaur. And in one corner she's drawn an elephant – inside a huge egg ... The flourishes of imagination, where do they come from? Children draw and paint, tell stories and listen to them. We all believe it's Katha's story pedagogy which takes our curriculum for life, the Me/We ideology places where a homogenized syllabus and curriculum cannot ever go. This, since 1990, has kept our children in the classrooms, and in formal education, preparing for a future they could well have missed out on. This year we touch intimately, the lives of 7000 children who might go without education if not for our teachers and their well-wishers.

In a country that is growing literate by the minute and where students have to break the barriers of caste, class and gender to help the country surge forward, the role of identity in the various acts of reading, teaching, and everyday living is indispensable. How a child interprets, values, and appreciates stories tells one a lot about the identity of the student and where she comes from. What Paulo Freire calls "the culture of silence" is created not so much by students as by teachers who are struggling with large classrooms and larger misunderstandings of what is culture, what is important about education. So reading for meaning, as Gandhiji wanted, or Sri Aurobindo or Gijubai Badeka or the many great teachers our country have had the privilege to know and learn from, is the task we set ourselves. And so hopefully, at Katha we daily teach ourselves how to come to a story knowledgeably.

This brings me in a round about way to our stories again. If with stories like the ones you hold, we discover one kind of India, with the children, we in Katha discover another world in India. You could say these then are our organization's reality check. Ours is a time for changes and transformations of a scale that can be merely humungous, troublesome and irritating, or can be magnificent, magical and magnanimous. The choice is ours, say the stories.

And for giving all of us this choice, I would like to thank – with all the love I can muster – our Nominating Editors for choosing these stories for us, for having taken the time and trouble to read most of all that has been published in these languages during the given years. We thank our award winning writers for writing these thought provoking stories, and the translators for translating them so well. I also take this opportunity to thank all those who have been involved in this volume, the fabulous Katha team, especially – Madhavi Mahadevan, Gita Rajan, Shoma Choudhury, Tirna Ray and Shalini Reys.

In these times, [to rephrase Mathew 19:24,] it is easier for a camel to go through the eye of a needle, than for a good book in translation to pass through the bookshop's teller. But the change is upon us and we thank you, dear reader, for buying this book and thus helping to usher in a quiet literary confidence in ourselves and for fostering the sustainability of linguistic multiculturalism. And, with these stories, we wish you fun and explorations as you discover anew for yourself the continent: India!

December, 2004   Geeta Dharmarajan

ॐ

SRIKANTH

THE SILENT SONG

TRANSLATED FROM TELUGU BY J BHAGYALAKSHMI
first published in Andhra Jyothi, November 2002, Hyderabad

NOMINATED BY AMARENDRA DASARI

Ajmat was up early and didn't want to waste a minute of the holiday. He collected the tools and went out into the small yard in front of the house. The children were already up. After brushing their teeth, and the morning tea, they were now playing in the street. As soon as they saw their father settle down under the neem tree, they came running and pushed open the gate. The boy squatted on his haunches with his arms locked around his knees. His bright, inquisitive eyes rested briefly on the tools and the heap of papers. Then they rested on Ajmat's face. "Will it be ready today, Abbu?"

Ajmat looked up from arranging his tools in the right order. He glanced at the shining four year old face and smiled.

"Yes," the daughter said, hands on hips, with the authority of one who, being two years older than her sibling, naturally knew better. "It will be ready today."

Ajmat's face was untroubled. "Shh!" he said gently. "You must not make a noise. It distracts me. Why don't you go in and see what your mother's doing?"

The mother, Ayesha, was in the kitchen, busy making breakfast. The four year old slipped his arms around her waist and asked eagerly, "Amma, will Abbu complete it today?"

Ayesha took the milk pan from the stove and turned around. She ran her fingers through her son's hair, and tilting his head back, smiled at him. "Didn't I say I would call you when the food is ready ... Why are you back so soon?"

"He saw Abbu and rushed back," the girl said. "He's sure to spoil it this time too ... just like the last time."

Looking deep into the boy's eyes, Ayesha said, "That was an accident, wasn't it?"

Two weeks ago, on a festival holiday, Ajmat had spent all day working under the neem tree. It was almost ready when the boy, in his excitement, had stumbled on it. Though Ajmat had been stoical about the mishap, Ayesha still remembered his face at that moment, the fleeting emotions that had chased across it.

At one time she had thought he was a little soft in the head.

That was just after the wedding, when he had talked about it for the first time. The idea had possessed him since childhood, he had said. She had thought he was joking. A few days later he took her into the room at the back of the house and showed her the tools, the huge paper heaps, the notebooks full of calculations. Suddenly, it wasn't funny any more. It was even a little frightening. Could she live with him for the rest of her life? Had her parents unknowingly married her off to a lunatic?

By and by Ayesha came to know him better. He was a mild tempered, undemanding man. He spoke little. Earned enough for their needs. Gave her a comfortable home, even though it was a rented place. Yes, he loved her very much. No basic flaws in his character except this – if it could be called a flaw at all. Certainly, it was a little bizarre. The neighbours talked about it. On every holiday they would see him working in the courtyard and would openly make fun of him.

"Don't pay attention," he told Ayesha.

"But they laugh at you! Do you even know what they say? That the eighth wonder of the world is right here in Hyderabad – you!"

He shrugged his shoulders. "Is that so? I don't know why they are so wonderstruck ... In our village it was nothing extraordinary, everyone was skilled in this art. Of course not many people got to hear of it because its ground rules were different. It worked only in rainwater and there was never enough of that in our village. But they were very good at it, the people of my village. They created such beautiful shapes. Did you know that?"

"I only know that I feel bad when they ridicule you. They make it a point to tell every visitor – do you know our neighbour Ajmat? He's a loose screw," Ayesha said crossly.

"Ignore them," he said. It left her very dissatisfied. That was in the early days of their marriage – when she had thought that this was just a passing fad. But now she was used to it and so were the neighbours. For three years now, Ajmat and Ayesha had been living in this locality and everyone had become used to seeing him working under the neem tree in the courtyard. When they came back from their holiday outings they would stop and ask in all seriousness, "How far have you got with it, Ajmat?"

The children were the most impatient. "Abbu, when will you complete it? When?"

They never doubted the outcome. The girl was keen to learn.

"Teach me," she said. He invited her to sit beside him. "Watch and you will learn," he told her as the mellow autumnal sun seeped in through the neem leaves. To Ayesha he said, "If I cannot complete this work, she will ... she has it in her."

One day, when Ayesha was pregnant with their second child, Ajmat told her about the antiquity of this craft. How in those days, people of his region used it to travel to other villages. Then there was a terrible famine. The sudden invasion of disease and starvation swept through the region and the clan was scattered far and wide. The traditional craft died out. Slowly, there was hardly anyone in the world who built these things anymore, leave alone travel in them. "I remember I was six when I saw my father build one. It was beautiful, it could carry two people. The one I make may not carry even one."

"But if your father used to build them, why didn't he teach you?"

"He was not allowed to ... Tradition decreed that the skill be passed through the women of the clan. My mother knew it and she taught my father. If a daughter was born, she acquired the skill and, when the time came, taught the art to her husband. To go against the tradition was a sin. The knowledge was never passed on to me. Whatever little I know, I learnt by watching my father. At times it doesn't seem enough."

Ayesha also knew something about paper boats. In the rainy days of her childhood, she too used to run out with hurriedly made paper boats and float them in the rainwater rushing through the lanes of her village. But she had never imagined that she would live with a man who dreamt of making a paper boat large enough for him to sail around the world.

One night, she teased him, "What else can you use to make your boats? Well, why not clouds?" Ajmat had promptly replied, "Oh, what a wonderful idea!" Two weeks later he said, dead serious: "But clouds have no weight, that will be a problem. I can somehow drag them down to earth. But you see, a boat has to be made in accordance with the density of the water in which it sails."

When they had moved into this house, the first thing Ajmat did was to take out his measuring tape and check the width of the street in front of the house. Then he sat down to calculate how much water would flow down the street if there was rainfall of average density. Then he crammed his notebooks with strange formulae and measurements. Once Ayesha even asked him, "Are all these measurements necessary?"

His reply was: "They are very important. If this attempt fails, I will know what exactly went wrong."

While Ayesha never talked about his passion, the children were just the opposite. When the class teacher asked, "What do you do on a Sunday?" The daughter proudly said, "I help my father with his paper boat."

Without comprehending, the teacher asked, "For you to play?"

"No. For him to sail in ... When it rains he will sail in it."

Next Sunday, the teacher and the entire class came to see Ajmat and his paper boat. The teacher said, "What a great idea, Ajmat bhai! When I was a child my grandfather would tell me about people who crossed rivers on paper boats. I thought it was a fairy tale. This is the first time I've seen such a person in flesh and blood. I wish you luck!"

The school children followed Ajmat's example and started making their own paper boats. The principal was flooded with complaints from parents. When he heard, Ajmat only said, "That's great! One day the whole world will make paper boats to travel around in."

Over the years Ajmat had researched a great deal on paper boats. He knew, for instance, that the ratio of length to weight must be absolutely precise. Second, the boat should weigh twice as much as him. Third, since he wanted to travel downstream, the boat would pick up momentum from the current; the wings beneath the boat had to be strong to control its speed. This was something he had learnt from experience, when a boat he had built had crashed just after sailing ten feet. The fourth and the most important point was that the floor of the boat must not act like a blotter and soak up water. After a great deal of trial and error he managed to overcome this problem by carefully layering the paper sheets with a thin film of sand. At last, the basic framework was ready, and he could now focus his attention on making a paper sail, a wheel, and a strong chair for himself.

"Is it done, Abbu?" the children asked.

"Almost," he replied, taking off the towel wrapped around his head and wiping his face with it. "Go, ask your mother to make me a cup of tea."

While he had his tea, he noticed that a cold breeze was blowing. Perhaps it indicated an early winter. The sun was less hot. He looked at the sky and saw the clouds. This could be the day, he thought. A thrill coursed through him. With renewed energy he attacked the remainder of the task. Ayesha watched him from the veranda. For nine years now, she had been watching him – his thin well shaped hands drawing, cutting, shaping, hammering; those eyebrows knitted in concentration; the slight tremor in his face as he drove the nails in.

About forty five minutes later, as the dark clouds gathered in the sky, he looked up and sighed with quiet satisfaction, "It's ready." As he was checking it one last time, it started drizzling. Quickly, he covered the boat with a plastic sheet and joined his family on the veranda. The clouds could no longer carry their burden, and the drizzle turned into a downpour.

"Abbu, can we launch it now?" the daughter asked.

"Not yet. We have to wait for some more rain. There should be enough water to make it float."

"Abbu, can I come with you?" the son asked, leaning against his leg. Ajmat did not answer. His heart was beating so hard that he found it difficult to breathe. The street was filling up. Would the level rise high enough? All that he had learned from his failed attempts had gone into the making of this boat. He was sure that this time he had spared no effort to get it right. Still, one never knew ...

Half an hour later the rain and the wind receded. With towel wrapped around his head he stepped into the street. The water was almost knee deep. A little more rainfall and it would be just the right level. Should he wait? While he was trying to make up his mind, his neighbour across the street, forty year old Chandram, called out from his window on the first floor, "Oi Ajmat, is your boat ready? Are you going to try it out today?"

Before he could answer, the girl replied, "Our boat's ready!"

Three boys from the next house looked out and said, "Best of luck! Today we'll see you sail."

Ayesha looked expectantly at Ajmat. He was still undecided. Shaking his head, as if brushing away all doubt, he smiled. "I am ready to start. I hope everything will work out, with god's grace."

Decision made, he did not waste time. Opening the gate wide, he placed a plank from the gate to the street. Next, he pulled off the plastic cover and with his family's help lifted the boat onto the plank. Then, rather gingerly, he stepped into the boat. "Give it a slow but firm push," he instructed his wife and children.

By now, word had gone around that Ajmat's four foot high paper boat was about to make its maiden voyage. Everyone in that narrow street came out and crowded into their verandas. The neighbourhood children were delirious with excitement. Ignoring their parents' cries, they ran out and stood in the rain, outside Ajmat's house.

Ayesha and the children pushed the boat. The front portion gave a slight shudder and slid into the water. The rest of the boat followed. For a moment it stood still. When Ajmat was sure that the boat could take his weight, he loosened the wings. Giving another little jerk, the boat moved ahead. There was a resounding cheer from the audience. Ajmat was completely oblivious to the noise.

His attention was fixed on the boat. It was gaining speed faster than he had imagined. It moved a few yards and he relaxed. His apprehensions melted away. He smiled. He had proved that he could sail a paper boat. Hand on wheel, he steered it away from the electricity poles. Wiping the rainwater trickling down his face he waved at the children standing two houses away.

Then it happened. Without warning.

The boat that had been so steady just a moment ago tilted to the left. Before he could recover, the other side was also submerged. Muddy brown rainwater swirled around his ankles, gently pushing him forward. The boat began to disintegrate. The wings floated away, the chair, the wheel and the sail followed. He stood there in the street, drenched, his jubba clinging to his skin, his hair plastered to his head. He watched the sodden pieces of his boat being swept away by the rushing water.

No one spoke. Then one man was heard saying, "I knew it would not work. Give up, I said. But he wouldn't listen. How is it possible to sail in a paper boat?"

There was no murmur of assent but no one disagreed either. Someone else said, "Don't worry, Ajmat. Better luck next time."

Without uttering a word, he turned back and walking against the stream came to the gate where his wife and children waited. Ayesha brought a dry towel. In a concerned voice the daughter asked, "What happened, Abbu? Why did it sink?" He looked at her, forced a smile on his face and shook his head.

Later, after dinner, when the children had gone to bed, he sat in a chair on the veranda, staring into space. The sky had cleared and the stars were peeping out. The leaves of the neem rustled in the breeze showering a light spray on the earth below. Ajmat sneezed. "I think I'm going to catch a cold," he told Ayesha. And then in a different voice, he almost cried out, "Why? Why didn't the boat hold out?" She couldn't think of an answer. He stood up and went into the house, pulled out his notebooks, turned page after page, pausing to study the measurements and his calculations. Two hours later he was still clueless.

That night as he lay beside his wife, his throat was sore, his head ached. His body was burning, still he shivered. Ayesha got up to fetch a soft towel and a dish of water. She sat up all night, soaking the towel, wringing it out and placing it on his forehead. Why? Why is he so stubborn? she asked herself, feeling a mix of concern, sadness and anger. What does he get out of it? For about half an hour in between she dozed off. She dreamt her husband was sailing away in his paper boat. The rainwater swelled into a huge wave that engulfed him. She sat up with a start.

With dawn the fever abated. As he slept, Ayesha went about the household chores. From the kitchen, she could hear him talking to the children. "Can one imagine that it rained so heavily last evening? See how bright the day is! Time to start work. Bring those notebooks from my room. Arrange my tools under the tree. I'm off to the bazaar to buy glue and nails." He calls out to her, "It's still quite wet under the neem tree. Could you spread out a plastic sheet, please? I will start work as soon as I return."

In the evening the wife and children sit in the veranda. People are walking up and down the street. Ajmat sits under the neem, making fresh entries into his notebooks. The neighbours look at him the way they do. Head lowered he pores over the figures, mumbling to himself like one singing a silent song.

ф

ASHITA

THE SUBSTITUTE

——◆——

TRANSLATED FROM MALAYALAM BY INDIRA MENON
first published in Bhashaposhini, March 2002, Kottayam

NOMINATED BY SUJATHA DEVI

A strong wind shook the tree in the garden. It scattered all its leaves and blustered through the window to snatch the letter from Yashodamma's hands. It finally left, noiselessly, through the door. In the fading sunlight, Yashodamma thought of her son.

The stormy arrival ... and the wordless departure...Yashodamma suppressed such thoughts with a deep sigh. Wasn't she used to her loneliness by now, communicating with it through sighs and silences?

The letter fluttered on the floor, not unlike the flutter of sorrow within her ... Yashodamma bent down to pick it up. It was Pisharodi's letter. He wrote, "For Yashodamma. I do not think I'll be able to come for the Saptaaham this time. My cataract troubles me much. I'm told that I need surgery. All is as god wills. But the Saptaaham need not be discontinued. I'll send a substitute. A capable man. Hope you'll do the needful for him. Faithfully yours, Pisharodi."

The letter had arrived five days ago. Yashodamma had gone through it countless times. No substitute can be as good as Pisharodi. Everyone knew that. "When Pisharodi speaks, even god listens!" Nambrathai Karunakara Menon often said when he came to look at the pandal being erected in Yashodamma's yard for each Saptaaham.

Like Aaraattu and Niramaala, the annual Bhaagwatha Saptaaham in Yashodamma's house – when the story of Lord Krishna's life is read aloud and explicated over seven days – was a major event in the village. People said it was held each year for a son who had left home when he was only sixteen. Nobody knew it for a fact. But for those seven days Yashodamma's house – that seemed lost in deep meditation, with a half-closed entrance door, so motionless and silent that even the sun, the wind, the rain, even the squirrels darting in to nibble at the paddy, stopped short of the front stairs – would open itself to colours and sounds.

It was at the entrance to this house on the hilltop that someone called late one evening. Yashodamma's eyes, dimmed with age, did not recognize him. She hurried out into the courtyard and asked, "Who is it?"

The reply was courteous and pleasant. "Pisharodi sent me. I am Swami Thanmayan."

At first glance, he reminded her of a grown-up child. She asked him in and looked again. "Ishwara, isn't he my Unni? Her heart lurched. The wind blew Pisharodi's letter out of her hands, and whispering in her ear, tugged at her thin upper cloth and disappeared. Tender mango leaves, new fronds of palms, lush paddy awaiting the harvest ... all this and more echoed in the wind's words and were quickly silent again.

Swami Thanmayan was coming up the steps, walking with a faint smile. Yashodamma felt the footprints of two baby feet on her heart. Her eyes filled with tears. She turned away, disgusted with herself.

After all these years, to feel so nervous!

Swami Thanmayan came close and looked intently, as if into her soul. "Pisharodi has told me everything."

His eyes were like a long precise coastline, unassaulted by even a single wave of memory with nothing but sand, and a stretch of integrity ... stretching to a distant horizon.

Is he who's come the same as the one who left? Why did he leave? What unfinished business brings him back? So many unasked questions fluttered in her mind, flapping their wings, scattering their feathers, as she served him dinner. It was only when she showed him to the room Pisharodi usually occupied that she could ask, "What did Pisharodi say?"

His reply echoed through the darkness of the room.

"Every one of us is in a constant act of penance, knowingly or otherwise. A mother brooding over a son who went away, has lived fourteen years with this annual Bhaagavatha Saptaaham. Go to her, Unni. Expound to her the essence of Bhaagavatham."

Yashodamma felt she was being sucked into an immense void large enough to contain a universe as wide as seven universes. It was only well after the Saptaaham vaayana had started that she could observe him closely. And the more she looked the more she felt that this was indeed her son. She searched for similarities – that glance, the slight turn of the head, that half-suppressed smile, the enchantment in his eyes. And that wound. The scar?

She deliberately shut her eyes. The truth always lies shrouded between two contending positions.

Seven days passed swiftly by. The Saptaaham continued to the point of uncertainty till it would change colour and he said this was indeed he.

On the fifth day, Thekkepaattai Bhagirathiamma, the oldest in the village, while taking leave, asked, "Yashodai, your son would've been this same age? Why don't you ask him if he's run into our Unni somewhere?"

Yashodamma felt a pang deep inside her. But she stood impassive as stone. I won't ask, she told herself stubbornly. As if I don't know.

On the seventh day Karunakara Menon took Yashodamma aside as he was about to leave after offering dakshina and namaskarams. "The vaayana was superb, even better than Pisharodi's one might say. But who is he? Where is he from?"

"I didn't ask." She repeated to herself, I won't ask. I don't want to know. A woman can bear this and more. What else is existence for?

The people started to leave one by one. When the last person had left, Swami Thanmayan came towards Yashodamma to take leave of her. Yashodamma wore a hard expression.

"Only you did not give any dakshina, nor did you say anything, Amma." His words had the softness of falling flower petals.

I have nothing to say. You did not consult me before you went away. You haven't asked my permission to return. Yashodamma's words smouldered for an instant and then crumbled. "Unni, you didn't even bother to send a line to tell me where you were!"

His reply had a winning calm. "I didn't ever realize we were separated. That was why I didn't write."

Yashodamma's resistance broke down. She stared at him, faith and misgiving battling in her gaze. The tears welled up. Her pain, murky from the years of suppression, surfaced and flowed with them.

"Where is the deep wound on your chest, Unni?"

"It may have been washed away by the tears of many mothers like you, Amma."

His every word as pleasing as a smile.

Yashodamma did not let go. Her faith needed proof, at least a small one to cling to.

"And the scar on your chin from the fight you had in the marketplace, the day before you left?"

"The soul holds no wound. Nor does love. Then which cut, what scar?" he asked.

Swami Thanmayan held Yashodamma's hands. "Ammai, life is faith strung together with small beliefs. But what purpose does mere commitment serve if it doesn't lead to knowledge? Deliverance lies there."

The cow lowed in its shed. While he slowly walked out of the house and onto the village pathway, Yashodamma felt her past uproot itself, and so too the anguish, her only asset for all these years.

Nambrathai Karunakara Menon, moving furtively in the dark, was disconcerted to meet Swami Thanmayan on the village road. To hide his embarrassment he asked, "Returning already? You must definitely come back for next year's vaayana."

"No," Swami Thanmayan replied. "There will be no more Saptaaham vaayana in that house."

"What! Why not?" Karunakara Menon sounded incredulous.

A kuyil sang into the late night. The moon rose. A strong wind soared upwards from under the earth and with a roar, whirled the dry leaves and flung them aside. His voice loud as the wind, Thanmayan said, "Yashodamma has discerned the essence of Bhaagavatham."

Then he disappeared into the moonlight and became a legend.

ॐ

MEENA KAKODKAR

EXPECTATIONS

———◆———

TRANSLATED FROM KONKANI BY VIDYA PAI
first published in Jaag, October 2003, Margao

NOMINATED BY VIDYA PAI

Nirmal passed away unexpectedly. Appa couldn't believe it. How could she leave so suddenly? She was here one moment. Brought him some tea, soaked a tub full of washing, bought some tisré for cutlets from the fishmonger. What else had she done? Appa thought hard. Yes, before she bought the shellfish she had set her cupboard right. She didn't normally do such things early in the morning. He had asked her what she was looking for, but she just brushed him off. "Oh nothing, really," she'd exclaimed.

What was she looking for? Appa sighed deeply. Did she find it? God knows. Appa sighed again. Now only god knew.

The neighbours came rushing when they heard him cry out. Phone calls were made, relatives informed. The house was full of people. But Appa seemed lost in the crowd, quite forlorn.

He spoke only when spoken to. He gave Anjani, his younger brother, Prabhakar's wife, whatever she needed for the rituals. He did as the bhatmaam asked. And all this while he imagined Nirmal was in the kitchen. That she'd respond if he called to her.

How could anyone see the turmoil in Appa's mind? He kept his composure as he responded to questions about what had happened. He never broke down. A sixty five year old man with tears in his eyes? No, Nima wouldn't approve.

Just the other day she'd returned from a condolence visit exclaiming, "Did you see the show they put on. While the old woman was alive no one had any time for her. Now it's a competition to see who can cry the most!"

"Some people cry." Appa had said.

"That's enough. She was really old and bedridden for ages. No one should live that long. But that's not in our hands. Her sons and daughters-in-law are over sixty themselves. Her daughters don't keep well. Everyone was worn out from caring for her. When someone like that finally dies, is this the sort of commotion one should create? I don't like it at all."

Nirmal always spoke her mind. Fragments of conversation from the last few days floated through Appa's mind. It was as though the words had been uttered in some distant past.

The bhatmaam was saying something to him.

Appa was torn apart. One half of him aware of his surroundings, the other half overwhelmed, lost in recollection. Which one is the real me? Appa couldn't tell.

His gaze drifted to the mango tree outside the window. There he was, their daily visitor – the crow.

Nirmal fed him every afternoon, just before lunch. And if, by chance she was late, the crow would make such a ruckus that Appa would call out, "Give him something to eat, quick. Must be one of our ancestors!"

"I don't know who this one is, but someday I'll sit on that mango tree and wait for you to feed me," she'd said with a laugh one day.

Appa suddenly remembered her words. Could this be Nima, then? In any case he couldn't let the crow go hungry. Nima wouldn't like that. He went into the kitchen and opened the fridge. Anjani followed him quietly wondering what her brother-in-law was up to.

There was some leftover rice in the fridge. The morning's milk was still by the hearth. Appa spooned some rice on to a plate and poured milk over it.

Anjani hurried to Prabhakar's side. "I think Appa's going mad. He's sitting there eating rice."

Prabhakar rushed into the kitchen and saw Appa mixing the rice with the milk.

"What are you doing, Appa?"

"See that crow." Appa pointed to the mango tree. "He's hungry."

"Crow?" Prabhakar was convinced. Vaini's death had upset the old man. Appa was losing his mind.

"All right, all right." He took the plate from Appa.

"But Nima always …"

"Don't worry. I'll take care of it," Prabhakar's voice was soothing.

Appa followed Prabhakar out. He told Anjani to leave the rice under the mango tree. She nodded. But as soon as he was gone, she threw the rice away and washed the plate.

The crow sat for a long time. Perhaps he was shocked into silence by the sight of so many people. Then he flew away.

Anjani went to Appa. "Can you give me one of Vaini's saris? A new one," she said.

Appa opened a cupboard. There were saris stacked neatly to one side. Some were folded over hangers. Appa and Nirmala had separate cupboards. He had never opened hers before. As he pulled the shutters apart, he was touched by her presence. A surge of emotion caught his throat as he looked over the saris. Some were familiar. Others he couldn't recognize.

I didn't pay attention to Nima's saris. She always tucked flowers into her hair. Appa remembered. Whenever we were ready to go out, Nima, all dressed up would stand there casually in front of me. But I was always so preoccupied, I didn't even notice. I knew my wife was good looking. She was always well dressed, so I paid no attention. Never complimented her. Just took her for granted, always.

Remorse washed over Appa. It's my fault, he thought. When she was alive things were that way. But now she was gone, and every little mistake came back to haunt him like some unpardonable crime.

Appa couldn't bring himself to pick a sari, so he beckoned Anjani who was hovering by the door. "Take what you want. She liked beige, the colour of figs."

Anjani ran her eyes over the pile of saris. There was a pretty fig-coloured one, with a golden-yellow border. She drew it out with some hesitation and looked up at Appa.

"Anything else?"

"No." Anjani was off.

Appa shut the cupboard door and sank down on a chair. He'd bought that sari for her. She'd loved it too. But she never got a chance to wear it. Fate had decreed that it would be draped on her lifeless body.

The smell of flowers and incense filled the air. The fragrance of past times now emitted a heavy, bitter scent that hung pall-like over the house.

Appa stared at Nirmal as she lay dressed in the fig-coloured sari, her forehead streaked with vermilion, her hair massed with flowers. Today he had the time to admire her. But where was she? She wasn't there to bask in his admiration. Still, he murmured softly, this sari looks good on you. It's setting out on its final journey too. Appa didn't register when the final journey to the cremation ground began, or when the last rites eventually ended.

No. He was aware of what was happening. He just held back. Like a stranger, not fully involved, Appa did as the bhatmaam asked. He went to the cremation ground, lit the pyre that bore Nirmal's corpse, returned home with the rest and took the ritual bath.

Prabhakar lit the oil lamp that would burn until the rituals were all done. Anjani set the kitchen in order. Mavshibai, who lived next door, brought tea for everyone. Suddenly Appa remembered the shellfish Nima had bought. What had happened to them? He wanted to ask Anjani. But what if she thought, "Look at this man. He's just lost his wife, but he's worried about the shellfish!" So he held his tongue. But he couldn't help thinking that Abole the maid could have been given the fish.

One by one the people began to drift away. Someone ought to stay with Appa, but they had their problems. Prabhakar's daughter's exams were coming up.

"If we stay here tonight we'll have to stay for twelve days. I don't think that's possible. But I'll come from time to time," he said. And Appa nodded.

Appa's sisters had their own difficulties. One's granddaughter was too young, the other's daughter-in-law was expecting. Minor issues. But how extraordinarily important they are being made to seem, Appa thought.

He didn't insist they stay, nor did anyone volunteer. What will you eat? How will you manage on your own? Nobody asked. They merely ignored the problems that were sure to crop up, and each person went his way.

What could they have done even if they had stayed, Appa thought. Would they be good company?

As darkness fell Mavshibai arrived with rotis and bhaji. She sat by his side, pressing him to eat. Appa wasn't hungry, but he ate some to please her.

"Why didn't anyone stay to keep you company?" she asked.

"My companion has gone. What company are you talking about, Mavshibai? Now it's time to walk alone, ekla cholo re."

"That's all very well Appa, but there's something called kindness and decency. This is a time of mourning. I'll send Gaja. He'll spend the night here." She retorted.

"No, no. I must get used to being alone. Anyway, once I fall asleep I'll only get up in the morning. Why would I need company?"

Once I fall asleep I'll get up only in the morning! The words came back to haunt Appa as he turned restlessly, with only the flame of the oil lamp flickering by his side. Memories of Nirmal floated up from the deepest recesses of his mind.

Do I really remember all this? Then why did I always say no whenever Nirmal asked if I remembered something from the past? Perhaps I didn't try hard enough. And today all these memories come unbidden. When emotions are charged the brain doesn't need to make an effort.

Am I upset that Prabhakar and my sisters didn't stay with me tonight? Appa searched deep within himself for an answer. No. When the ties or bonds that should hold the family together have worn so thin, how can one expect anything? How can one complain? Nima and I tried so hard. Yet each one drifted further and further away. And now, it is the people to whom we have no ties of blood who come to our aid.

Nima always said, "Don't ever expect any help from strangers. You can't complain about their behaviour. One can only complain about a loved one. One can only expect something from one's own."

"In that case you have me and I have you. We can complain about each other," Appa had said. Who could he complain about, now?

Early next morning, Mavshibai's grandson brought him some tea. Then she came over with coffee and something to eat.

"Why do you take so much trouble? I'll make something for myself," Appa protested.

"That's enough, Appa. Not another word." The old woman wiped her eyes as she took the empty dishes away.

Nima was an excellent cook. Anything she turned out was delicious. I didn't even have to make myself a cup of tea while she was around. "Now look here," she'd say, "a man should know at least enough to keep his belly filled." But Appa paid no heed. I didn't let Nima teach me how to cook. Now I'll have to learn from Mavshibai. Just rice and curry. Enough to keep body and soul together. Appa mused.

He returned to the present with a jolt, shaking his head. Nima went only yesterday. And here I am worrying about filling my stomach.

Horrible. How upset Nima will be. What if her crow spirit form refuses our offerings? Appa decided not to dwell on anything that might upset Nima. He would do nothing that might displease her.

Mavshibai had set out his lunch. But Appa was still waiting for the crow. What had happened to him? Nima was gone. Did the crow think that there was no one there to feed him?

Maybe it wasn't so late after all. Appa only thought it was late because he'd been waiting so long. As he glanced out of the window the crow settled on the mango tree. For an instant Appa wondered if it was Nima. Maybe she was joking, but hadn't she once said something like that?

It was the same crow. But today Appa saw it differently, searching for some sign that might indicate to him that it was indeed Nima who had arrived. Appa didn't believe that a dead man's spirit takes the form of a crow. Nor did he have much faith in rituals like the kakol. Even then, after Nima went away, he saw the crow as a link with his dead wife. He was terrified that this link might suddenly snap.

"Here. Eat your fill," he said, placing the saucer of rice under the tree.

Mavshibai was sitting beside him when Prabhakar phoned.

"I did say I'd come, but I don't think I'll manage. Sprained my back."

"Go see the doctor," Appa advised.

"Yes. And my wife's not too well either." Prabhakar's litany of woes droned on.

Appa listened in silence. The same familiar excuses. What could he say? Don't feel bad, he consoled Nima.

We both know these people. We mustn't expect anything from them. Then there'll be no cause for complaint. But don't worry. I'll see that the rituals are performed correctly. I don't need anyone's help.

Nirmal had always complained that he never paid attention to anything, he freed himself from domestic responsibility by dumping everything on her shoulders. You'll never manage on your own. I worry about you. She grumbled.

Appa began to fret as he remembered. What if her spirit, bogged down by these worries, refused the kakol offerings on the twelfth day?

Prabhakar's voice whined on and on.

"Let me see what I can do. If it's possible I'll drop in sometime."

"All right." Appa set the phone down.

"Who was that?" Mavshibai asked.

"Prabhakar."

"So, when is he coming? Tomorrow is the third day. You have to collect the ashes from the pyre."

"He can't come."

"Can't come? What do you mean?"

"Sprained his back. Everybody has their own problems. What can he do anyway?"

"Now look here, Appa. It's not a question of what he can do. At a time like this it's good to have one's own people around. Gives one courage."

Appa was tempted to ask what she meant by one's own. Family members who behaved like strangers, were they one's own? Or people, unconnected by blood, yet tied by close bonds? He would gather the ashes of the one closest to him, the one person he called his own. What need had he for anyone else? But Appa didn't voice his thoughts.

He went with the priest to the cremation ground and came home with Nirmal's ashes bound up in a piece of cloth. Such a tall, strapping woman and now this. He struggled to stem the tide of emotions that threatened to overcome him.

Some advised him to immerse the ashes at Nasik. Others said go to Narsobavadi. But Appa wasn't happy with that. Nima had set off on her voyage to the Great Beyond. But these ashes should remain somewhere close by. Appa sat in his armchair, his eyes closed.

That afternoon as he placed the saucer of rice before the crow he said, "I won't go to Nasik or Narsobavadi. Just somewhere close by."

Appa's voice caught in his throat. He said no more. Nima would understand how he felt. He was certain about that. When he sat in the hall, he told himself that Nima was working in the kitchen. Or that she was somewhere inside the house. She was gone. He knew that. Still, he tried to deceive himself. The thought gave him courage. Helped him get through the day.

Days passed. The baravo rituals, performed on the twelfth day after death were due soon.

"Appa, where will the baravo be done?" Mavshibai asked.

One must be practical. Not get too emotional, especially in one's old age. One might wish to do many things, but one might not always find the support one needs. A man should be able to manage in any situation. Nirmal always said. What guarantee is there, that circumstances will allow one to act on one's convictions?

Appa, head bowed, was lost in thought. The twelfth day rituals should actually be performed here. Nima's spirit, hovering over this house for eleven days, should find salvation at this very spot. But who will help me organize everything? I must be practical, like Nima used to say.

"Appa, where will you perform the ritual?" Mavshibai asked again. "You might want to do it at home, but I don't think Prabhakar's wife will be of any help. They should have stayed here with you during the mourning period. Your sisters at least should have stayed. You have done so much for them."

Appa shook his head. "No, Mavshibai. Everyone has their own problems."

"That's enough, Appa. There is such a thing as duty. Not one of them has come to see how you'll manage the baravo ceremony. Self-centred creatures. Like parrots!"

"I don't want to hold it at Harvale. Don't think I can manage at home either." Appa tried to change the subject.

"Why don't you perform the ceremony at Dadu bhat's place? He does everything in a proper, traditional manner. Just tell him how many people will be there for lunch."

"In that case I'll do it there."

"Phone Dadu bhat. Or send Gaja to his house."

The matter was discussed with Dadu bhat and the plan for the ceremony got underway. Prabhakar and Anjani dropped in the next day, possibly worried about what people would say.

"You'll have the baravo at Harvale, won't you?" Prabhakar asked as he walked in.

"No."

"What do you mean?" Anjani cut in. "Where will you have it, then? I'm not well. Who's going to take on all that responsibility?"

Appa almost laughed out loud. She was talking as though she'd personally conducted all the rituals so far. Prabhakar didn't like his wife's tone, but he tried to smooth over the matter. "It's not easy to organize the baravo rituals. Better have them at Harvale. Not much work, and so much cheaper."

"No. Not there either."

Anjani glanced at her husband. Didn't I tell you? Appa'll decide to hold the function at home. I can't do all that work, her look said.

Appa was aware of what was going on. He didn't leave them fretting too long. "I'll hold the function at Dadu bhat's house."

"Will he organize everything?"

"Yes. Just need to tell him how many people will be there for lunch."

Prabhakar turned to his wife. She held up two fingers, relieved.

"We will be there."

"Alright."

Appa wouldn't have been upset even if they'd said they couldn't come. They left soon after. Neither asked Appa what he had eaten, nor how he'd managed. In fact, Anjani didn't even step into the kitchen.

No. No. I'm not complaining. Appa said to himself.

Appa thought long and hard and bought all the things that Nima had loved. He didn't forget the braid of mogra flowers.

"Everything must be perfect," he said to Mavshibai. "None of Nima's wishes should be left unfulfilled."

"Don't worry Appa, everything will be just fine. Mark my words, the crow will swoop down on the kakol in a matter of seconds," she assured him. But Appa wasn't convinced. He had an uncanny feeling that the crow wouldn't appear at the right time. So, he kept watch on the mango tree.

Please, don't be late. Take the kakol at once, he implored.

Dadu bhat got everything ready, just as Mavshibai had said he would. And when the ceremony was over Appa took the kakol out into Dadu bhat's garden. It was quiet. He couldn't hear a crow cawing anywhere. Our crow must be waiting on the mango tree at home, Appa thought, as he placed the vada on a strip of plantain leaf on the garden wall. He had barely turned away when a crow swooped down and carried the kakol away.

"He's taken it – taken the kakol away!" Dadu bhat exclaimed.

Taken the kakol away? Appa was amazed. He hadn't seen a single crow anywhere around, then how did one appear at exactly the right moment? He turned around to see a horde of crows at the garden wall.

"She's accepted your offering Appa," Dadu bhat said.

"Good. Vaini's wishes have all been fulfilled," Prabhakar exclaimed.

"So? Did the crow accept the kakol?" Mavshibai asked when Appa got home.

"Yes. The moment I put it down."

"Didn't I say he would?" Mavshibai was pleased.

"Now we know that her spirit has left no unfulfilled desires behind."

It was late, but Appa tossed and turned in his bed. The rituals went smoothly. Nothing went wrong. The lunch was delicious. The baravo wasn't held at home, but the atmosphere in Dadu bhat's house was warm and cordial. It was good to see the crow swoop down on the kakol.

Everyone was pleased.

Dadu bhat was happy.

Prabhakar was happy.

Mavshibai was happy.

I was happy ...

Appa was lost in thought. Was I really happy? Nima went away, leaving me to fend for myself. My heart is restless. I don't know where anything is in the house. I can't find anything. I've told Mavshibai that I'll do my own cooking. But it will take some time before I manage that. Nima's reminders are driving me crazy. When I think of getting through life without her by my side, I'm terrified. Whom do I confide in from now on?

Nima was the only one I could call my own in this whole, wide world. Who do I have, now?

Can you feel this churning in my heart, as you sit up there? Appa spoke to his wife. This man has gone to pieces. Who will take care of him? Who will support him? Shouldn't you be worried about it? You've deserted him halfway. Shouldn't you be sorry about that?

I thought you wouldn't accept the kakol. That I'd have to plead with you. Nima, don't worry about me, I'll look after myself. Go. Go without a care. Only then would you accept the offering. That would have shown me that you were still concerned about my welfare. It would have given me the courage to cope. But you swooped down on the kakol! Don't you care about me any more? How could you, Nima? Why? Why?

All that was in Appa's heart welled up and flooded his eyes. And the night, soaked by his tears grew darker. And darker, still.

ச

CHEZHIAN

THE HARMONIUM

———◈———

TRANSLATED FROM TAMIL BY RAMIAH KUMAR
first published in Kanaiazhi, September 2002, Chennai

NOMINATED BY VENKAT SWAMINATHAN

One evening I met the respectable Mr Hasan Pandit. Walking through the narrow lanes amidst tall buildings and climbing the near-vertical stairs, I finally found the mansion's room number seven. At the entrance was a name board that said, Harmony Music School. A withered garland of assorted flowers and leaves adorned it. A pair of worn out slippers lay in front. From inside the room came the fragrance of udubatti and the music of the harmonium.

"Vanakkam," I saluted in formal Tamil.

With his eyes he signalled me to sit. The pandit's fingers, which were caressing the keys of the harmonium, gradually came to a halt. The resonance of the music permeated the entire ten by twelve foot room before it died down. Udubatti burned below the pictures of deities of all religious faiths.

"I wish to learn music."

"Sit down. Where are you from?"

"Sivagangai."

His fingers seemed to search for something as they moved noiselessly over the keys of the harmonium.

"Mmm. Tell me. Where did you say you are coming from?"

"I'm from Sivagangai. I want to learn music."

"What do you do for a living?"

"I am looking for a job."

"Day after tomorrow ..." his fingers were calculating as his lips murmured, "is the eighth day after the full moon. Thursday is new moon day," he said adding, "you could begin on that day. Classes are held every Monday and Thursday. Twice every week. The fee would be two hundred rupees. Have you taken music lessons before?"

"No."

"Has anyone in your house studied music?"

"No. I am the first."

"Why do you want to learn music?"

"I just have a desire to learn."

Pandit Hasan smiled.

I took leave saying, "I will start from next Monday."

As I moved past the room and started the descent down the stairs, the music of the harmonium once again wafted through the air. I visualized his fingers halting, jumping, sliding and retreating over the keys in pursuit of music.

It was beginning to get dark. Pandit was also dark, like the beginning of night. His hair was backbrushed in the style of a bhagavathar. His eyes were small but sharp. His face was clean shaven, and his countenance had the characteristic radiance of a musician.

I was delighted by the very thought that my evenings which used to be spent vacantly watching the clouds from the open terrace, would now resonate with the notes of Hasan Pandit. Just thinking about starting my classes on Monday filled me with joy. I bought two long notebooks with unruled pages.

Monday, two other middle aged persons with long notebooks were also waiting there. The teacher asked me to wait till their lesson was over. The pleasant aroma of baking bread wafted in from the bakery next door. One of the students picked up the harmonium from a corner of the room. It had a green rexine cover. That was when I realized that there were three harmoniums, of which Pandit Hasan's was the biggest. Both of them took their seats in front of the teacher, and the practice began.

"Play the jandai varisai."

Starting with sa-sa-ri-ri-ga-ga-ma-ma, they adjusted with ease to Hasan Pandit's moving fingers and the beat of his hand. The dancing notes frolicked and swayed like the multicoloured ribbons held by little girls in the Independence Day parade. The music filled the room like electricity and turned the very place into a fantasy world. When they finished, the vibrations gently settled into silence that engulfed the room. Telling them to write down the lesson, the teacher turned to me.

Taking my long notebook he opened the first page. After closing his eyes by way of a brief prayer, he placed the traditional Pillaiyar suzhi, as invocation to Lord Ganesha on top of the page after which he wrote my name in large letters.

There was silence in the room.

He began with the story of music, how Stone Age man blew out music through bones that lay in burial places. As he spoke with the adeptness of the skilled artist, assisted by facial expressions and movement of the fingers, the contours of the room faded and I could hear the sound of the beetles boring through the bones lying on the burial mounds, producing the music of a flute which whirled and spread out like smoke, creating an inexplicable sadness. His dark fingers, habituated to playing notes, artistically simulated their movement over the keys of an invisible harmonium in the air. In the dark dense forest, the peacocks are calling out – from it originates the note, Sa. The krowncha birds are singing. The male elephants that had found and eaten the bamboo shoots in the moonlight are loudly trumpeting the pleasure of dominating their mates, the sounds penetrating the very rocks. The notes come alive with movement. At Kailasam, not content with dancing alone, Shiva, with his seven heads is singing seven different songs, each with a different rhythm. The sage of music Narada's veena strings, vibrate on their own.

Sa, Ri, Ga, Ma, Pa, Da, Ni – the seven notes. The father of Carnatic music theory, Venkatamahi's organization of ragas into twelve groups of basic notes. The seventy two perfect ragas. The seventy two mother ragas, as it were. And their countless children. In the genial streets of Tiruvaiyaru, Saint Thyagaraja's tanpura resonates music. The nagalinga flowers that fall into Kaveri river come alive and take flight. The experience of Shyama Sastri's raga rendition. The mastery of rhythmic patterns from Muthuswamy Dikshithar. The sharp writing tool of Tulsidas moves, making impressions on dried palm leaves. The basic note patterns for the learner, the sarali varisai. The harmonium's smooth continuous sounds aligned with Gandharva's voice.

When I got back to reality, the chair in front of me was empty. The smoke rings from the incense sticks were gently revolving together before breaking into streaks that dissolved in the air, like the silent rendition of a raga.

"Melody is the mother of music, and rhythm, the father. The note and the rhythm conjoin over and over again. They break off, meet, touch and embrace – their pace sometimes fast, sometimes normal – in the air, through the air. And their union becomes music. All else disperse as streaks of noise. Air is music. Air is life. Music is life. The capacity to concentrate in music is meditation. It is also the ultimate wisdom. A crore of mantras in repetition equals meditation. A crore of such meditations equal layam, the merger with Oneness. Grasp the layam, which is the beat of the rhythm. There are seven of these – the seven princes. And there are seven celestial maidens – Sa, Ri, Ga, Ma, Pa, Da, Ni – the seven fundamental notes. The seven horses of the seven princes come galloping, each following a different beat of the rhythm. Five syllabic components of music formation, dextrous like the footwork of the dancer, become the base for colourful garlands. In the air, in the unperceivable formless space, the garlanded princes and the celestial maidens revel in the joy of union.

"Whatever one hears is a note. Whatever one hears is rhythm. When the rain falls on the roof with the noise, chatta chada chatta chada, there is a grammar of rhythm in its sounds. After the rain subsides, when only drops of drizzle are heard from the yard, there is again another kind of lyrical grammar in it. When a baby moans there is the smooth curve of music in the lower octave and when the baby screams, it is the elaboration of music in the higher octave. Like a magician producing strings out of sheer sand, there is magic in music spun out of air. If you have ears, listen. If you can compose, then it is wisdom. Listen to the voice of the air. Begin right away."

I was returning home by bus, seated next to a window with the cool breeze fanning my face. Ever since I met Pandit, all the windows in my being which had hitherto been tightly shut, seemed to be opening of their own accord. The days passed, rising and falling like the waves of music. And it was already Thursday.

Again the sandalwood smell of the incense sticks. And the smell of yeast-rich soft bread baked in the oven. The Harmony Music School.

"Vanakkam."

Hasan Pandit who was seated behind the harmonium writing some course details, looked up.

"Just a minute. Be seated." He spread out his fingers over the harmonium's keys pressing them soundlessly time and again as he continued writing. Over his head a yellow framed picture of the three saints, the Carnatic music trinity, adorned the wall.

"Did you go over the lesson that was taught last time?"

"Yes, I did. It was very good."

"What is the name of the note, Ga?"

"Gaandharam."

"Good. I had given details of practice in sarali varisai. Did you practise them?"

"No. I haven't yet."

"Why? Practice is very important, isn't it?"

I told him I did not have a harmonium.

"That is all right. But you must buy one. If you have an instrument, it will facilitate practice. As we go along there are going to be too many details requiring practice. One can postpone the purchase of an electronic keyboard. But, as of now, do buy the harmonium – even an old box should do."

In my jobless condition even attending the music classes was proving difficult. How could I dream of buying an instrument? "It is said in the Koran that music is haram, something not conducive for spiritual progress, hence avoidable. For that reason people in my house didn't allow me to learn music. I was nineteen then. There was a pandit called Srinivasa Sastry. He lived near the temple of Meenakshi Amman. I learnt music by offering every kind of service to him. I am saying all this to make the point that if you have the will you will find the way. Will he, who gave you the interest and the ability, conceal the needed instrument? You will surely get what you need."

That day I wrote down the remaining part of the basic lesson, as he dictated it to me. He then turned his harmonium towards me and asked me to play.

"This is the lowest note, Sa. Use your thumb. With the left hand, operate the bellows. The pressed air goes into the inside chambers. When you press a key the trapped air passes through a hole. On its way out, it makes the tongue-like reed vibrate. That is the sound of a note. Now ... play the note, Sa."

Excited, I pressed the key with my thumb, operating the bellows with my left hand. It was like the thrill of grey sparrows taking flight from a bush. Next came the lower level of the note, Ri. As my fingers continued with the keys for the higher Ga, the lower Ma and the Pa, I could sense the varying tones in which the harmonium was trying to talk with me. How could I ever describe the joy of it?

"All sounds are notes. This I have said already. And all sounds in the world can be resolved into the basic seven notes." He put down his glass of tea on the desk with a light sound. "This is a note." The window curtains fluttered in the breeze. "This is also music."

It was raining as I returned home in the bus. What a great musical instrument is rain! How many strings in this violin! What a big disc of music the ever revolving earth is! The reflection of the moon in the tank's water moves up and down, like the strings of the veena in motion. Each object has its own music. I was lost in amazement. When the eyes close, the world of the ears opens. "Listen to the voice of the air, the carrier of all sounds. Begin right away."

Monday and Thursday followed by another Monday and Thursday went by in succession, filling me with music. I was still unable to buy the harmonium. In the meantime, I had progressed with my lessons to more complex patterns in which the notes leapt from one level to another as in a dance. Shankara Koti, who also came to the classes on the same days that I did, had bought a new keyboard for ten thousand rupees just the day before. It could accurately produce the roar of the ocean's waves or even the ringing sound of a late night beetle. My emotions swung between wonderment on one side and despair at my helplessness on the other. I felt disheartened at the thought of continuing the lessons without the instrument. I walked aimlessly along Madurai's Koolavanigan Street.

"Hello, sir. How are you keeping?"

"I am fine, Shah Jehan."

"How come you are here sir? Please get into my car."

As the car picked up speed, the sweat evaporated from the back of my head – a pleasurable sensation. At the fruit juice joint on Town Hall Road we drank a glass of apple juice each.

"Where are you working now sir?"

"I am jobless, Shah Jehan. No work at the moment."

"What are you doing in Madurai with your shoulder bag and all?"

"I go for music lessons. I am learning to play the keyboard." As I was unemployed, I felt a mild sense of guilt in telling him about my music classes.

"Oh! That's interesting! Can you play songs?"

"No. I have just completed my first month."

"I am also interested in music, which you must be aware of. I also took music lessons for ten days. That was all. I always seem to leave things midway. Well. Which instrument do you have?"

"I am yet to buy one. I am on the lookout for a second hand harmonium."

Shah Jehan laughed.

"Very well. Let's go. Come home with me."

"No, Shah Jehan. Maybe some other time."

"Get into the car. You haven't visited me since I moved into my new house."

He seated me in his drawing room and went in. When he came back he was carrying a small wooden box. It was obvious that it was a harmonium. Placing it before me, he wiped the dust from the top. The case had a hinged lid. When I opened it, it looked like a Carnatic musician smiling sadly with his betel stained teeth. It was a very old instrument. The white keys had mica pasted on them. Their corners were chipped and the white had turned yellow with age. On either side of the harmonium, there were bronze handles of intricate workmanship. In front there were four stops which open the air chambers and regulate the volume of the sound. To facilitate the pulling of these stops, there were white marble knobs on them, resembling large buttons. Looking at it I knew at once that it was a single reed instrument. Like a child I lifted it up with both hands in order to check the bottom for any damage. Everything looked fine. As I placed it back, noticing something engraved between the two marble knobs, I wiped the dust with my hands. It read: Pitch Level Eight, Muruga Sikamani Bhagavathar, Kandaramanikkam.

Over the harmonium's mid octave black and white keys were stuck small square pieces of paper with the words – Sa, Ri, Ga, Ma, Pa, Da, Ni – written on them in order to identify them. A box made of superior teakwood and containing reeds made in Germany. It was in good condition with no leakage of air from the bellows.

"It is a very old box. Do all the notes have voice?"

"I don't get you."

"When you play the keys, do they all produce sound? Or are some of the keys defective?"

"Try it out yourself. It's been two years since I've even touched it. Once in a while I bring it out and wipe the dust off. Even that I haven't done for a month. You see, there are no houses around here and my mother wouldn't allow me to play it as she feared that it would attract snakes. Hoping that at least snakes would be attracted by my music, I would go to the terrace and play it. Muruga Bhagavathar taught me just one song. And I have forgotten half of that song now."

As I drank the cardamom flavoured tea served by Shah Jehan's wife, I caressed the keys of the harmonium with my right hand. They moved smoothly and did not get stuck at any point.

"Just try playing it. Or, pass it to me. I will play it for you." Turning the harmonium to his side, Shah Jehan sequentially pressed all the keys beginning at the lowest end. Perfect notes, strong and clear. No trace of discord.

"You can hear its sound seven houses away. That Bhagavathar treated it like a treasure. He saw that I was very enthusiastic. He suffered from asthma and was so poor that he could not buy medicines. Finally, he gave it to me."

"How much did you pay for it?"

"I won't tell you that. But when he gave it to me, he said, This is an instrument that I am used to. It is my deity. I am giving it to you only because you have a desire to have it. Don't allow it to collect cobwebs. This is the goddess Sarasvati. Take it. Play it and acquire fame. Now I want to give you the same advice. Take it. Play it and acquire fame."

The way he said it was very touching.

"If you tell me what I should pay, in a week's time ..."

"All right, give me a hundred rupees. A musical instrument should not be given free of cost."

"No. You must tell me the right price."

"I bought it for just that amount. Are you happy now?"

He accepted the money and demonstrated his acceptance by playing the prelude of the only song that he had learnt. His fingers were stiff and lacking in facility. He wrapped the instrument in newspapers, using a nylon chord to tie it up. He touched it with both hands and reverently brought them together in a gesture of prayer. He then held out the harmonium to me, handling it gently as if it was an infant too young to hold up its head straight. When I took leave after thanking him and came out, the moonlight had enveloped the metalled road. I felt the weight of the harmonium on my hand. With the nylon chord hurting my fingers, I transferred it to the other hand. The silence of the musical instrument was heavy. How deep would have been its meditation as it lay in the darkness of the room, in the silent company of innumerable ragas and notes, with no fingers to play it! What are the feelings of musical instruments when they are not played?

I sat at my preferred window seat on my way back. With the harmonium in my lap like a sleeping baby, I felt a new sense of responsibility. Just as the good angels in the magic tales, told by grandmothers, collude with the lesser spirits, creating a veritable tornado which relentlessly pursues the heavenly prince seeking marriage, the breeze that fanned my face pursued me and my harmonium, clamouring that we transform it into music.

When I carried the harmonium into the house, its strangeness drew everyone's attention. Placing it in the middle of the drawing room, I unwrapped it. The arrival of the harmonium caused neither joy nor sorrow to anyone. Making the habitual gesture of reverence towards it, I considered playing the basic lesson in music. Our home was a small one. At this hour of the night, who would tolerate an unemployed youth playing the harmonium? I picked up the harmonium and proceeded to the terrace.

A day before the full moon, the moonlight was soothing. The next music lesson was three days away. I drew the harmonium close to me. I played the note, Sa, of the lower octave. I felt as if I was unlocking the door of a room which had been confined to darkness for long. With my middle finger I pressed the Pa key and with my little finger the Sa key of the middle octave. Together the three notes sounded like the buzzing of a bee hovering around a garland of mixed flowers. I tried to align my voice with the sounds of the harmonium. To begin with, it was slightly discordant. It gradually improved and when the matching became perfect, it was an exhilarating experience.

All other aspects of my being are dissipated, all that remains of me is my disembodied voice alone. And soon I find my identity slipping away completely in the presence of pure notes in harmony with one another.

Hesitantly I begin with the basics – first at a slow pace, then a medium one and finally the fast pace. Now I progress to jandai varisai, the repetitive note patterns in which each note seems to be followed by its own shadow. My fingers are now at ease and the effect is good. The ascent is progressive, starting with the lower notes, deliberating over them, gaining impetus and leaping to the higher note at the right moment. And then it is the descent, like a piece of cloth being blown by the wind. A few moments of rest now at Sa and back to more ambitious ventures, to relatively complex patterns. My fingers move over the keys with more and more ease transporting me into the ocean of music. The harmonium is floating in it. My feet are transformed into the tail of a mermaid and I begin to swim in the ocean. The stars above touch me and swim along beside me. Another huge wave envelops me. It breaks against the violet coloured door of Harmony Music School and scatters into water droplets. The door opens into a desert expanse. Only sand as far as the eyes can see. The dusty breeze slaps my face. From afar floats in the sound of a hymn in Arabic. Undulations made by the wind on the surface of the desert look like impressions made by the movements of serpents. Mirages of the simmering air. In space and on the sand are impressions of the air. At a distance are two harmoniums.

The sand is being blown into the air. What is Hasan Pandit doing there with his hands buried in the sand? As the wind blows away the sand, the buried harmonium slowly becomes visible. His fingers are continuing to play.

"Pandit Sir, can you play Tansen's famous raga Deepak?" Hasan Pandit's fingers pause and hesitate. His fingers move in the air rehearsing it and then he starts to play. As he plays, sparks of fire emerge from the Pa key. They break into flames. The harmonium begins to burn. The air shudders. Pandit Hasan's fingers catch fire, like the wicks of candles. Before the harmonium is completely burnt, I pull out the keys. Growing larger in size, rings of smoke rise and disappear. I speed across the sand dunes, my feet slipping in the process. The keys which I hold tightly keep falling until I am left with just one white key. On it is a small square piece of paper with the note Ga written on it. "How can I compose music

with just one note, Panditji? Especially when that note happens
to be the higher Ga? Is it possible, Panditji?" Strewn all over the
desert among the snake like undulations are my own footprints
and the keys of my harmonium.

There is someone lying there, covered in green rexine. I awaken
him. A bhagavathar with matted hair.

"Sir, I have only one key with me – the one which produces the
higher Ga sound. Could you exchange it with me for a harmonium?"

"Yes, I will."

When the green rexine cover was removed, there emerged a white
harmonium made of ivory which was so small that it could be held
in the palm of one's hand.

"This came down from the sky during a hailstorm. Do you want
to have it?"

"Yes. But isn't it far too small?"

"As you keep playing it, it will grow larger in size. I will give it to
you. But you have to give me something in return."

"What?"

"You have to give me all your fingers." The fingers of the speaker
had been burnt entirely and both his hands looked like the edges
of two harmonium keys. On his forearm was tattooed the name
Muruga Bhagavathar.

Calling out the name of Panditji, I begin running into the mirage.
My feet are sinking into quicksand. In front of me are green coloured
waves, roaring and whirling as a bid by the sea to overpower the
desert. The expanse of sand is disappearing. Clutching the solitary
key in my hand, I scream in fear. As a wave strikes my face and
passes, I find myself surrounded completely by the sea. I swim
along with the seahorses. The key in my hand turns into a fish and
slips away from me. From the bluish green expanse of the sea, a
harmonium floats towards me dispersing bubbles on every side.
Holding the harmonium close to me with my left hand, playing it
with the right hand, I swim in the ocean at a depth beyond the
reach of sunlight. In the mountain ranges deep below – which are
encrusted with slabs of salt – are engraved the symbols of Western

music. Wearing a miner's lamp on his forehead, Hasan Pandit is busy rapidly noting down these notations.

"Today is Monday, Panditji."

"So what? This is a music class for the submerged cities."

I woke up making a stroke with my legs as if I was swimming in the ocean. The ocean had dried up and I was back on land. I was lying on the dew drenched cement floor of the terrace. All that remained of the sea was the still water in the glass in front of me.

Going down, I found everybody was asleep. I was exhausted. Supper had been left for me in the kitchen.

Tomorrow morning I should practise the taattu varisai – the leaping patterns of notes. The white keys of the harmonium have collected dirt over the years. All the screws have rusted. The bellow needs to be cleaned and attended to. With these thoughts I fell asleep. In the morning I took the harmonium to the terrace. Muthu Vinayagam happened to be there.

"Hey! Are you intending to become a Carnatic musician? These things only herald poverty in the house."

I ignored him and plunged into efforts to give my dear harmonium a facelift. I brought a screwdriver, some old cloth and a small mugful of water. After wiping off the dust I moistened the cloth and cleaned the white keys with it. Not having been played for ages, they were dirty like the dark night. Patches of dirt all over, appearing like stains. No amount of cleaning seemed to make a difference.

With effort, I unscrewed the rusted and stubborn screws. I took off the wooden lid above the key panel. Now dismantling the keys became easy. Below them were strands of cobwebs, dust and tiny sesamelike droppings of insects. Neither blowing off nor wiping could get rid of the dust. I placed all the black and white keys on the floor in their right order. Placed on the floor, the row of keys looked very attractive.

The brass reeds inside the harmonium had minute engravings that said, Made in Germany. Beginning with the smallest and increasing in order of size, the reeds were finely fitted. I slowly removed the stops which regulated the air flow into the many chambers of the harmonium, chambers that looked like the separate containers for condiments used in the kitchen. The wires were so rusted that pulling them out was quite difficult. Inside the harmonium chamber two silverfish were alive though they looked very pale. Perhaps they had once been nurtured by the vibrant music of Muruga Bhagavathar. Or, perhaps they were the remains of the ragas that came alive with his music. In any case, how wonderful it was to live in romance with music in the darkness of the harmonium's chamber! When I tapped at the sides, both the silverfish, which were still dreaming about the lost era of music, scrambled out, unable to bear the sunlight.

I wiped the dust from inside the air ducts. Now the harmonium was in pieces – the keys, the knobs, the screws, and the lid. Both outside and inside, the wood which the harmonium was made of had lost its natural appearance and looked faded. Looking at the keys reminded me of betel stained teeth again. The colour was detestable.

It was then that an idea struck me, Why not paint it to make it look new?

I bought fifty millilitre tins of black and white Asian Paint, some varnish, a small brush and sandpaper with fine grains as suggested by the shopkeeper.

I gently rubbed the surface of the keyboard pieces with sandpaper. In order to ensure the right order during the reassembly, I marked the numbers with a pencil at the back of all the pieces. I then carefully applied paint over the black and white pieces like my elder sister applying nail polish on her fingernails. I varnished the harmonium's case and left it to dry in the shade. I had bought new screws to replace the old ones. It was eleven when I finished it all.

Today is Monday. There will be a music lesson in the evening. The paint has to dry up before that. Surely it will. I should take my new harmonium today and demonstrate to Hasan Pandit the lesson on basic notes.

By three in the afternoon, the keys were dry. The varnished harmonium looked beautiful having regained its natural wood colour. I refitted the stops and assembled the keys in their order. With every step it looked more and more appealing.

It is now a brand new harmonium. How beautiful it is! I longed to play it just once, to complete one cycle of ascent and descent. The very feel of the keys now seemed like soft bread. It was now five in the evening. Normally I should have left for Madurai by half past three. Hurriedly I put the screws back in their place. There was no time to play it. I now felt that it would be appropriate to play it to Hasan Pandit and get his blessings. He would surely be happy with that.

I wrapped the harmonium with an English daily and tied it with nylon chord. I boarded the bus to Madurai with it in hand.

By the time I reached Hasan Pandit's room, it was seven o'clock. He was absorbed in the photocopy of a book in English on music. On seeing me he removed his spectacles, closed the book and smiled.

The aroma of soft bread and the sandal fragrance of the udubatti in the room were enticing.

Before he could enquire into reasons for my delay, with bubbling enthusiasm I volunteered that I had bought the harmonium from a friend. Hasan Pandit helped me undo the knots of the nylon chord. I unwrapped the harmonium.

"Instrument with reeds made in Germany. A very old one. That's why ..."

Showing understanding, Pandit Hasan laughed. I sought his blessings. With those dark fingers that make music, he touched my head.

"Sir, there is a call for you," came the voice of the mansion's manager from below. Hasan Pandit said, "Start playing. I will be back," and walked towards the stairs.

I looked at the framed picture of the trinity of Carnatic music.

Dwelling on the meditative ambience of the room filled with music, I closed my eyes and prayed. After touching the harmonium with a reverential gesture, I pressed the bellows with my left hand and the Sa key of the middle octave with my right thumb. There was absolutely no sound!

Operating the bellows with a little more force, I now pressed three keys simultaneously – the lower Sa with the thumb, the Pa with the middle finger, and the higher Sa with the little finger. All the notes were mute. They did not produce any sound. With rising panic, I worked the bellows fiercely, as I pressed the keys of the lower Ri, higher Ga and the lower Ma. In place of raga Maya Malava Gowla, there was only the hissing of the air. I pushed the bellows even harder, desperately pressed several keys – the black and the white, the higher and the lower octaves. None of the notes came alive, there was no sound at all. My dear harmonium, whither have all your clear and distinct notes gone? Like the parting breaths of Muruga Sikamani Bhagavathar when he was dying of asthma, the harmonium was only emitting puffs of air. The world was darkening before me. Smoke rings from the udubatti grew larger and larger as they moved relentlessly towards me.

ॐ

MADHURI MOHAN SHANBHAG

JUNGLE

———◆———

TRANSLATED FROM MARATHI BY PARNAL CHIRMULEY
first published in Vipulshree, October 2002, Pune

Chitra woke that morning feeling a little befuddled. The window wasn't in its usual place; and an unfamiliar birdcall filled her with sudden joy. The usual clamour of honking vehicles and clanking metal was not with her today. Instead there was the eerie stillness of the jungle and the indefinable scent of clean air. Lying there, she recalled her journey by train from Mumbai to Londha and from there, the jeep ride en route to Goa, the turn off the highway into stacks of wooded hills, to reach the village at the base of one. By the time they got to the tiled cottage on the hilltop, it was nearly afternoon. They had eaten and rested, wandered about, and returned in the evening.

Chitra stretched languorously then, bringing her hands together, she murmured the sloka that she always said, first thing each morning, since childhood: "karaagre vasate Lakshmi, karamuule Sarasvati, karamadhye tu Govinda, prabhaate karadarshanam." She slipped out of bed and, so as not to wake Kishor, moved noiselessly to the window. She remembered having opened it to let in the night breeze. Kishor must have closed it some time in the night. Gently she slid back the latch and spread the shutters wide to let the morning in. She filled her lungs with the damp green smell of the jungle.

Since she arrived yesterday, she had been overtaken by this smell, this air, this greenery. Deep down inside her there was something that throbbed awake with this jungle, making this place her own. Like one possessed, she kept saying to Kishor, "It's such a beautiful forest – as if no one has ever even lost their way in here. We must stay here for at least four days."

"Chitra! You know the Katekars won't agree. We have to go to Goa. Two days here and four in Goa."

"How about if just the two of us stay on? I really like it here. It's, it's like meeting an old friend."

"And to think that you spent your whole life in Mumbai. Have you ever seen a forest before, apart from the one in the Khandala ghat on the way to Poona, and the one full of people in Lonavala?"

"That's just why. We can go to Goa some other time. Please Kishor!"

"Let's see. If they don't agree, let me see if we can go down later, by bus."

The joy on her face had cheered him as well. It made him happy.

She let the morning air wash over her for a while. In the sky, far to the right, a ray or two of red seemed to waver over the black and brown hilltops. Everything was still shrouded in darkness so you could see the shapes of the trees but not their colours. She simply took it in for a few minutes, until her eyes adjusted themselves and the shroud melted away.

This spacious cottage with its seven or eight rooms was quite secluded. It belonged to a friend of the Katekars. The hill sloped away just outside the cottage. At its base were little houses with red, orange, and brown tiles, either crowded together wherever there was space, or loosely spread out. A winding dirt track went down the middle of the hill, all the way to the bottom, where the slopes of other hills rose abruptly. Here it met the tarred road that led to the highway. And right there in the cleft, was a happy little waterfall, scurrying along, spraying a mist of droplets like clouds of cotton wool, as it passed under the road and disappeared into the valley below. A little bridge there had steps that led down to the shallow pool beneath the waterfall.

Chitra strained her eyes in its direction. In the soft morning light, it looked like a jagged line of milk, this waterfall that flowed only in the rains. Last evening they had driven back to the base of the hill. She had stood under the waterfall. Oblivious of passers by or of Kishor she waded through knee deep water to stand there under the flow. She raised her face and was caught by its fine spray. Only the Katekars, their children and the watchman of the cottage on the hilltop were there. Plus a few noisy travellers who'd stopped especially to see this waterfall.

She moved into the waterfall. The force grew stronger. Kishor was signalling to her not to go further. He was moving towards her.

Chitra, stop. You'll catch a cold. And she had moved deeper into the intensifying flow.

From the moment she arrived it was as if the jungle had cast a spell on her. She simply could not express this to Kishor. Stray thoughts came floating through her mind: I am a schoolteacher. My husband Kishor – is a bank clerk. It is our responsibility to get his two sisters married, so we have no children. Each day moves along the ordained pattern and ends at the bedside in the predictability of the next day. Such a joyless routine, a tedium caught only by the skilled poem of a Vinda or a Mardhekar ... And I'm here today because Kishor's LTC would have otherwise lapsed. The Katekars had organized this trip and invited Chitra and Kishor – so they could split the expenses. A four day change. But something had changed forever the moment they arrived.

Chitra stood wantonly under the torrent. That little waterfall drenched her body, pounding down, it flowed and flowed right into her being. Her body moulded to its surge, her chest, her belly, the torrent infiltrated her skin with its tender, yet powerful blows, permeated blood, sinews, bone. Chitra was enthralled. She embraced the water, bore its onslaught. A jungle grew inside her, surrounded by green hills, changing her before a ray of light could penetrate the not very tall, but dense and stocky jungle. She had no idea of the tangle inside her. The falling stream of water had awakened the jungle.

Bit by bit it had begun to course inside her. She felt the voices of the birds and animals within. A searing thirst smouldered deep in this jungle. Strange notions that she could not quite articulate thrashed inside her. Would surrendering herself to the waterfall slake the thirst? She moved a little further in.

The water could beat down on her back. She did not want anyone to see her, the ravenous expression of her face. Gently she received the stream on her breasts. Then, turning, she arched her back and took the flow on her midriff, her belly and further down, then her thighs, feet. It must happen. She was in deep now, up to her thighs, and the waterfall was all over her. She shut her eyes to conceal her pleasure, her restlessness clearly visible on her face.

"Chitra. Come out now. What are you doing there like a mad woman. Everybody is laughing at you. There's a current. It will carry you away. Come out."

K ishor's calls broke the spell. On the plinth by the highway stood someone with a camera. Someone else had got off a truck and was filling a water bottle at the fall. She quickly climbed out of the water. The cool breeze raised a welter of goose pimples. Her padar clung to shapely dark breasts, nipples erect, all hidden by the dark purple sari, the goose pimples around them only she could feel. She turned away, pulled the padar slightly off her body, wrung it, and wrapped it neatly around herself again. She took the towel from Kishor and hid her ears and face in it, flushing hot in spite of the cold. She climbed into the jeep without a word. Guilt embraced her on the drive back. Guilt, and a little fear. Ever since her arrival, she had felt a deep connection with this jungle. The falling stream had reaffirmed this with its touch. The sound of the jungle inside her, the half-awakened beasts within, made her shiver.

"I told you not to stand under the waterfall like that. You are shivering so."

She just sat there without speaking. The jeep wound up the hill and stopped under the porch at the cottage. Chitra still did not raise her head. As she got off Katekar vahini said kindly, "Change your clothes and have a hot cup of tea. I'll ask the watchman's wife to make some. Have you brought a shawl?"

"Uhmm. Hm."

"Then put it on. The chill will be gone in a minute. Little children are used to playing in water. But we women fall ill at the slightest excuse. Besides in Mumbai, water flows only from the taps. There is that big sea, the chowpatties, but who has the time to take a dip?"

Lowering her voice, she said conspiratorially, "And if the chill does not go, you have Kishor. You don't even have children."

Kishor must have overheard her as he sat there on the veranda, waiting for the tea.

Without replying to Katekarbai, Chitra lowered her head and made straight for the bathroom. By the time she came out, drying her wet hair, the jungle was asleep.

The watchman's wife brought hot, steaming tea and upma. Katekar was saying that they should go into the forest the next day. About two hours by road, apparently one could spot herds of deer along the way. If they could leave by nine thirty, baths and breakfast finished?

Kishor turned towards her and said gently, "I told Katekar about your idea. He said it would be better as we would spend a lot less. We stay in Goa on just the last day, and take the train that night. It seems it is possible to see all the temples in one day.

That night Kishor held her close. Then, the nightly marital ritual over, he fell asleep. Chitra lay tossing, like a ravenous beast that had been thrown a handful of straw.

And now, standing by the window, she could vaguely make out the milky line of the waterfall. She stood there till the colours of the morning spread across the sky. The outlines of the trees and houses grew sharper, the birds, louder. Wisps of smoke from the huts below dispersed into the sky. The thunderous waterfall was now clearly visible – like arms spread wide and beckoning. Quickly she closed the window and went over to the bed.

"Come on Kishor, wake up. It's such a lovely morning. Let's go for a long walk."

"What time is it?"

Chitra bent over to look at his wristwatch on the side table. The blinking hands said a quarter to six.

"Quarter to six. Come on."

"Give me a break! Last night was so tiring and here there's no rush to get to the office. I am not getting up till eight."

"Okay, I'll go for a little stroll then."

"Don't go too far. Stay close to the bungalow. And come back soon. We'll have breakfast. We have to visit the Siddheshwar temple remember? Don't go standing under the waterfall like a being possessed, like you did yesterday."

"Oh all right. How many times are you going to nag. I did say I was sorry didn't I?"

He turned over and wrapped the sheet around himself.

She pulled on her shoes, wrapped a shawl around the sleeveless maxi, and set off.

A ll the windows were closed. The cottage had just seven, eight rooms. The watchman lived in one. A kitchen, dining room, one hall. The Katekars had the room next to theirs. Someone had probably come in last night; a Maruti Gypsy stood next to their jeep.

All kinds of plants and shrubs sprouted by the compound wall. She plucked a bunch of white flowers. As she came out on to the road, their harsh sweet smell had seeped through her palms to her nostrils. She decided it would be better to take the road going straight down than to walk round the house. The little path was visible. She had seen the watchman's son go scampering down it. From between the dense growth, this dew drenched, red-earth path beckoned. She could barely see the colour of the tender grass on the verge but she could imagine its feel. There was the waterfall through the tangle of shrubs and trees. In the east were clear signs of daybreak but the trees made it seem like it was still dark.

She picked up a slender fallen branch and, brandishing it, she stepped briskly into the fragrance of wildflowers and the little pathway. Her feet sank into the red earth of the slope. Both sides looked deserted. As she walked on another path branched off downwards. The road below was nowhere in sight, but Chitra was not afraid now. She'd caught the trick of walking through dense trees rather than along a road.

It was brighter now.

When the broad flow of the water caught her eye, she left the road and took the narrow path. She was eager to cross over, to stand there and watch the waterfall. The jungle with its crashing waterfall that had come awake inside her strained to meet this jungle on the outside. Her breath caught, stifling her.

Just then she turned to the sound of footfalls behind her. A broad palm clamped down firmly on her mouth. Another arm came up from behind her. In an instant she was lifted gently and carried off the path, towards the darkness of the trees. Set down against a low branch, a weight pressed heavily against her, and a pair of thick, hot lips crushed hers. She got no time to scream. Gathering all her strength, she pushed against the body trying to break free. But legs bare to the thighs locked her tight. And then her resistance waned. She let the touch wash over her like the gush of water. The jungle inside her met the torrent and yielded to its force.

Like two serpents entwined, biting hissing tails erect, moving apart only to come together again. To love like this but To love like the beast To reach that note in the blood With the strength of many past lives ...

The remembered poem pulsated through her body. She relinquished every element of her being to its power, as she had to the waterfall. She bore it all and called out for more. She felt the jungle inside her throb with all its creatures wandering unfettered, wallowing in the surge.

She looked closely at his face as it moved away from hers and could only see its outline in the morning light.

In a satiated voice he said throatily, "I saw you under the waterfall yesterday and was obsessed. Forgot myself. On the highway, I had stopped for a cup of tea. Some tourists spoke of a waterfall three or four kilometres from the fork. I turned my Gypsy around to take a couple of pictures. Stopped the car at the road. At the railing I saw you, wet under that fall, flaying like a hungry snake. I took a picture or two. You didn't notice. I saw the water fall in your lap and I decided to ditch the journey. Through the night you were before my eyes, getting drenched, possessing me. When I woke up and looked outside, you were at your window, arms spread wide. Thought I would swoop down and carry you away, like a kite snatches its prey. I saw you come out. And immediately guessed you would go to the waterfall. I followed. You left the road and took the path and I lost control. You crossed the road and I ran after you. Do you understand?"

A sigh escaped her.

"I am sorry ..."

Chitra shut her eyes. Yesterday, as she emerged from the water she had felt a pair of eyes on her. She had felt them flit over her as she squeezed out her padar and wrapped it around herself. Butterfly wings had passed through the towel Kishor handed her, peacock feathers brushed over her limbs to make her hair stand on end. She'd not met those eyes yet the chase had begun. Relentless and restive, now the hunt was finally over. Here were those eyes. The awakening jungle inside her had bewitched them, drawn them here.

Chitra opened her eyes. The silhouette was gone. She gathered up her clothes and pulled them on. She could see scratches. Faint teeth marks. She could remember biting those sinuous arms, thighs, back. The corner of her mouth was bruised. The bite on the thigh was black and blue with coagulated blood. She ran a tentative fingertip over it and pain shot through her. She wrapped the shawl around her and stood up. Around her all was quiet as if they had witnessed nothing. A morning sun played on the treetops. She turned to look at the waterfall. It was crashing down, but perhaps a little slower. She listened carefully and thought she heard its song of joy.

She walked slowly back to her room. Kishor was still wrapped up in the sheets. Under the shower in the bathroom, as she stroked her body, every tight snarl of a benumbed mind came undone.

"Come on out, quick, the tea is ready."

Mechanically she went through the motions of getting dressed. Everyone was having breakfast on the veranda.

"Come, the pohé's real good, you must be really hungry na. You're back from a walk so early?"

She swallowed the lump in her throat and pulled the plate towards her.

"Look, your upper lip is swollen."

"Arré, something must have bit me while I was out walking."

"Wait, let me get the cream from my bag. Sometimes these insects are poisonous."

As Kishor stood up to go inside, Mrs Katekar asked in a soft knowing voice: "Are you sure it was an insect?"

Kishor reddened. Tears began to gather at the corners of Chitra's eyes. "It really burns, god knows what kind of beast that was."

Katekar called to the watchman and asked, "Did someone stay in the other room last night?"

"Hahn saheb."

"Then go call him. Maybe he wants to come to the Siddheshwar temple. We can all go together. It will be company, and the expenses will be shared."

"No saheb, that saheb seems a little eccentric. Yesterday at the waterfall he asked if there was a room up here. I said yes. Are these people staying there? I said yes."

"Then?"

"He came with me. Ate in his room. Said he was a photographer. Was out scouting locations for an ad agency. He said, Tomorrow, I'll go to the Siddheshwar with these people."

"Arré, why didn't you tell us?"

"God knows what happened in the morning, saheb. He gave me a huge bakshis and said he was leaving. If I stay, the jungle will gobble me up, he said."

"The jungle?"

"It does have wild animals, but they rarely come close to our houses. Occasionally they drag off cattle, but mostly there are only deer."

"Chitratai, you were chattering away yesterday. Today you are totally silent."

"Yesterday's soaking has given me a heavy head."

Kishor put the tube of cream in her hand.

Throughout the journey she was quiet. In the Siddheshwar temple she sat on the cold floor, the puja was performed in the sanctum. The smooth black pindi shone in the light of the freshly lit lamp. Next to her sat Kishor reciting a stotra.

Her mind raced as she listened to the words. The dry and routine lovemaking of two years of married togetherness. Kishor, sensitive, loving her more than he did his own life, yet ... The madness of the morning's experience possessed her once more, silencing the jungle and its beasts. That accident. If it had not come her way, she would never have known the jungle inside her. But the jungle stirred, how could she remain in the embrace of this discontent forever after. The sanskar of husband and domesticity were torn asunder in just one half hour, and now life would pass in its eternal shadow.

If only she hadn't come here.

She shut her eyes. The intensity of the morning's experience looped under her lids, over and over again. Tears gathered.

"Kishor, I ... I feel really unwell."

He put his palm to her forehead and said, "Yes, it does feel a bit warm. I have a Crocin. Take the tablet and lie down quietly. Get into the jeep."

"Kishor, this jungle is beginning to scare me. Lets go back."

"Crazy girl! Yesterday you said you wanted to stay here, that you liked it, and now ..."

"I think I am getting a fever."

"I kept telling you ... You were soaked yesterday. Look at me. We'll see how it goes. If the fever doesn't come down with the Crocin, we'll go back to Londha. We'll see if we can get tickets to go back. If not, we can go to Belgao and try for bus tickets. Now stop worrying. I'm here."

She held on to his hand and sat quietly. She'd lead a life hiding this jungle within but first it was imperative to get out of this one. As an anchor, there was that faint touch. Just a touch ... the steep climb ...

She let go of the tear at the corner of the eye.

crp

JHARESWAR CHATTOPADHYAY

THEIR ONLY ONE

———◆———

TRANSLATED FROM BANGLA BY TIRNA RAY
first published in Sambad Pratidin, March 2002, Kolkata

NOMINATED BY DEBES RAY

Nirmala fastened the loops of the mosquito net on the bedposts and sighed.

Paramesh lay on the bed, on his side, his face buried in the pillow. Quiet. Nirmala undid her hair, setting the bangles and shankha around her wrist tinkling. Paramesh turned over to look at her, and Nirmala said morosely, "Here are we lying in the comfort of a mattress. And he in that narrow iron bed."

"That's the way hostel beds are."

"But aren't they a little too cramped?" Nirmala asked, tucking in the net.

"Hmm."

The memories ... still so fresh and abundant. Even the day before they left for this place, Nirmala tucked in the mosquito net for Suman. Today at the hostel, has the boy tucked in his net ...

"The bedposts at the hostel are so wobbly. Will he be able to fix the net?"

Paramesh feigned confidence, reassuring her. "Three boys together in a room. They'll manage, don't worry."

The hotel room. Grills behind glass sheets, heavy curtains against the windows. A night lamp suffused one corner. In the soft light, Nirmala ran her fingers through her hair. The boy, she thought, was so studious. At home, he didn't care to eat unless she nagged him. Like a child. Every time he misplaced a shirt, pants, books, he screamed, Ma-a-a-a ...

"Ma-a-a-a." The cry caught Nirmala unawares. She rushed to the window. The curtains rippled. There were ripples in Nirmala's heart. Who! Was Suman outside the window?

Nirmala jerked the curtain aside. On the main road, the streetlights dozed. The huge Life Insurance hoarding was lit by bulbs in a wire frame that set its logo – the flame in the safety of cupped palms – flickering. The tall buildings looked bleak with deserted attics. The D V Campus, the school grounds, its residences, the hills, its boulders – all were heavy with night and darkness.

About two kilometres away was Suman's college, opposite which stood the hostel building – a solid structure of cement and stone, each one by one-and-a-half-foot wide – massive.

Asleep in the old block and new block were six or seven hundred first, second ... fourth years. The departments of Mechanical, Information Technology – all in one block. Computer Science, Metallurgy, Textile, Management in the other. Within the campus, on a stretch of grass, stood a big tree with clusters of red flowers. On so mild a night, it slumbered, its leaves drooping.

Dew misted the halogen lights on either side of the hostel gate. Nirmala's eyes grew misty.

Paramesh asked softly, "Can't sleep?"

Listless, Nirmala rested her head on the pillow, next to Paramesh's. And then, suddenly, she was hugging him, saying softly, "Listen ..."

"Hmm?"

"If we had another one ..."

Her eyes glistened. Her cheek on Paramesh's chest, tears – warm and sad – soaked his chest. The appeal was poignant, but there was no passion in the embrace. A dying fire, a moving submission.

Paramesh's entire body was rigid, reserved.

"Remember those times? So many family responsibilities. Even if we had had another one, could we have brought up the child properly?"

"Perhaps not."

"Then?"

Paramesh wasn't sure whether his question reflected restraint, or was merely evading the sense of loss. Despite the apparent warmth of the embrace, her voice was sad. "It would have been a financial strain. It would have been hard, but now, it is even harder."

Paramesh didn't try to find an answer. Decades of rationalizing shattered in one blow. Nirmala's tears melted his heart. "Maybe it is a bit too late ..." he whispered, gathering himself together, trying to focus on what needed to be done the next day.

Then, he said gently, "Sleep. We'll have to catch the train tomorrow ..."

Geyser water in the hotel bathroom. After a quick bath, Nirmala went up to the terrace to dry her synthetic sari. Beyond the houses and factory chimneys, beyond the coconut groves that graced the neighbourhood, lay the lush fields. The floating clouds engulfed the farmlands that cultivated leaf food for the caterpillars that made pure silk. A wedge of sun swept aside the wet clouds in the eastern sky. The synthetic sari basked in the warm breeze.

Nirmala gazed at the massive Nandi Hills as she combed out her wet hair. How they stooped, enduring the stony burden of centuries, their corrugated peaks distributing the load on knees, elbows, neck and back. Black clouds hovered behind the white before engaging the crests in a misty game.

Nirmala felt the sting of brittle raindrops on cheeks and hands.

From the staircase she called out to Paramesh, "Can you come up?"

Towel and pyjama in the big bag; paste, brush, soap and razor in the bag pockets, Paramesh was packing.

He came to the door. "Coming."

"Lock the door behind you."

The terrace: only a few steps from the third floor. Nirmala drew his attention to the peaks. Black, knotty clouds spread eagled against them. The thirsty stones seemed to soften, as if to wring out the old water sucked up from the heart of Nature over the centuries.

"Remember the trip the college organized on Suman's first day, when parents and freshers went around the place? Did we visit this mountain cradle?"

Paramesh, in full sleeved shirt and a light woollen jacket, adjusted his glasses to look into the distance.

"Mudenahalli village ..."

"Hmm. Where we saw the museum – his coat-pant, books, glasses, pen."

"You mean, M Vishweshvaraiya's? There are any number of technical colleges named after him."

Nirmala's forehead wrinkled as she tried to picture the hill-village. "Vishweshvaraiyaji was just a village boy, son of a farmer. Wasn't he?"

"Yes, his life story is engraved on the marble slab."

"A farmer's son grew up to be such a successful engineer!"

Paramesh laughed. "Just a successful engineer? He even gave Gandhiji moments of worry. When Gandhiji appealed to the nation to spin the charkha, produce khadi, Vishweshvaraiya's inspiring line was: Industrialize! Or else, a country with crores of people will just lag behind ...

But Nirmala was not listening. She stood gazing at the village against the hills. "Maybe not as big, but even if our Suman could be a little like him and do something with his life ..."

The sky, framed by the bus window. Nirmala looked at the floating clouds and said, "It might rain." The road piggybacked on a reddish-pebbled way. The bus crossed the steep slope of the road. Paramesh said, "The sky here is so unpredictable ..." Before he finished, the conductor rang the bell, "College-stop." They got off. "Aich." The conductor mashed the word between tongue and palate. The bus moved on, towards the city.

A bag on Paramesh's shoulder. VIP suitcase in Nirmala's hand. A cloth festoon across a tree: Cyber Stop. New comp lingo on the tree's worn out, age-old bark.

Here was the iron gate. The engineering college campus. Fenced gardens, fields, tar-coated paths, a sprawling three storied

Sir Mokshagudam Vishweshvaraiya (1861-1962) was a gifted engineer. During the colonial days, when there was little infrastructure and no government support, he was the brain behind several engineering projects including the huge Krishnarajsagar Dam in Karnataka. About a mile and a half long and 140 ft. tall, it has 711 doors that open or close automatically depending upon the water level. Amongst his other engineering achievements are the automatic doors for Khadakwasla Dam near Pune (the Panama Canal borrowed the design from it) and the control systems on the Moosi river that protect Hyderabad even today.

building. The white house behind was the workshop. Looking at all of this for one last time, Paramesh was lost in thought. "Living so far away was the boy's destiny, away from his parents ... food habits ... language ... state ... was everything preordained ..."

Nirmala glanced at the empty college premises, the guardhouse. In a few hours we'll be going back, she thought, we'll leave this place, this state and return to our own territory. But Suman ... he'll continue to stay on ... Till yesterday, he tossed his bag on the bed as soon as he was home from school, and shouted, Maa ... give me something to eat. Here at the hostel who's going to do all that for him?

Nirmala's eyes were brimming over.

Quite a few private cars and KSTC buses went by. Paramesh said, "Come, let's cross. Let's go to the hostel."

The bag on Paramesh's shoulders was heavy. So was his heart. Suman-ré, if only you had managed to rank well in the West Bengal Joint Entrance exam. Down on the list, lost, everybody advised: You'll just about manage to get him into one of the new engineering colleges here. Try outside Kolkata. It would be a wise career move. Well Suman, you've made it to a good college, a good branch. But ...

Nirmala and Paramesh wiped their shoes on the thick rubber mats. Just as they wanted to wipe so many things from off their minds.

The watchman stopped them at the hostel entrance. "Where to?"
"Room number 104."

Paramesh knocked at the door. The bolt was sliding back. Nirmala rushed in asking, "What are you still doing here? Don't you have a class?"

"Yes."

"Why aren't you ready yet?"

"Loo and brush over. Now I'll take a bath."

"When do your classes start?" Nirmala asked while checking Suman's mosquito net. It was still draped. She started unfastening the loops from the stands. Paramesh stopped her. "Let him learn to do things for himself. Can you do that for him everyday?"

"I know, but at least as long as I am here ..."

Paramesh pointed to the other two beds. "Then do it for them too."

One was Bharat Prakash's. He was from UP. The bed on this side, still a mess, belonged to Ritesh from Bihar who said, "Aunty, please, I'll manage."

"You'll have to, in any case. But let me do it for you today since your mother is not here."

"Thank you Aunty." He was in a wet towel and a little self-conscious about changing in front of aunty.

Paramesh looked at Nirmala, "Let's go. He's uncomfortable."

As they stepped outside, they bumped into the pant-shirt gentleman. His middle-aged wife, in a green shawl and sweater, was beside him. They had bags in their hands and on their shoulders. Paramesh paused a little and asked, "Leaving today?"

"What else?"

"Which room is your son in?"

"125."

"Branch?"

"Mechanical."

"Your room number?" asked the man.

"Right here, this one."

The wife asked, "Branch?"

"Telecom."

"Good. We got our son into the mainstream."

"Right decision, but ..."

The couple looked at them quizzically.

"Our only child. Leaving him here is a little painful ..." said Paramesh lamely.

The gentleman thrust his hands into his pant pockets and said gravely, "No choice. We have to leave them for the sake of their future."

Paramesh accepted his logic. "How many children, Dada?"

The green shawl, fair mother looked pale. "Only one child."

"Oh." The words were a balm on Paramesh's heart. "Where do you stay?"

"Durgapur." The minutes were ticking away on the dial of the watch. The man took two steps forward on the mosaic floor and said, "Okay. Thank you."

The corridor took a turn after room 106. Within a few steps another couple called out from the other side: "What news?"

"All's fine. How come you're here? We thought you had a daughter."

"We just met her at the town hostel. A friend's son has got into Information Technology. We were here to see him."

"Room number?"

"Umm ... new block," said the wife.

Paramesh walked with them. "You are from Salt Lake, aren't you?"

"Yes. Near tank number eight," the husband mumbled.

Paramesh asked in a low voice, "How does it feel to leave her behind?"

The man stopped walking. Face to face with Paramesh, he looked him straight in the eyes. "Actually, our only child. Painful ..."

"I know." Paramesh's voice was gruff.

The wife dragged a button into the buttonhole of the sweater, trying carefully to hide the twitching pain in her chest. "What to do? Shouldn't we help her stand on her own feet? In Kolkata, even if you raise an objection they don't care to show you your answer sheet. And here, they give you a copy of the answer script at the exam hall itself. So modern ..."

"Absolutely. Besides, everything here is computerized." Paramesh, walking with them, reached the veranda office room. A few parents were sitting anxiously on the chairs and bench. A burnished bench with a backrest, stuffed with foam. The day's dailies, *Deccan Herald*, *The Times of India*, *The Hindu*, *Pragyabani* in Kannada were strewn over the centre table.

An electronic clock on the wall. How much can these mere dials absorb from the orbit of eternity? It can at best keep ticking and convey the half-nibbled truths of our roots to contemporary experience.

8.40 am. Students from the old block and the new block rushed out in shirt-pant-shoe-tie, some clutching files, others, with textbooks, practical notebooks and graphics-scales stuffed into carry bags. A few parents walked alongside their children.

"Don't skip your meals. Eat properly," Nirmala urged Suman. There's a shop outside. You can buy fruit, eggs and milk from there, but ..."

Paramesh said, "Suman, you're here to build your career. To become capable. To stand on your own feet. Don't get led away by friends. Don't waste your time. Stay out of trouble."

Suman slowed down to look at his father, and said, "Okay."

"We will be about two thousand miles away. We can't see you or guide you. You have to make your own decisions, what's good and what's bad." They crossed the deodar trees and the neatly trimmed plants in the garden.

Nirmala said, "Come, Suman let me help you cross the road. The way I did when you were in KG."

A childish smile flashed on Suman's pensive face.

"Always be careful. The traffic here is heavy." Paramesh was still talking when the road ended at the college gate. Suman stretched out his hand. Paramesh passed on all his dreams and hopes as he took the hand of his only child. The contact ripped through his soul leaving countless gaping holes. Its warmth, chilling him to the bone, as something inside him died.

Nirmala pulled Suman close. "Take care," she said tenderly. "We'll leave now ..."

The Godavari's swelling waves welled up in Nirmala's eyes even before her words found voice.

The platform. The afternoon train was in. Paramesh checked the reservation list before they got into the coach and sat down. Side by side. Paramesh looked out of the window.

"If Suman stayed with us he'd have at best done Maths or Physics honours," he said.

"What else."

All well-rehearsed, rationalized responses were thanks to relatives and well-wishers who had lent them their best over the last few months.

The train whistled and jerked to a start. A blaring announcement: The Brindaban Express is leaving from platform number one.

The window's sky flaunted a thick curl of clouds. Nirmala touched her forehead in prayer. Now, even if I want to, I can't take a bus to Suman. The platform is far behind. So is my precious one. Alone. Out of sight. The thought cut through Nirmala's inner self, jolting her entire being, and all promises and possibilities, career viabilities, campus interviews, fluency in Hindi and English in six months, a guaranteed job, new avenues – everything was washed away, rinsed clean.

Paramesh wiped his eyes. The passengers opposite sat staring at them, quietly. The train crossed a couple of stations. The modern houses, changing skyline, green landscapes and the irregular contours of the far away hills gradually gave way to an illusory calm. Paramesh called to Nirmala softly, "Listen ..."

Nirmala looked up with wet eyes.

To draw her out of her just-devastated world, Paramesh attempted fables, proverbs, chronicles, but nothing worked. He recalled the last few days. So many people, parents, understated human touch in a tech-savvy world. He began to narrate those stories, the psalms of this newfound world. Didn't you see. Almost all of them ... so many ... so many of them, with just one, their only one. However many, they are all leaving their only child behind.

अ

SIBANANDA KAKOTI

THE LAST MEAL
ON THE WATER FRESCO

———◆———

TRANSLATED FROM ASOMIYA BY PARISMITA SINGH
first published in Ajir Asom, October 2002, Guwahati

NOMINATED BY PRADIP ACHARYA

The man has been standing for a long time, gazing at the river's sinuous current. The serenity of his person is wrapped in a pristine white shawl, the edge of its length almost grazing the earth. The gruelling progress of the afternoon hour has often seen the shawl's end trail the ground. The knot of the flowing wide dhoti falling to his ankles, quivers every now and then in the gentle breeze, rather like a flag. But the man is as if oblivious to the minutes spent all afternoon, watching the river. Waiting.

It is the end of the Bhaad month. The rains are over. The narrow stream, a tributary of a larger river, grows swollen with rampant currents only during the rains, the pregnant waters seeming to rise up to both banks. It carries no trace of mud from the heavy rainfall. No, even in this season its waters are never muddy, as if its moving waters must always be white. At the shore of this white water, the man stands today, in his khaniya sador and dhoti. Silent, absorbed.

A small carbuncle has troubled him since yesterday. Today, its throbbing is no greater, yet it shows no sign of healing. He is not able to discover any irritation or discomfort, but it has kept the man's mind and body on perpetual alert. Even when he tries to ignore it, it quickly slips back into notice. The man runs his hand around the spot where this tiny uninvited guest sits. At his touch, the tender carbuncle seems to swell, as if beseeching forgiveness for causing inconvenience, inevitable though its presence is. The man strokes the agitated area for a long while, very gently, tenderly, invitingly – with deep understanding of why it is there. And now, it is as if he wants no longer to contemplate it. Nor the pain.

A boatman passes down the middle of the stream to the place thick with reeds.

The man begins to walk along the shore of the river, unhurried, calm. But after only a few steps, he stops, to breathe deep and long. He looks at the river once more. These rivers have given him so much companionship all through his life. It is as if he has by now lost count of how many times he has been up and down these rivers of his country. Yet on every voyage, on the shores of each river, by dawn or by dusk, alighting on or off their banks, he has always felt that all the rivers are one. The one river of the one land, diverse veins and arteries of one body, converging to make a whole. As a child, he has swum from bank to bank, sandy shore with an unbroken line of kahua grass to opposite shore. And now here he is waiting before this river at virtually the last moments of this life ...

What is his connection with its ambrosial waters?

He grows pensive. Mortal man even when immersed in the waters, the sky and the sandbanks, in all this, remains the same. All of humankind remains the same, constant in the midst of this creation. Only in time there is a carbuncle on the body.

The pain begins.

A shy smile plays on his face. He turns to wait again, gazing at the majestic river before him, vivid and swift. He has meditated long on their vast banks, on many things, has been beholden to them. How nicely the soft earth of the river has mellowed him.

The man breathes deep, thinking that perhaps he must walk a little now. He's barely taken a few measured strides, when overhead a flock of fishing eagles flew whistling past. White clouds fill the blue sky in every direction. No rain clouds. The skies seem to reach down to softly kiss the encircling green hills. The man stands waiting. The flying eagles soar over the river to disappear between the hills and sky. Their song continues to echo in his ears.

He is amazed once again at how harmony and rhythm, raga and taal, resonate in nature, pervading the very universe. In its reverberations and silences, its cadences and crescendos he hears the ragas and songs of years gone by. Some time ago, on an afternoon stroll along the shores of another river he had composed the prelude of a new song. A noon raga, it was a deep breath like a pranayama that had been sharpened by the discipline of inhaling and exhaling – ke-sa-av-a-a ... powerfully drawn, and then, with equal intensity, the omkara, with an ooukara – to turn finally, always to the chant of siba-siba. On which bank of which river had he composed this respectful union of raga, controlled breathing, nature and devotion? He cannot recall anyone else singing it correctly in this, an alien country, nor the prayer house reverberating with it.

But then, the man does not especially want to remember any of this. Not today. Now and then, the small carbuncle troubles him. He waits by the river, as if yearning to return with its flow. A thought comes: Why go back? Why turn to look at the past? Has he not told himself every day that being able to let go of one's self in the fluid currents of the river is life itself, its highest essence? But now, each time the carbuncle enters his consciousness, he wants to turn back. He wants to disregard it, let the impersonal present take over.

This mundane pain stimulates reflection.

But reflect on what? What could he bring forth from the river to consider? It is as if all is blurred.

Gradually the rotund sun is caught by the river. Refractions of light spread outwards from its centre, like a circular carpet. As if the long colourful rays have thrown a broad kuhila mat over the water. In the middle of the river, he clearly sees a watery fresco, still and tranquil, with enough room for the man and a few of his disciples to sit, legs crossed, in a circle. As if he wants to sit on the mat of the water fresco, in the brightly flowing waters of the river, as if he wants to sit someone down before him and converse, not about religious texts or life's spiritual truths – no, none of that – he moves.

What seems important today, more than spiritual truths, life's essence, dharma and other such serious issues, what was most important was: what did I do in my lifetime – what did I leave undone?

At the thought of deeds unaccomplished, another face immediately came to mind. Just a few days ago, on the banks of another downstream river, the man had spoken to this other who was overcome with grief immeasurable, who had come to bid him farewell: If I do not return, compose a volume of love and devotion recounting numerous good and godly deeds. It is time you assumed responsibility for the world, considered its welfare. Write down the ten thousand names, he had said, the *namaghosha*.

He had walked back down the river and suddenly a hundred thousand transgressions and sins of mortality came to mind. He could not write about them himself. He looked at the perpetual river before him in great distress. How could he bring those immersed in the ocean of sin to salvation. To prayer, devotions, a stirring of the conscience. He could not forget the sins and sinners of the three worlds as they came crowding into his being.

He walked step by step down the riverside, greatly agitated.

The water fresco gradually became more distinct. In the sun's bright rays, his white clothes blazed. But this afternoon he had no interest even in nature's intensity. He was in a deep meditation.

A sudden question arose inside him: Have I been able to transcend sorrow as I have the pleasures of the flesh? Perhaps some unconscious sorrow gnaws at my subconscious? Perhaps a crushing grief for the battle yet unresolved, has weighed him down ever since he discovered this raw carbuncle. But he is powerless to either grasp or contain it. Restlessly, he walks on.

Each time he reverently touches the carbuncle, strokes it, as if offering a prayer, each time, those whom he couldn't bring to belief and harmony, appear.

The water fresco lightens. He looks towards the middle of the river. Perhaps he could have chosen a few singers from the wide, circular mat and rendered a hymn to Nature's colourful mats, placed so carefully on the heart of the river. And he thought once again: Or perhaps we could have dined in the middle of the river. Who would he invite to this meal? Who would eat what? What would he serve whom? Who would have wanted more and of what?

This time, walking downstream, on the sands of another bank, he had savoured a meal. In the shimmering water of the downstream current, he had suddenly said: Do you see any fish? And they saw that the water was full of fish. The Thakur with them had said, Don't catch them. Let them be. But he had. They had prepared a meal on the sand. After a swim, he had taken his son and lit a fire under the earthen pot. The air was fragrant with the smell of katla fish, of tenga, pepper, mani. Everyone had eaten with relish. Even the Thakur; he had not realized that river fish could taste so good.

He had been able to share a meal on the khagarikata sandbank.

But a meal at a water fresco in the middle of the river? How do we eat it? Whom do we invite? He imagines the mani, peppers and hari dwar he would have used to cook today's meal. The bhagawats sitting on the wide mats of the river fresco, pure of spirit, free of sin, whom would he invite to sit with him – to share this meal?

The word bhagawat once again disturbs him. As if another problem is there before him.

Once he had to answer to the king's question – and that, in court. What is the sign of the bhagawat?

And he had recited the thirty two marks of a bhagawat, including a rounded forehead, curly hair, fine nose, red lips, almond eyes, hands that reach to the knees. He had explained this very naturally and simply.

The whole court, the king, courtiers, the Brahmins and everyone else there had examined themselves. They had stood mutely, heads bowed. Then the king, with great courtesy, had asked him to stand. And he had stood.

And even the king cried out in alarm. Where else but here were the thirty two marks of the Almighty!

Immediately after the meal, it was ordained – that he would be provided sanctuary until the next day. Shelter with the learned men until tomorrow.

Disillusioned, the man just stood there. Silent in the royal court. How could he initiate a king so intent on worldly pursuits, into the Vaishnavite dharma? Countless crimes may have been committed, though he cannot remember who committed which, when. The man walks as if he can no longer put his troubled mind to rest. But even then, he knows with certainty, he knows well, that he would never be able to welcome the king into the Vaishnavite sect.

What is the refuge of a righteous king?

Why does the king who provides sanctuary to others himself need asylum?

How could he say all this to the king?

And realization dawned that like all physical pain concentrated in the carbuncle, its cause is transitory.

He sees before his eyes again the day he came downstream. He had given precise directions to another man waiting on the bank. He had asked him to complete the writing when he returned. As if the man knew exactly what must be written. That is why he now repeatedly recalls the friend he has left behind, whose words might have held him spellbound as he fires the stove or cooks the rice or serves the food in this water fresco. Perhaps there could have been an exchange.

And whom else would he invite to share this transcendental non attachment? Would he be able to find in his son or another, one worthy of his trust? He could not think of anyone.

His eyes flew to the distant prayer house. The small straw seat was waiting by it, all alone. More than the occasional love he has for his son, it is pity that wells up within him. Perhaps he rebukes himself for his failure as a father. Perhaps it hurts him to be unable to seat his son close to the carpet on the shimmering water. Does anyone belong to my son? And he desperately searched for a disinterested, dispassionate, unselfish thought to defuse these feelings.

Uninvited, sadness comes to him. Why cannot he invite his own son to eat a meal in the middle of this water fresco? Or his wife?

And he thinks up answers to his son's likely questions. Suddenly, if his son were to ask him for everything, he had an answer prepared for that as well. What else does he have left to give his son? As if the son is a stranger to the father. He could not find his son to give him the most precious thing in the world. Could not find the father. Where is the father, where the son?

The river's fresco is slowly beginning to ebb away. The question of mukti, the ultimate release never once entered his mind. Neither did he think of the being's salvation or his union with the almighty, of being away from crime and sin. It is as if he wishes to renounce salvation and attain release from the desire to live amongst these men for infinite births. He has great love for man. An all encompassing love. In this love, is his maya.

The bright light has disappeared. The river flows as always. In the sky, flocks of homing birds crossed the shore and homeward bound, vanished into the hills.

One flock alights – another takes off. Again, they come and again they go. The river flows beneath.

He passes his hand tenderly over the unhealing carbuncle, its pain increasing.

On another bank of another river, a small boat floats to the edge. A man waits there, a horizontal gamoosa of bereavement on his head. The other man's heart misses a beat. In an instant, the ground slips away from beneath his feet. The pestilential darkness of the country overwhelms him. An unintelligible sound escapes his mouth – wrenched from the innermost recess of his heart.

Unfathomable sorrow ...

Medieval India saw the birth of Bhakti, a religious movement that emphasized devotion to god as the primary path to salvation. It left a profound mark on Indian life, thought and culture that has lasted till today. Many of the religions and cults like Vaishnavism, that we practise today were born in this crucible. Some of the important people of the Bhakti tradition were women.

Sankardeva, born in the mid-15th century in Assam, led the movement there during the time when the Cooch king Naranarayana (1528-1584) ruled in Western Assam, and the Ahom King, Chuhumung or Swarga Narayana (1497-1593) ruled over the Eastern part of the Brahmaputra Valley. The Ahom rulers of Eastern Assam were followers of Sakta priests and considered Sankardeva a heretic. Sankardeva fled to Paat Baauxi in Western Assam. The enlightened Cooch king, Naranarayana, offered him refuge. Naranarayana's younger brother, Chila Rai, became a disciple of Sankardeva. Naranarayana also desired to be one. Sankardeva did not want to accept the king as his disciple because he wasn't convinced that the king with all his worldly attachments could pursue a spiritual path. But the king had given him shelter, so how could he refuse the king's ardent pleas? He looked for a way out. Hence the carbuncle.

Sankardeva's son was not a follower. When he finally turned to his father, it was too late and Sankardeva pointed out to his disciple, Madhava Deva. Hence it is that the son carries the news of his father's death to Madhava Deva. The horizontal gamoosa signifies a messenger of bad news.

ꯛ

KENGBA YENGKHOM

DREAM TALE

——◆——

TRANSLATED FROM MEITEILON BY PRAVABATI CHINGANGBAM

first published in Chumthang, January 2002, Manipur

NOMINATED BY I R BABU SINGH

As soon as the bus stopped at the crossing, Oja Madhu signalled to me. I was in the seat behind his. He got up ... I followed him ... we got off the bus. He said to the handleman, "Ibungo, please get that thing down." I went and stood by his side. The handleman quickly climbed up to the roof of the bus, untied the rope and said, "Oi, catch it!" and Oja Madhu replied, "All right, drop! We're ready." Together we intercepted it.

The bus left. Oja Madhu lifted it on to his head. It appeared heavy. Could have contained all the belongings of a man.

We moved off the pucca road on to a footpath heading east.

I said, "Oja's load seems quite heavy."

"Indeed it is," said Oja. "The drama props I talked about earlier. This is not all of it, there are many more. Sad, isn't it? People don't understand the importance of props in theatre."

I smiled.

He smiled back.

"The carpenter was amazed. Unable to understand my words. Only when I made a sketch and showed him could he get the correct shape."

Truly, I had never seen such a thing before. Appeared to be made of glass. Yet I could not even begin to fathom what was inside it.

"What is it Oja? What drama is it for?"

"Can't tell you yet. You'll find out tomorrow while you watch the play."

"Oja, how secretive you are! Will telling me make the play less spectacular when staged?"

"Why ask if you know it?"

We laughed. We walked on.

"There on that hillside is our theatre, what we call our Sangam Kala Kshetra."

"You mean we have to climb a hill!"

"We must. What to do."

"Your load must be quite heavy, Oja. Why don't you transfer it on to my head?"

"Yes, do help me," saying so he lifted it and put it on my head. What a weight it was! I looked up at the steep climb up the hill. Daunting. Though I did not say so.

Wd e climbed on, I stolidly. Let alone converse, I couldn't even think. My head ached. I felt warm, queer. Sweat trickled down. In the scorching sun the incessant singing of the cicadas drove me mad. To the point of wanting to cover my ears with both hands.

After a while Oja Madhu sympathized with my state and said, "You must be tired. Here, pass it to me."

Taking turns, we reached the big building of the Sangam Kala Kshetra.

The sanglen was like a mandop. Very big. Huge pillars of solid wood. What made it different was just this: A mandop is open on all sides. The sanglen was walled with veranda on all sides.

As we approached it I told Oja Madhu, "Oja, let us rest for a while."

"Haima," he exclaimed, "must we rest? I shall go in."

He turned towards the southern veranda. I walked up the eastern side.

"I shall be here," I said, "enjoying the cool breeze. Do come out after keeping that thing."

I sat down. How cool and restful it was after the steep climb uphill beneath the scorching sun. The large pines swayed and danced in the breeze. Migratory birds called sweetly, incessantly. Even the sound of the irritating cicadas now seemed pleasing! "How rightly it is said that a person's temperament changes with the place and time."

My thoughts swerved. "Oja Madhu has been a long while, what could have happened?"

Then I heard it. The sweet strains of a woman singing. I perked up my ears. The voice seemed to come from within the hall. Accompanying it was a musical instrument. Then slowly the singing faded. The instrument picked up speed and sound, on and on and on till it was frightening. All of a sudden, a thunderstorm! The sky darkened. Thunder struck. And beyond the covered walls of the sanglen, frightful beasts tramped and raised hell.

My hair stood up, I was petrified.

"What what? Is Oja Madhu a ghost?"

My fear grew.

The animal sounds became even louder.

I got up hastily and walked towards the southern veranda, down which Oja Madhu had earlier gone.

But there was no one. Just a path moving west. At the back of the sanglen it branched. One went down the hill slope. It was well trodden, lots of footprints. The other climbed up the middle of the hill. Untrammeled. But there was a light far away in that direction.

For a moment I paused. Which way should I go? That very instant the terrifying sound of a powerful beast preying upon a lesser beast came from the direction of the path that headed up the hill.

My hair stood up on my head and on my body. I opened my eyes. The terrible sounds seem to echo in my ears even now. I brushed my palms down my head, face and eyes. I chanted to myself, "Haré Krishna. Haré Krishna. Haré Ram." Is this dream or reality?

❦
NEELAKSHI SINGH
ONCE UPON A BUJHVAN
———◈———
TRANSLATED FROM HINDI BY RACHNA SETHI
first published in Tadbhav, October 2001, Lucknow

NOMINATED BY SARA RAI

There was news: The frontiers of science had been extended. Karl Peter Giese, a British scientist who led a team of researchers at the University College of London, had unravelled the mystery surrounding human behaviour. He'd discovered why we suffer memory loss and gradually stop learning in old age. And the culprit? A part of the brain called the hippocampus.

Once this was found, Giese sir and his team worked on developing mice with defined mutations, to discover what went wrong in humans. Saying that the study of learning and memory cannot be framed solely at the molecular level, they incorporated approaches in their research that allowed them to take advantage of a number of other strategies to manipulate brain functions in rats and mice. They derived genetic mutations. Some that affected learning in mice, and others that only affected their memory. Mental activity, said Giese, depends on electrical signals between nerve cells in the brain. In old age, the channels on the surface of these neurons, through which the current flows, become "furred up," and they take longer to send an electrical charge.

This success geared Giese Sir and his team towards more vigorous research on unsuspecting rats. They worked on human mice. They declared that they would produce a memory pill to rejuvenate neurons in people above the age of 60. They announced a pill that would arrest memory loss in the elderly. It wouldn't restore things already forgotten, they explained, but once the medication started, it would ensure that one forgot nothing from that moment on. The media and the medical fraternity took notice of the invention. Amazing progress, they said. Once again one human mind had gained control over another.

But sometimes nature plays tricks with man's strivings, and this is one such story.

Once there was Bujhvan ... old man of the village, Bujhvan. Bujhvan's special quality was that his brain was like Giese sir's modified rat. The neurons of his hippocampus were active even in old age. Without the memory pills.

Bujhvan belonged to that section of society that had to dig a well each day for his water. And when unable to do so, he satisfied his hunger and thirst with thoughts of water. He was one of those living below the poverty line. From the day his voice broke and his moustache bristled shyly, from youth and middle years to old age, Bujhvan was rich only in his name, Raj Mistri, Royal Mason.

Bujhvan had laid the foundation of all the pucca houses in the village – of each and every one built after independence, people said. The skill of his deft hands testified that he was the modern avatar of those ancient architects and master builders. When joint families broke down and walls came up to partition these houses, it was Bujhvan's hands that were considered first. If it was auspicious to have Bujhvan lay the foundation of a house, then, if his spade was the first to strike when families were divided, all disputes would be settled amicably. He was impartial. And a professional through and through.

Now, in this late modern age, villagers feel it's enough to have knowledge of the last three generations to solve internal disputes. So they've agreed to start their history on a day fifty years ago and, as in Indian history, they had divided these years into three clear eras: ancient, medieval and modern. Please remember that Giese sir's rat had a third and most important function: memory. Bujhvan's brain was an incredible storehouse. It never forgot anything! This further made him the most reliable member of the village Panchayat to settle all disputes. The history of the last seven and a quarter decades was locked in Bujhvan's grey cells. So he actually remembered the village's prehistory, a time long lost when nobody in the village could read or write. If somebody turned to question Bujhvan, he promptly came back with an answer. The finest details of important events like births and deaths – which child came from the womb, hands first; all the woman's children, living and dead; who was the last dying man to ask for Gangajal; and which son's name he called as he breathed his last; and, most interesting, who had rehearsed the last scene how many times.

Bujhvan was barely four and a half feet tall and how all the people of the village depended recklessly on him. They never heeded the advertisement broadcast before the 8 am Hindi news on All India Radio, Delhi about the legal obligation to register births and deaths in the family. So what if the proof of their past would be gone the day Bujhvan fell silent? There was time enough for that.

Now you might think it strange that Bujhvan who had such a stock of information about the most trivial aspects of the lives of other people, didn't know the actual time or circumstance of his birth. So people aged him as they pleased. Some said he was eighty five, others claimed he was ninety. Fragile old age came nevertheless, and he could see but dimly, things near or far misted over, skin wrinkled like unironed clothes. When he walked, he swayed like the hood of a snake. Rice-eating teeth tottered and fell in the same order in which they had appeared. His body shrank and shrank, till people wondered how Bujhvan's massive brain resided in such a small body. Like most deaf people, he started feeling that all ears heard only words that were shouted. He had learnt to use his eyes and lips to listen. So when someone spoke, he blinked his eyes in rhythm and kept the lips open. His hands trembled while lifting bricks and the spade, which once felt light as mehendi flowers now weighed like a fruit-laden tree. His tongue twisted words after two or three straight sentences. And sometimes even a small bidi brought on a bout of cough that yanked the entire chest off the body map. Body parts lost their edge. Only the bowels still demanded their regular fees. Teeth gone, the tongue acted dictator and the gums marched ahead, chewing and swallowing, demanding additional wages – a tasty feast. Sulking over sattu, asking for rice to go with tangy green vegetables, green banana curry, potatoes.

But ai bhagwan! The daughter-in-law had such a foul mouth! She banged the sattu down before the old man, and when he complained she retorted, "Ai budae, is the house being run on the pittance you get from your astrology? (Stupid bhauriya, mistaking tales of history for astrology, mistaking the past for the future.) Put money in my palm and the demands of your tongue will be met."

Bujhvan's middle aged wife pounced on bhauriya and roundly cursed each member of her bahu's family. The enraged daughter-in-law returned the compliments in no uncertain terms. Bujhvan's wife sat watching her old husband tackle the sattu, his gums and tongue valiantly struggling with coarse flour rotis made of parched grain.

She sat in a corner, hot tears pouring down worn cheeks, repaying with interest the love received from her husband. Bujhvan continued to eat without looking at her till one salted, old tear dropped on the sattu entering his mouth. Tongue and gums stopped for a moment, then joined ranks with his wife's tears.

Bujhvan's first wife had died a suhagin after giving birth to seven dead children. Bujhvan was middle aged but despite the pressure from relatives, he didn't remarry. But as he grew old, he understood the advice of old people: Old age is an insurmountable mountain without support. He married again, a wife so young that even if her age was stretched thin, she would barely reach half his age. But the woman was faithful. She gave him a healthy heir. Bujhvan opened the bundle of his love and assets before her. The woman ran the house parsimoniously, brought up their son strong and healthy. So what if his hands lacked the skill of his father, or he wasn't interested in masonry? He left it to pull a riksha. Bujhvan hoped that when his body grew tired, his son would be able to pull the burden of the household along with the riksha. And so it came to be. But then bhauriya came, with a tongue as sharp as her features. She pulled all three – Bujhvan, wife and son – into her grip and held them there, squirming.

By this time, the bright young men with their ultra modern ways and shaven moustaches, rejected Bujhvan outright. Was this because everyone loves a handsome tall man and Bujhvan was neither handsome nor tall? The old master mason got some attention in the houses where ageing fathers ruled the roost. They called Bujhvan in as the supervisor and he'd sit in a corner, rubbing tobacco into his worn palm, giving instructions to young workers.

For some time the workers would enjoy this, but when Bujhvan felt that his instructions were being ignored, he'd swagger in with his trowel, mix sand and cement, four to one and slap it on the walls. The workers snapped at him. He'd pay no heed but soon, too soon, he'd be forced to back out, and he'd retreat, head bent desolately. Quiet would prevail. Others too would turn quiet and only the rhythmic folk-song rumble of the cement mixture and trowel would be heard. Then someone would walk up and ask for tobacco. Someone would tease, the situation would become lighter, but Bujhvan would still remain quiet. Till a mutter would rise from his throat and the whole process would be repeated. This lasted till he'd take leave of the master, blessing him with all his heart, clutching the money earned, the ten rupee note in his left hand, the five in his right. The left hand's earnings belonged to bhauriya. The right was solely his. To buy a handful of bidis. Kachoris at five for two rupees for his dear wife. Tying the gift to his dhoti, Giese sir's Indian rat would skip and trip all the way back to the house.

On one such hard day of dry sattu and hot tears, and Bujhvan not having got a contract for a couple of days, two earthshaking bits of news reached him. Related to one another, yet so different. One painful, Thakur saheb was on his way to the other world; the other, pleasurable, the sons wanted the property divided before his death. Bujhvan quivered at the latter news. He would earn a gift if his was the first spade to hit the ground. But God ... what an age to die ... sixty two!

Thakur saheb had no trace of zamindari left except his name. His ancestors had left behind a pucca house, a flower garden, backyard and a big grove at a little distance from the house. But three fourths of the garden had fallen into the hands of the government for the new prison. The rest was mortgaged to marry off his six daughters. There were two sons. As they grew, Thakur saheb's circle of influence dulled. A bull had thrown him ten years ago, leaving him paralyzed. Forgiveness, they say, suits only a poisonous snake. Anger too. And a helpless Thakur saheb found both forgiveness and anger unseemly. Suddenly, he had been declared the most useless thing on earth, next only to the mahua tree in the backyard. The sons, Trilokinath and Chanderinath, did not get along. The daughters-in-law fought day and night. Thakurian was caught in these disputes of the household. At suppertime, they served the Thakur bitter words along with roti and vegetables. No different to the practices of contemporary society. One day, things became too loud and violent and then only one solution was left – division.

Thakur saheb was caught in the illusory tangle of the past. He trembled at the thought of dividing the property entrusted to him by his ancestors. He gave up food and water. What else could he do? Some old men called the Thakur's sons and advised them patience, at least till Thakur saheb's last rites were performed. This division alone will kill him, they warned. But the sons said that it was all Thakur saheb's fault. Anyway, nothing would happen to him, and even if it did, death was preferable to this painful life. Both brothers would contribute equally for his funeral ceremony.

Giese sir's rat was appointed panch by both sons. They invited him to come with his spade. They proposed fifty one rupees and a dhoti from each side. Two dhotis, thought Bujhvan. Enough for the rest of his life. Money too was ample but ... There was a strong argument behind this "but."

1945. A fire had razed all the thatched houses to the ground. Thakur saheb's father had built the pucca house. Bujhvan had got his first contract as head mason. Pucca house, chabutra in front, Shiva temple by its side. The first expression of Bujhvan's architecture in the village. After that, under Thakur saheb's reign, he continued to get contracts as head mason for innumerable reconstructions and constructions. Thakur saheb had a lot of influence then. How one blow had changed his destiny.

But Thakur saheb still needed Bujhvan. Only his role had changed. From a mason working with his hands, to a worker of words. As a storyteller who kept tales of the past safely locked in the fine vessels of his brain. Lying on his bed, Thakur saheb would call out for Bujhvan day and night. Bujhvan would come, and Thakur saheb urged him to take out a long forgotten incident from the graveyard of memory. Bujhvan told his story to Thakur saheb who listened, his eyes closed. Behind the closed lids, a fervid imagination gave the stories shape and form. Bujhvan's memory and Thakur saheb's imagination built magical minarets upon the ruins of the past. Strange that Bujhvan's first handiwork and now the magical towers constructed by the memory, should both have something to do with Thakur saheb.

Other dying people also needed Bujhvan. They wanted to relive their youth. Bujhvan's eyesight was weak, but he gave others a rare vision that allowed them to savour the memories of bygone days. Look! ... this is your past. The dying forgot their pain in the labyrinth of the past. And the modern young men with their education smiled and said, "After Khadi Gram Udyog, it is old Bujhvan's udyog. The government should designate him Virasat Udyog for professionally making deaths easier for old people."

Bujhvan's eyes filled with tears as he lay thinking about all this. When he turned to wipe his tears, he saw his middle aged wife sleeping nearby. Her worn out sari was torn from the waist. What would he do with two dhotis? One would be for her ... this woman in a blue sari. Why did Bujhvan wipe away a single tear – there was now a stream of tears ... two ... three ... four ... this is the limit!

Giese sir's rat, with his four and a half foot thin body, carrying the burden of a spade on his shoulder, was walking towards the gate of Thakur saheb. A virus was trying to break into his computer-brain. He was in a terrible state of confusion. He walked nonstop, till he reached Thakur saheb's pucca house. Thakur saheb's bed was moved from the veranda and placed on the chabutra (because the veranda was to be measured and divided into two after the partition). The twelve members of the panch were seated there in order of rank. Amin babu was present with a measuring tape. A seat of sacking was placed there for Bujhvan, separately, not because he had been appointed head panch, but because among the twelve Rajputana panch, he alone was a low caste. Thakur saheb's two daughters-in-law had posted themselves at the doors opening towards the veranda. Thakurian – what purdah does one practice at her age – was sitting at the top of the veranda stairs. Thakur saheb was still fasting. His face had shrunk. His eyes darted from here to there, his neck and right foot moving in rhythm. His mouth was clamped tightly shut, as if his spiri. was ready, bag and baggage, waiting to slip out on the sly as soon as he opened his lips slightly. Even in the absence of any evident and apparent charge, Bujhvan sat shrinking into himself, believing himself to be the culprit. His eyes trembled so much that they would not even lift themselves to look at Thakur saheb.

First the panch did a close survey of the geography of the house. The division was straightforward. The two brothers were to get exactly half each. The two rooms each on the left and right side of the house were easy to divide. So too the veranda, garden and backyard. One was to get the bathroom and the other the toilet. The two would alternatively take up the responsibility of Thakur and Thakurian for a month. One would perform the last rites of the mother and the other of the father, or they would do it together – all these matters were simple and lawful. But there was one difficulty, the main cause of conflict.

The small kothri in the middle of the house, whose window opened onto the backyard. Both daughters-in-law were firm on having it as the kitchen. The panch offered various alternatives. For example, they said, the one who gives up her claim would be given an equivalent area in the garden or backyard, and the other brother would share the construction costs. If that didn't please, they said, a larger portion of the front veranda could be hers. But both were obstinate. So, a wall was to be raised in the middle of the kothri. Peace at last, thought the panch, when a piercing lamentation was heard from the top of the stairs: "Do not divide the kothri of Iya, Bujhvan ... Thakur saheb will not survive it ..." Thakurian ran up to her husband and, covering him with her arms, she started sobbing. There were no tears in Thakur saheb's eyes.

They were just gaping fissures and crevices ... full of shadows ...

Bujhvan sat frozen. Thakurian had heard each of the tales of Thakur saheb's past, of his childhood, adolescence and youth that Bujhvan had been narrating for the last couple of years. Not ostensibly, but while she bustled around, as if busy with other work. Her ears would twitch and turn towards the stories. She knew that the tales helped Thakur saheb connect to his past, especially to his deceased mother, Iya. Thakurian's sobs turned into a huge wail by the time it reached Bujhvan. His nerves crackled like dry burning wood ...

Before the fire of 1945, this house was made of tile and straw. Iya's small room sat where the present kothri was, a chest in one corner with a variety of ornaments and things, tied neatly in a small bundle. Iya's life was in it, for besides the bridal sari, a gold necklace, her first gift from Thakur saheb's babuji was in it. Iya was young, fair and beautiful at that time. It was husk at Sutwatoli's Rambechen that started the fire. It was rushing to engulf Thakur saheb's house in the summer afternoon of the Jeth month, driving men and women out of their compartments. Suddenly Iya fled back into the house while everybody looked on. Babuji followed, screaming after her. The flames had reached the outside of the house and people were shouting. Iya took a key from under her pillow and opened the chest. She turned things over in the trunk even as babuji was pulling her out by her waist. When the shouts became wild, the delicate Iya pushed away the heavy babuji, "Run away, run away, run away ..." Other people had already come in and they pulled babuji away. Iya found the bundle. She clutched it and could have run away when the lid of the chest fell ... Iya's sari ... When everything had turned cold and the ashes were removed, Iya's necklace was seen amidst the heaps, shining.

When Thakur saheb's babuji built the new house, he had placed Iya's kothri at exactly the same place, and of the same size. Bujhvan built it. Bujhvan set it up. Bujhvan narrated its tales ... to Thakur saheb and Thakurian.

Trilokinath grabbed Thakurian, shaking like a mynah caught by its wings. The two women tucked behind the doorway abandoned their sense of modesty to pounce upon their old mother-in-law. How dare she try to emotionally blackmail the panch! The panch tried to mediate, but by that time Thakurian had been disgraced. Chanderinath started shoving her inside the house, but he was stopped immediately by panch. The sons, Trilokinath and Chanderinath, were ready to take a miserly piece of that kothri, but were not ready to give it to the other and instead take land of equal area and money. So the decision remained unaltered. Amin babu immediately began the work. It was a square plot, so there was no problem. Measurements were taken quickly and areas marked out. Chanderinath was reassured, he turned to one of the panch members and informed him that he had given the brick seller an advance. In an hour or two, five thousand bricks would arrive at the door.

The division had been settled verbally. Now the proceedings. Come Bujhvan baba, start the digging. Let's start from the veranda, get the spade.

Bujhvan's brain stayed in control and instructed the eyelids to rise. He lifted his eyes, turned his neck ... Thakur saheb's pupils were fixed on the line drawn across the middle of the veranda. The neck did not move, nor did the feet. The pressure of his lips had weakened. Panch members sat on their seats, because they thought that the lips could open any moment and Thakur saheb's spirit would escape through it. Any moment ... probably when Bujhvan got up ... probably as he would lift the spade ... when he struck it ... Bujhvan pushed away the thought of the spade from his mind. No. Thakur maalik ... he would not be able to do it.

No, then what ...? If he refused once, then who would call him again for such work? From where will he get the cash reward ... the pair of dhotis? The blue sari will continue to tear ... what will he eat ... bhauriya's rebukes ... Bujhvan quickly laid his hand on the spade. If he did not strike the spade, would the division not take place? Chanderi maalik would immediately pick up his spade and strike. He had so much energy that he would lay claim to the division on his own. Bujhvan was not called because he was the only one skilled in this art or because his hands were auspicious. What is auspicious? When the mind is willing, everything is good.

The masters had merely kept his honour by calling him. If one Bujhvan did not raise his spade, then it was certain that several others could be raised, and one of these spades would hit Bujhvan in the stomach. No, no ... Bujhvan stood up. Picked the spade, put it on his shoulder.

Giese sir's rat was now standing in the middle of the veranda. He turned his head to look at Thakur saheb. No! Maalik was not looking at him ... he was looking at the mark on the veranda. Thakurian was crying at his feet. Bujhvan looked at the panch. With bated breath, everybody looked first at Bujhvan and then at Thakur saheb. Bujhvan picked up the spade. People looked at Thakur saheb. He had been saved. The lips were the same as before. A nerve was throbbing in his hand. The spirit was still within. Thank god. Oh ... People turned to look back ... the spade was lifted, but had not struck as yet! It was still held in mid-air ... Giese sir's rat was falling down, right at the mark in the centre of the veranda.

Bujhvan's soul was running away, to appeal in the court of Giese sir that India's old people would be happier with their past forgotten. No memory pills please, Giese sir.

ॐ

KHOIREN MEETEI

RETRIEVING THE HOROSCOPE

—◈—

TRANSLATED FROM MEITEILON BY THINGNAM ANJULIKA
first published in Naharolgi Thoudang, December 2002, Imphal

NOMINATED BY I R BABU SINGH

Mother was sad. "Your horoscope says you are destined to have children. But all these consultations with so many expert doctors during the last three, four years have been of no use. Agree, child. The panji who is coming tomorrow is a famous astrologer. He makes no mistakes. And we can arrange a puja after seeing your horoscope. Don't have doubts."

Ima's words nourished the regret within. The new horoscope I had asked khuri Yaima to cast, spoke of children. Did khura Yaima put it in? I had told him all that Ima had told me about me and the various predictions made for me. I asked him to leave out nothing from the calculations – not even the fact that as a child when I was given my first solid spoonful of rice at the Chawumba ceremony, I had reached out for a book and everyone had promptly seen a government job lurking somewhere in my future.

I was not married at that time. So I hadn't asked my mother nor discussed children with astrologer Yaima. Now I just had to know what my original kuthi had in store for me. Children, yes. And the other prediction of a government job. Since my mother proudly says it will, frequently, it cannot but come true. But government jobs ... I have crossed the age limit by a year. The OBC or the Other Backward Caste certificate is a must. And it might take six months or so ... so the job was a year and a half away. I am no BA or MA, can't dream of being an officer whose signature holds power. The kind of job that I, a matric fail, would probably get would be the job that comes with a table-less stool or a creaky chair without arms, placed near an officer's door and close to the wall.

To procure me a government post with a table and chair, my stars would have to be so strong as to force the government to give out a new recruiting order: numerous people to man the many mobile paan shops that will be advantageously placed where a Suman Leela is being staged or where, on moonlit nights of Holi, the thabal chongba is being held. Imagine such strategically located markets. Any day, one run by a beauty will rake in profits, hence recruiting women for such jobs under the government's economic development programme would make sense. But my horoscope cannot be false. I remembered the guaranteed groom's seat in my life. Ima, being a professional dresser of brides, a potloi dresser, had kept such a luhong plan at home hoping that that creaky old thing will bring her luck. In my childhood I had played a lot on this seat. Maybe that's why the prediction was nullified and I was unmarried, I thought then. It was then that I swore by my deceased father never ever to sit on a creaky chair and stool.

But a horoscope has to be right, right? It was written in the kuthi of Chaoba (he who lives in the northern leikai) that he would become a minister. And he did become one. An auspicious number in his horoscope rested on the elephant's head, elders said. In your case, khura Yaima said, glancing at my horoscope, that number rests somewhere around the elephant's rump.

So this famous fortune teller was coming to study my kuthi tomorrow. I wanted him to look at my original horoscope. But it was not with me. I'd been wanting to retrieve it for a long time now, and decided that, right that minute, I would ask my friend Tolmu to help me. I had no doubt that I'll get the original horoscope back, but was worried about the oath I once took, one Krishna Janma day. Lord Krishna's birth was being celebrated and I, holding a lotus-fruit with big seeds, had said, "Today, this thamchet being witness, I, Ahanjao, will not wed any except you, Mangallei!"

Was that a real oath? Would an oath taken in the middle of the road bear the same results as one taken inside a temple with bells ringing and which is followed by seven rounds of the temple? I didn't think about or question that oath then; I regret it now. I tell you, for the sake of the young, local clubs or the government should put up signboards in hoards that say, "*Pakhangi wakhalshing e-phing phingga-nu, replay yadaba punshini,*" – *Warning all young men not to be hasty, as life cannot be replayed.* I'd like to see these signboards at restaurants, in every nook and corner of Loukoi Paat, the dating grounds, the entrance to the Govindajee Temple. The signboards with drawings of new models of cars, gold chains and earrings must carry borders with helpful information – like AIDS safety measures – like the jingles do, in the radio news.

While I was thus engrossed, the clock struck half past two. Ima was already at the market to buy stuff for the next day's puja.

No one knew the real facts about my horoscope except my friend Tolmu; and since he did, his wife Jamini knew too ... all husbands and wives tell each other everything, don't they? The moment they see a fault, they blurt it out, no matter if the other wants it or not.

At Tolmu's, I waited for him to change his clothes. Tolmu's father, Rajen, was sitting in the porch, puffing away at a hookah. Born to wealthy ancestors, he made sure, without doing much work, that his children stayed together.

"Ibungo," Tolmu's father called out, using the affectionate term that an elder usually used to address young boys. "Do you also have problems making friends in your locality. Tell me truthfully now."

"Pabung," I replied, for like Tolmu I too called him father, "call it inability to make friends or the lack of time, but please tell me how do fathers know that?"

He took his time to answer. "My son," he said finally, "Your friend here cannot make any friends in the leikai. This amazes me. The two of you are close. You are also like my child Tolmu, na? Where are you two going now?"

"Just going to meet a friend."

"Why don't you tell me the name and address of this friend so it would be easy for the police to find you." He laughed loudly. He was waiting for an answer but I didn't offer one. Tolmu came out. We had crossed the courtyard, pushing the cycle, when Tolmu's father called out in a loud voice, though not angrily, "Don't go too often to the houses of those friends whose name you don't want to reveal."

Smiling embarrassedly, we walked out. Pushing hard on the pedal of the cycle, Tolmu said, "What made you give the horoscope to her? You're great. Lovers give letters to each other, we gift clothes at the beginning of the year and other occasions ... but giving her your kuthi just because you love her! Are you not *mad*?"

"True yaar, at that time I was truly mad. Love is ... bhai, how do you say it in English?"

"M-A-D, mad. All right, go on."

"Truly yaar, love is Mad and happened to me. I wanted to do all that she told me. That I come from a poor family, she knew from my clothes, the shredded mudguard above the front wheel of my cycle and my trousers with its frayed bottom. And that I am illiterate ... One day we were sitting at Loukoi Paat and some irritated looking commandos came by after an exchange of fire with insurgents. They grilled me about my name and address. Not satisfied, they asked about my educational qualifications. I answered truthfully. I could not have been more honest. From that day on, she hasn't written, as you know. You don't have to remember, so you forget."

Tolmu asked again, "But why did you give her the horoscope? Proof of age or what?"

"I haven't told you till this day. Listen. One day she asked me about my zodiac sign. I am a Virgo, I said. When's your birthday she asked. And I asked in return, In English or in Meiteilon? She laughed heartily. I had said what to me was the truth. A day starts after midnight in English, so if I say it in English, I was born on a Sunday. But since in the Meitei tradition it is still the previous day until you can see your body-hair, I was born on a Saturday. When I explained this, her laughter died down slowly, leaving just the shadow of itself on her face. Her face was like some twenty, thirty sharp spears piercing my heart. That day, I touched the statue of Netaji Subhas Chandra at the INA Memorial, right at the spot where Netaji's army placed their flag on Indian soil for the first time during World War II, and took the oath that I will give her my horoscope. That was why I handed my kuthi to Mangallei. But not many days after, she married someone else."

"All right, but we cannot easily overlook the oath you took that day. Try to remember the exact words – did you say, With the lotus-fruit as witness, or, did you say, With the lotus-fruit I am holding as witness."

"I said, With the thamchet I hold as witness. And the thamchet witness was so nice with big seeds that we shredded it and ate it up. Bhai, was it a sin eating up a thamchet that had acted as a witness?"

"No sin at all," said Tolmu seriously, "what we have to do now is to get your kuthi from Mangallei. So let's plan what we should do when we reach her house. I will engage the people in her house in small talk. You talk to Mangallei."

Since we didn't go there often, her house seemed far though it was barely twenty kilometres from my house. But all the talking and thinking made it seem as if Mangallei's village was next door. Some kids were playing before a nice bamboo gate. We went up to a kid who appeared intelligent and asked, "Do you know Mangallei's house?" The child started shouting "Ima, Ima," and ran across the courtyard. Trust me to ask a crazy kid. But then the gate was Mangallei's and the kid was one close to Mangallei. This made my pulse race. Mangallei called out from a corner of the courtyard, "Come in, come in. Such a surprise ... where all have you been to? Please come in."

Tolmu and I went in. In a corner was a table and some chairs. When I surreptitiously pressed down the chair, the hinges appeared a little loose. But there was a table too, so I dared to sit down. Mangallei went in to make tea. Two, three children were playing ball. The ball bounced up to the tin roof and got caught in the gutter and the kids started looking for ways to get it. They turned their eyes towards us. They came and grabbed the edge of the table and pulled. But I swung both my feet around a leg of the table. The children heaved and I fell, the chair coming down after me. My forehead connected with the edge of a stone. It started bleeding. People rushed out of the house.

"Nothing, nothing," I said, embarrassed.

Mangallei came near me and asked, "Sure you don't want some medicine applied on it?"

And I replied, "I came to take back my horoscope."

"Oh?" said Mangallei. "Didn't your mother tell you? I returned that horoscope to her the very day you gave it to me. Ima wanted to go to khura Yaima's to have it read, but when we went there he said he was busy and kept it with him. Did she tell you that it was lost?"

One hundred rupees and a thousand troubles. But khura Yaima's horoscope had to be correct! I decided not to worry about my fate any more.

I looked at Mangallei. "Three days after I gave the horoscope to you I went to him, saying that I had lost my horoscope. I gave him a hundred rupees and asked him to write another one that was exactly like the original. Khura proudly told me that he had cast my kuthi, exactly like the original."

Ish! If the children had whisked away that table without my knowledge, I wouldn't have been able to get a government job.

क

SANTANU KUMAR ACHARYA

ANOMA'S DAUGHTER

———◆———

TRANSLATED FROM ORIYA
BY BIBHAS C MOHANTY AND THE AUTHOR
first published in Kadambini, July 2002, Bhubaneswar

NOMINATED BY PRATIBHA RAY

There is a river. In front of it is a house that opens to a limitless horizon. It is the same limitlessness to which the river expands in the rainy season. And there in the veranda of this, his ancestral house, is Raghumastré with his daughter Chitrotpala and son, Ramanatha, their school books open. Chitu, as sharp and intelligent as her brother, is ten years old. Ramu is seven. And Chitu asks,

"Bapa, tell me, is Bihari the robber an honest man? In the newspapers it is reported that Bihari robs the thieving rajas and zamindars and distributes the booty among the poor."

Raghunath laughed. This daughter of his never ceased to amaze him. Look at the way she talked, balancing opposites with ease: The thief is honest while the honest thieve. The rich are poor and the poor, rich. Heroes are murderers, and plunderers, heroes. Like Alexander and Napoleon.

Without answering Chitu's question Raghunath asked one of his own. "Can you tell me the ancient name of this river?"

Ramu came back promptly with an answer: "Old name of Chitrotpala? It's Anoma!"

Raghu looked up at him, pleased. "Now, where did you learn *that* from?"

"From you, Bapa!" Chitu said. "You told Deba mausa when he came in search of Bihari the robber. He was here for lunch, remember?"

Chitu launched into a long account of Deba mausa's last visit. And Ramu promptly joined in with minute details of the rough khaki police dress Deba mausa had worn that day, the way his dun coloured horse flicked its tail, and of the red turbaned policeman dafadar and the brisk chowkidar running behind, hurling shouts and abuses at the village children.

Suddenly there was a loud noise from the western side of the riverbank.

"Ei!" Ramu was the first to react, "It's Deba mausa!" and, before anyone could stop him, he darted off to join the procession tagging after Deba mausa's horse.

The train came to a halt outside the renowned village teacher, Raghumastré's house. Dafadar Raju Jena, tall as a palm tree, with skin as black as a moonless night, held the horse's bridle from one side. On the other side was the wily-faced Jadu Mallick, perkily dressed in the green coat of chowkidar. It took both men a few minutes to calm the excited horse enough to allow their master, police inspector Dibyakishore Das, to dismount with practised ease.

Seeing Raghumastré standing in the veranda, the handsome police officer called out, "Ei Raghu my friend, where is my bahu? I'm inviting myself to lunch at your house. I have much to discuss with you."

Striding up the ten stone steps, he enfolded his childhood friend, Raghunath Kalama, in a bear hug, lifting him clear off the ground. He turned mastré around as if he were a ten year old and then set him down.

Ramu asked, "Are you going to talk about the Anoma again?"

Dibyakishore laughed. "Maybe. So friend, tell me. How far has your research progressed? Did you learn anything about the history of the Anoma from those revenue maps I sent you? Can't imagine how you've stayed such a student all your life. Ei baba, what do you gain from all this history-fistory, research-kisearch?"

Raghumastré grinned at Dibyakishore as he walked him into the house. Chitu of course would have disappeared to hide herself behind her mother, deep inside the house, the moment she heard Dibyakishore bellow: Where is my bahu?

Last time too Dibyakishore had arrived quite suddenly. He had come on tour but when he found out that his old friend Raghunath Kalama still lived in his ancestral village, he had stopped by and impulsively stayed for lunch. He had seen Chitu for the first time and, "Arré, Raghu!" he had exclaimed in his loud voice. "This cannot be your daughter! Now where have I seen you before? Where? Was it in the puranas? The history books? Arré, you're none other than Janaki, the daughter of Mother Earth, right, Bhudevi's daughter." And he had set a bewildered Chitu down to turn to Raghu. "You dare to proclaim a girl of such unparalleled beauty your daughter?

I protest! Won't let it happen! This girl's been born in your family specifically to come into mine. Arré yaar, do you know the name of my son? Ramakishore. It is Ramakishore. Raghu, I am reserving this daughter of yours for my son. From this day on, she is my daughter-in-law."

Deba mausa had lifted Chitu in his arms. Patted her and asked, "Maa, what is your name?" Chitu was then barely six years old. Looking him straight in the eye she told him her name. It was Dibyakishore who had done all the talking from the time his booted feet had touched the ground of Keshanagar, Raghumastra's village. Now, Chitu took over, talking nonstop with her new friend as old as the river, Deba mausa. Dibyakishore had placed five ten rupee notes in her tiny palm which Chitu accepted with alacrity.

But today was four years after that first visit. And an older Chitu was suddenly bashful. Like a frightened fawn she ran through the three inner courtyards of the house to take shelter behind her mother's kani.

Padmavati had just started cooking lunch. "What is it, Maa?" she asked. "What was all that noise outside? Is it the zamindar of Kalikapur riding along the riverbank?"

Shyly Chitu said, "He has come again."

"Who?" "The one who gave me money last time, Deba mausa!"

"Deba mausa? Aalo aalo!" Padmavati felt her hands and feet suddenly turn to wood on learning the identity of their guest. She rummaged in the containers for flour, sugar and tea even as Raghumastré called, "Padma! My friend has come and is sitting in front of me. Arrange for some tea and snacks. And yes, he will have his lunch with us. He is a saheb, isn't he! Send Ramu to Banchha fisherman's house. Just this morning I saw him catch four big jalangas in the river." Padma quickly changed the menu and pushed Chitu out of the kitchen saying, "I'll make puris. Now you run get me some brinjals from the backyard. Tell Ramu to go to Banchha fisherman's house quickly, or all the fish will be sold out. And one minute, tell him to buy some tea on his way back. There is none left. Now, what do I do!" But the chairs and tables were immediately arranged in the middle courtyard so that Raghunath could seat his guest there.

Though Raghumastré was an ordinary teacher of English and History in the village high school, anybody who happened to see the layout of his ancestral house would notice that this was no ordinary schoolteacher's house. Standing on the bank of the Chitrotpala, it looked, at first glance, like an ancient matha. The high veranda of an ancient monastery, with typical stone walls, massive pillars, wide open cobbled courtyards and the range of clustered living units, each with its own entrance under a neatly thatched roof. The Kalama house sprawled within a compound spread over an acre of land. The main entrance was a wooden door made from heavy sisam wood so old, that this strongest of woods sagged and had to be manually lifted to be opened or closed. On the main panel of this door were painted pictures that a discerning observer would instantly recognize as Buddhist art – but in this mofussil area on the banks of the Chitrotpala where could one find such an observer?

Raghumastré made up for the deficiency with his long term research on his ancestors. And when now and then a rare guest like Dibyakishore chanced to visit, he would show them around the house. On his last visit, Dibyakishore had noticed the colossal walls of the house. His attention was drawn to the extensive artwork on these walls.

"These pictures seem very old," he said, not taking his eyes off the murals. Their colours were now faded here and there. "Raghu, this house of yours must be of ancient times. Was it ever a matha? Who has drawn these pictures on the walls? How old would you say they are?"

Raghumastra had the air of one about to pronounce the statement of the century. "Mark," he said, smugly, "mark the style, colour, texture and themes – what do they remind you of? The frescoes in Ajanta? Ellora? See the richness of the colours? These paintings are probably from the sixth or seventh century AD."

"Ei bandhu, remember what that scholar Ananda K Coomaraswamy said," Raghu was quizzing him. "Almost all that belongs to the common spiritual consciousness of Asia, the ambient in which its diversities are reconcilable, is of Indian origin in the Gupta period. We all know that Ajanta is important today because of the Buddhist legacy, because it fostered and supported the best creativity from the second century BC to the seventh century AD!"

Deba babu examined one painting closely. It covered an entire wall. Despite being faded in some places, the colours by and large were vivid. The wall was made of mud. But what kind of mud was this that could stand for so long without crumbling? And the paintings! It seemed like there were a hundred walls and pillars that unfolded the whole drama of human persistence and endeavour. Princesses and saints, sadhus and kings caught in actions of a thousand kinds. The colours of the forests and the jungles, the peahen and the tiger were still vivid, and through it all flowed the Anoma, sacred river of the Buddhist legends. What grace and beauty unveiled themselves before Dibyakishore's eyes. He saw them again now and wondered why it had taken him this long to return to his friend.

"Wouldn't you say, a perfect combination of power, self and passion," Raghu was saying now, his eyes glued to his paintings, as if seeing them for the first time.

"Sixth or seventh century, you say?"

Raghumastra chuckled. "Bandhu, the wall is probably older."

"Meaning?"

"Just push the date back by another twelve hundred years or so. Sixth century BC ..."

"You must be joking." Dibyakishore turned away abruptly. That stupid old habit of Raghu Kalama was rearing its head again. There had to be some limit to exaggeration!

They had studied together all those many years ago in Queen Victoria High School in Cuttack, he and Raghunatha. One day, the History teacher had talked to the class about the Barabati Fort. "What can you tell me about this remarkable example of ancient technological skill of Orissa?" he had asked. "Who can tell me about this nine storied palace on the bank of the River Mahanadi?"

Raghu stood up and said, "If you say that there was a nine storey building in the Barabati Fort, which is just a mound of clay today, then do you mean that our Cuttack was once bigger than Kalikata?"

The teacher had gone on to wax eloquent about the history of the Oriya people, even though the textbook makes no mention of Orissa ... "you study the history of Great Britain!" he concluded.

"There isn't a nine storied building in Kalikata even today," Raghu Kalama had added quietly.

The class snickered behind lowered heads and closed mouths.

The teacher had asked, "What is your name, balak?"

Standing erect like a hero the boy had replied, "My name is Raghunath Kalama, sir!"

A gale of laughter greeted this announcement. Raghu's name never failed to amuse his classmates. This unusual surname of Raghu makes everybody laugh. But the History teacher – Deba babu could not for the life of him remember his name – looked at Kalama with awe. He asked, "What did you say?"

"Raghunath *Kalama.*"

"Come here, Raghunath Kalama."

From the teacher's tone it was clear that this was a serious matter. Raghu would probably get caned. But to everyone's surprise the teacher stroked the boy's head, and for the benefit of the class said, "This surname, Kalama. Did you know that in the sixth century BC in Kalinga, there was a rishi named Alara Kalama."

The teacher added that Bhagwan Buddha had chosen Alara Kalama, at Vesali, as his first guru. Kalama at that time had had 300 disciples in his ashram and it was he who took the Buddha through the first steps of meditation and the theories of the Atman.

"After his long and arduous search for Enlightenment, the Buddha spoke of only two of his teachers during his discourses to his disciples. Alara Kalama of Kalinga was one of them. A thinker who had generously taught him all he could. The teacher said, "Gautama not only mastered Alara Kalama's complex philosophy, but he carried forward the understanding of meditation that his guru had helped him understand. *Akincannayatana*, the sphere of nothingness. Note it down," he had said.

The class turned silent.

Turning to Raghu, the teacher asked, "Kalama, where is your village?"

"Keshanagara in Cuttack district, sir, on the bank of the River Chitrotpala."

"Oh! Keshanagara?" The history teacher stroked Raghu's head again in a gesture of blessing and said, "A very sacred place indeed. Do you know that the ancient name of your village is Keshapura or Keshaputta?"

"Let me tell you a story. Once long ago, after Rishi Kalama had passed away, the people of Keshaputta Township, the Kalamas, were very troubled. Many religious teachers passed by their village. They preached to those who lived in the village of Rishi Kalama, each convincing them that the only truth was what he told them. The Kalamas could not decide what was right and what wrong. Then one day, the Buddha came to their village. The Kalamas brought their problem to him. And the Buddha said, Do not accept or believe anything right away, just because it fits with what a lot of learned people say. Explore. Examine. Understand. Do not become an intellectual slave to anyone, not even of the Buddha! And he taught them what is now known as the *Kalama Sutta*." The teacher paused. "We are today like the Kalamas of two thousand years ago."

Emboldened by the teacher's interest, Raghu said, "Sir, on the wall of our house there is a very old picture. It shows a prince. He is cutting off his own hair with a sword. The picture also shows a very wide river. A horse stands on the bank ... Maybe it is the prince's horse?"

The teacher listened with great interest. He said, "And this picture is on the wall of your house?"

"Yes sir."

The teacher's eyes, Dibyakishore still remembered, were shining. "Gautama's horse Kanthaka with Channa clinging to its tail. They say that Kanthaka jumped across the river just in one leap. Then he took off all his ornaments and gave them to Channa, his charioteer. Then he cut off his hair and beard with his sword and tossed them in the air ..."

"That's what we have!"

The teacher could no longer contain his emotion. He embraced the boy and said in a choked voice, "You are singularly blessed my boy!" Then he composed himself and enquired, "Is there really such a mural on the wall of your ancestral house? Then that must be the treasure house of human history! Is it a pretty large building, like some ancient matha where gurus taught their disciples, in old times?"

"Yes, sir. I do not know who my ancestors were or from where they came. My father says we were Buddhists for generations. Later, somebody from the family became a Vaishnavite. But recently we have been eating fish and meat." Having said so much, Raghu lowered his head in sudden shyness.

The teacher said, "The clues to your family's history probably lie buried in the foundations of your house. Just as centuries of brave Kalinga's history lie buried in the hillock below Barabati Fort. Dig it up and you might bring to light archaeological proof of the glorious history of people now forgotten. Remember beta. The Bengalis take pride in showing off to the world the post-British Kalikata of hardly a hundred and fifty years vintage. They are looked up to all over the world. And we? The Oriyas have never learnt to be proud of their past. The time has come to change this mindset, especially in the light of the new archaeological discovery."

Asking Raghunath to go back to his desk, the teacher continued. "Do you know that there is a controversy amongst the historians about the birth place of Bhagwan Buddha?"

There was a collective murmur. "No."

"Then listen ... So far, the history books have maintained that the birth place of Bhagwan Buddha is in Nepal. But this will soon be amended. About a year ago, in 1928, an ancient stone edict was found in Orissa, not far from Bhubaneswar. It was discovered buried under a village called Kapileswar. Now who can tell me the birthplace of Gautama Buddha?"

"Lumbini." Someone volunteered the information in a low murmur.

"Right! And the edict has Lumbini written on it! According to some researchers this is the truth. I am not aware of the arguments for and against, but I know this: The place that has at least two well known temples to Shiva and Lingaraja – the name of that place is Kapileswar. And the Praganna name of Kapileswar is ... Lumbei. The stone edict found in Orissa was recovered from under the earth of Kapileswar village!"

After the class was over the students had surrounded Raghu. Pulling his long hair, they had teased him, "You are nothing, but wild Kalama shaag."

Padmavati was adjusting her sari to cover her head as she emerged from the inner section of the house. She was carrying a very large bell metal thali. On it were arranged freshly made puris, crisply fried brinjals, cut lengthwise. Fried fish and a variety of sweets.

Deba babu laughed. "Samuduni, do you think I am Bhimsen? All right, I will try to do justice to this spread, but tell me, where have you hidden my daughter-in-law! Do call her."

Padmavati went inside. She came back dragging Chitu by the hand. Dibyakishore delved into his pocket and took out a small jewellery box. He took out a gold necklace and slipped it on Chitu's neck. The gold gleamed brightly in the sunlight.

Padmavati bade her daughter to touch his feet in respect.

Chitu did so. But who knows why she stood up crying aloud and fled from his presence.

Deba babu said, "Samuduni, do sit down. Don't feel shy. As you know, I am a childhood friend of your husband ... Has Raghu ever told you that instead of becoming a schoolteacher, he could have been a police officer like me? Has he ever told you about that? No? The fact is that both of us had got job offers in the police department at the same time. We received appointment letters from the government. And we started on our jobs together. On our way to join up, this patideb of yours asked me, We'll have to chase thieves and dacoits in a police job, don't we? I retorted, Why? Do you want to chase women? And you from the Kalama family of ascetics, sanyasis and mahants? He grumbled all through the journey. Do you know what he feared most?"

Raghu babu interrupted. "You know my reason well enough, Deba. We've all noticed how the sepahis used to thrash the satyagrahis. I used to look upon the policemen of the British Raj as if they were the messengers of the very Yama, God of death. It was around the time of the Lavana satyagraha. Remember how the police packed congressmen into jail vans as if they were sheep. Then – the lathi charge, firing and tear gas. I had a feeling that, if ordered, I would have to do similar things to my countrymen."

Ignoring him, Deba babu said, "Samuduni, this husband of yours is a sadhu baba ... He went with me as far as the office of the SP. There he chickened out. Finally, I went ahead into the office on my own. I submitted my joining report. This stupid fellow kept standing outside the SP's office, looking in. The SP was a white man. When his car passed through the gate the guard saluted. I was watching the whole scene ... And what do I see next? The very next moment I saw Raghunath Kalama's cycle speeding down the road. Within a twinkling of an eye our bahadur police sub-inspector designate vanished from the scene. Almost like a hunting dog going for toilet in the middle of the hunt. Hee, hee, hee! What a coward!" Dibyakishore laughed. Raghu babu joined in to lighten the atmosphere and Deba babu asked, "Samuduni, is he less timid these days?"

Padmavati's veil had slipped halfway revealing her face. To

Dibyakishore she looked like any other village housewife – the kind of wife a man like Raghunath Kalama would have, he thought. Large eyes. The pala singers describe such women as mrignayani, the doe-eyed. Padmavati said artlessly, "Only he knows what he keeps doing. He's digging a hole. Ask him and he'll say he's making a tunnel under the foundation of this house. He has been doing this for more than two years now."

"A tunnel?" Dibyakishore stared at Raghunath. "I thought you were a policeman at heart. So you're a thief! Thieves dig tunnels under other people's houses. So why are you digging into the foundation of your own house?"

Padmavati replied in a complaining tone. "He says that there is a treasure there."

"Gold? The wealth of your ancestors?" Dibyakishore stood up. "Let us go and see where and what kind of tunnel you are digging. Or don't you want me to see it?"

With as much good grace as he could muster, Raghu led Dibyakishore to the back of the house. There was the large wildly dense walled courtyard with trees of baula, kadamba, mango and jackfruit – the kind of trees that were always found in the mathas of earlier times. The air was fragrant with the scent of blossoms.

"It is here," Raghunath pointed to a hole in the middle of the large courtyard. "This tunnel was probably an old one but it was buried under the earth. I am reopening it. The work is not yet over. Let it be completed. We'll see what my ancestors have left for me."

Dibyakishore bent down to peer into the dark tunnel. The inside was filled with sand.

Before taking his leave Dibyakishore remarked jokingly, "Well! Whatever hidden treasure you may retrieve, do make it a point to pass it on as your daughter's dowry. Let it be a condition. What do you say, Samuduni?"

Raghu babu said to his wife, "Deba always speaks like that. But the man has a good heart."

Two

It took the Second World War about three years to reach Keshanagar from its confines in the western parts of India. All of a sudden one midnight, fire rained on Pearl Harbour. It was as if the Pacific Ocean was on fire. The American warships sheltered in the vast harbour burned high before sinking into a watery grave. This was followed by a strange sense of fear emanating from India's eastern horizons. Till that time it was Germany and Italy who were fighting in the Second World War as enemies of the allied forces. Now because of Japan's entry into the war, the Second World War seeped into the daily lives of ordinary Indians. One midnight Japanese aircraft bombed the Paradip-Kujang area, a few miles away from Raghumastré's village. The next day, a long line of army trucks was seen crawling along the metalled Cuttack-Kujang road. The sight of those trucks sent a wave of fear through the quiet hinterland. All sorts of rumours were doing the rounds. As if lending weight to them, dafadar Raju Jena and chowkidar Jadu Mallick went from house to house alerting everyone.

"A bunch of Japanese spies have landed on the beach near Paradip. They have come in a submarine. Their vessel has been seized. But no one knows where the culprits have gone. There is a manhunt on for them. Beware. If you get any news, inform us immediately. There are instructions from above. If a foreigner is suspected to be hiding in somebody's house, we will raid that house. The house owner will be arrested and sent to jail. Now do you see the danger? If you come across anybody even remotely like a foreigner moving around in your village or orchards, inform the authorities immediately."

Apart from the fear of Japanese spies hiding in the countryside there was a new rumour spreading terror in the villages – that strange objects were falling out of the sky. They descended without warning on farmlands and barren fields. Some had even fallen into the river. It was said that when these objects landed on the ground they burst open releasing fantastic animals with half human half horse forms that ran about the countryside, abducting normal human beings. Some fifteen villagers had vanished in this way. Knowledgeable people said that the mysterious flying objects were in reality, giant rubber balloons. Wherever they fell, a lot of paper was scattered around. Something was printed on the paper. There were also pictures. It was not easy to decipher them. Most of the writings were either in English or Japanese.

Chitu and Ramu had heard all these rumours. They kept their eyes peeled for these strange flying objects. Ramu said, "Dei, suppose one of those things falls from the sky in the orchard behind our house. And a few of the four legged horse-human creatures come out, then what shall we do?"

Though Chitu was frightened, she concealed her fear, and adopting a sensible tone said, "An animal with four legs can never be human," with false confidence. "If it is not human, it can never have the intelligence to match us. Bapa says we are the most intelligent creatures ever created. We can control those four legged animals, don't worry!"

"But how?" Ramu persisted. He did not believe that he had enough intelligence or strength to control a horseman or an elephant-man.

Chitu mulled it over, then said, "We will do satyagraha. Just like Mahatma Gandhi. Bapa says the Mahatma is on a fast, Quit India or I will starve to death is his ultimatum to the British. Bapa says the government is getting quite nervous. We'll just follow Gandhiji. If a horseman tries to kidnap us we will immediately sit down cross legged and say that we are starting our Anasana satyagraha. Then he can do whatever he likes." Chitu was rather taken by this idea of hers.

Ramu just laughed. "And he will just lift you up on to his flying saucer. As if any anasana or fanasana will help!"

Chitu said, "Let him do whatever he wants. On my part it will be noncooperation."

Ramu knew nothing about Noncooperation but as the man of

the house, thought it best to caution his sister, "In times of great danger it is better that girls do not move about outside. From now on you keep indoors. I will bring you news from the streets."

Chitu said, "Shut up! As if you were the great Alexander! Do you know who killed the brave conqueror Alexander? Bapa said it was a woman. What do you know about the strength of girls? You are a boy and all you know is to use your hands and legs. If you had even a mite of intelligence would you not have realized the strength in the satyagraha of Mahatma Gandhi? Wait and watch. By the time this war is over, the white man will leave India and run away. Mahatma Gandhi will triumph without a fight."

"The *Englishmen* will leave? What hope! So even if they do leave out of fear of old man Gandhi, what about the Japanese? They are marching in from the East. If the white men lose the war, the Japanese will win. Do you think they will also go back to their homes shit scared of Gandhi?" Ramu's main worry was the strange stories he was hearing here and there about the debacles faced by the Japanese. He was instantly scared if he heard anyone mention "Jap spy."

Those days they saw quite a bit of Deba mausa. There was a reason. Dibyakishore had information that there were Japanese spies hiding in the Mahanadi-Chitrotpala delta, particularly in the vicinity of Wheeler Island, where the lighthouse stood. It was believed that they were scouting for a convenient place where they could get a foothold on the eastern seaboard. On these visits Deba mausa looked preoccupied, but he always made it a point to stop at Raghumastré's house. Chitu always felt his eye run over her, head to toe, as he gave her one small present or the other. He would say, "In two to four years. After my son Ramu passes the BA examination, I'll finalize the wedding. This daughter of yours is reserved only for my son. You understand, Raghunath? You don't have to worry about her. Her responsibility is all mine."

He also made it a point to ask about Raghu's archaeological research. "How far has your tunnel progressed? Have you started hearing any resounding clank of gold?"

Raghunath would smile. "My ancestors were not rich. They were spiritually inclined – sanyasis, Vaishnavites – but with families. I don't expect to hear any thon-thon noise. But there is definitely something beneath the foundation of this house."

"Sure it's not a skeleton?" Deba mausa laughed.

Raghunath said, "Maybe. If not a skeleton then definitely some kind of bone or hair or teeth!"

"What are you are talking about, Kalama? One of your ancestors was a dacoit maybe?" Deba mausa smiled.

"Never! It'll anyway not be bone, hair or teeth of any ordinary person. It'll be a relic. If such a thing is found it will send a ripple around the entire world." Raghumastré went happily into his pet theory.

Dibyakishore was a practical man. He thought, This Raghunath is a born schoolteacher. Once he gets on to a subject he goes on and on. On every single visit to this house he had heard only the same useless thesis from Raghu. The subject was deeply entrenched in this poor schoolmaster's brain, and its roots spread far and wide, destroying Raghu's brain just as a banyan or peepal seed, dropped into a crevice of a huge building by a passing crow.

Finally Dibyakishore could take it no more. "Raghu, have you gone mad?" he asked. "How does it matter if Gautama Buddha came south from the north or went north from the south? Why are you after the Buddha?"

Dibyakishore got up to leave. Once again he called out to Chitu. Placing his hand on her head in blessing, he said, "Study well. Clear the matric exam. I will take you to Cuttack. There you will study in Ravenshaw College, as my daughter-in-law. It appears to me if you stay in this house for too long you will also lose your head. Maa, do you notice how this father of yours is obsessed with the name of Buddha? Arré! This is the twentieth century. The age of science. What did the Buddha achieve? Do you know the mantra of those times? Let us all leave our homes and turn into ascetics – bhikshus and bhikshunis. Bhiksham Dehi! Bhiksham Dehi! He destroyed India and now one more Buddha has appeared. These stupid fellows call him Mahatma. He also follows the same principle. Let us all become male and female beggars, damn them! You take your studies seriously now. I am going to make you a scientist."

Dibyakishore mounted his horse and set off along the riverbank. Dafadar Jena and several red turbaned policemen ran in his wake. Following them to some distance was the usual caravan of village children and barking dogs.

It was a Sunday. Raghumastré could barely wait for dawn to break, then, armed with spade and shovel, he started on the tunnel. The mouth had been widened considerably. As he progressed through the days, it became evident that this was indeed a secret passage of olden times. The question was: Where would it lead? Was his house really a matha of historical and archaeological importance, or was it merely the exterior portion of a stupa? Raghumastré flashed the long five-cell flashlight that he always carried into the tunnel. Though the war had led to a scarcity of cells in the market, he had managed to procure some from Cuttack. When cells were not to be had, he would take a lantern with him. He was aware that the arrangement was not without danger. Like in deep wells, it was possible that there was a gaseous deposit inside the tunnel.

On that day Raghumastré had barely started work when he had a strong feeling that he was not alone in the tunnel. There was something coiled and heavy, something staring at him with cold, hypnotic eyes. A python? His heart pounding, aware that he was facing death, he spun around, even then desisting from shining the flashlight in its face.

Hot breath fanned his ears. A voice in a strange yet beautiful language whispered,

Ujum Janapado Raja Hemabantassa Passato
Dhanaviriyena Sampanno Tosaleshu Niketino

Raghunath Kalama was dumbfounded. The lines were from the Sutta Nipata or the "Sutta Collection," an ancient, probably the most ancient, part of the Buddhist Suttas. A current of excitement ran through his body. Verse 422! His heart was filled with a unique sense of elation. A thousand lotuses inside his head opened their petals with lightning speed. He knew the words – the language, the sound, the rich meaning of these mysterious utterances.

Very humbly, in a voice choked with emotion, Raghunatha asked, "Mahatma, who are you? What brings you here? Are you a deity or a man? From which universe have you come into this dark sunless hole?"

"I am a Buddhist monk. From Japan. They are looking for me because they think I am a spy. My life is in danger. Please let me shelter inside this tunnel for today. I will go away as soon as it is dark."

This sudden transformation, from the exalted to the earthly, was a rude shock to Raghunath. The lotus petals of his sahasra closed all of a sudden. "What do you mean?" he demanded. "Are you a Japanese spy hiding here adopting the language of a Buddhist monk?"

"I am not a spy, Vatsa Raghunath!" the fugitive replied in a grave voice.

Raghunath was surprised. How did this man know his name? It must be a trick. Spies make it their business to find out everything. He must have collected his information in advance. Therefore, in an effort to outwit the visitor, he asked, "When did you manage to

---

Ujum ... This quote is from the dialogue between king Bimbisara and Gautama. Bimbisara met the young sanyasi on the outskirts of Rajgriha and asked his identity. Gautama's reply is contained in this quote. In the original Sutta Nipata sutra the words were Himavnta and Kosala, not Hemabanta and Tosala. Himavanta means the Himalayas, Hemabanta signifies the mountain of gold. Kosala and Tosala are different geographical regions in ancient India. The former is in the north, in the proximity of the Himalayas. The latter is a part of Kalinga, almost identical with the present Bhubaneswar of Orissa.

learn the literature and the language of this place? You must have been left here by the Japanese submarine four to six months ago, that is immediately after the bombardment at Kujang?"

"See, Raghunath!" the stranger said in a pitying voice, "the very truth about the Buddha which you have been trying to find for so many years from the womb of the earth, has been gathered by me. I am a monk, a traveller. Do not look upon me with the suspicion of an ordinary ignorant man. The police suspect me as a spy. If they catch me, they will torture me both physically and mentally. I don't want to be a prisoner of war for years together. If you wish you can provide me shelter at least till the evening ... I am terribly thirsty, Bhadra Raghunath. I seek your protection."

Raghunath did not waste time. He came out of the tunnel and went back into the house. To Padmavati he whispered, "We have a guest. Arrange for some food quickly. And yes, please see that nobody else comes to know of it."

THREE

Chitu whispered to her brother. "Listen Ramu! Don't tell anybody about the guest in our house."

Ramu had already had a good look at the man. He hides in the tunnel all day and comes out after dark. He eats in the house and then sits talking to bapa for hours. Sometimes he speaks in Oriya and Ramu can catch a bit of what he's saying. But mostly he and bapa converse in English. They laugh together. His appearance is puzzling. He looks like he's from China or Japan. He dresses like a sanyasi, in a long saffron robe well below his knees. He carries a cloth bag on his shoulder. Inside the bag is a small drum. The man holds the handle of the drum and slowly beats it with a small stick. He also chants a mantra. Ramu tries to understand it. But the language is completely unintelligible.

Ramu asked Chitu, "What mantra is he chanting?"

Chitu said, "I don't know. Father says this prayer is sung everyday in the prayer meeting held in the ashram of Mahatma Gandhi. This is a Japanese prayer to Bhagwan Buddha."

"Is Mahatma Gandhi a Buddhist? Is he not a devotee of Rama?"

"Rama and Buddha are the same, silly. Ishwar and Allah are the same."

"Then why is this man not praying to Rama?"

"Don't you dare laugh." Chitu said angrily.

After a while Ramu said, "Who is the Buddha? Was he not born in Nepal? Why is this person hiding at our place instead of going to Nepal? If the chowkidar or the dafadar see him he will be arrested."

"Ramu, Buddha was not a Nepali! How many times must bapa tell you!" Chitu burst out. "He was an Oriya. Pure Oriya."

"Shh! If the man hears you he might get angry," Ramu warned her. Ramu never lost any opportunity to assert his superiority over Chitu. After all he was a male child. According to him, it was the man's duty to keep watch on the females and discipline them. This idea had already taken form in Ramu's mind over the last few years. Thanks to the World War there were too many green fruits ripening precociously on the trees.

"I am only repeating what he has told bapa." Chitu said, adding, "Since when have you started understanding English? Tell me what is the meaning of Stop, Look and Listen?"

"As if you know a lot of English! Don't show off. Just because you are to become the daughter-in-law of Deba mausa you don't have to already feel so proud. Wait! I will go and tell everyone in the village that you're talking to a Japanese spy. You take him some breakfast in the morning! I'm going to announce in the bazaar that you are bad, bad!" Ramu shouted.

Chitu slapped him on the cheek. Ramu cried out aloud. He raised his hand but before it could find its mark, Raghu babu came running to intervene. He was haunted by the fear that the secret would be out any time and desperately wanted to avoid attracting attention to his house.

As expected the secret didn't remain so for long. One day Dibyakishore's horse appeared on the riverbank. The dogs started barking. The village children raised a commotion. "Police! Police! Police!" The dafadar and the chowkidar arrived in advance at Raghu babu's house. A drummer came – dhaon dhaon – making a loud proclamation, "Beware! Orders from the government! Raghunath Kalama's house is to be searched. Those inside stay where you are. The police will fire if you move an inch. There is a Japanese spy hiding in this house. Anybody providing him shelter will be arrested with all his family members. His wealth will be forfeited to the government by virtue of the war laws."

Raghu babu was stunned. Before he could react armed guards had already surrounded his house. Chitu and Ramu who were observing the whole scene through a crack in the window saw Dibyakishore's horse stop at the foot of the steps to the veranda. But this time, Deba mausa did not dismount. Instead he ordered, "Start the search!" Immediately the armed sepahis forced their way into the house. Two of them held Raghumastré's arms and dragged him before the police officer. The officer continued to sit on horseback.

Not wasting his breath on a preamble, Dibyakishore said in a harsh tone, "Raghu! Where have you hidden that Japanese spy? Tell me frankly. Or else I will be forced to arrest you."

Raghu babu was silent.

Dibyakishore cautioned him again citing the wartime law, "Under this law, there is provision to send you to Kalapani, Raghu. You will choose to go to the Andaman jail rather than hand over this spy to the police?"

Raghu babu said, "There is no traitor or spy in my house, Inspector saheb. He is a Buddhist monk. His name is Kajyoyoda."

"Where is that yoda or bedha? Tell me where have you hidden him."

"Listen, Inspector saheb," Raghu babu raised his voice. "My guest has done nothing wrong. I cannot hand him over to the police just like that. My conscience doesn't allow it. Give me whatever punishment you like. But I will never hand over an innocent man."

"You won't do it? Do you know what you are saying?" Dibyakishore looked at Raghumastré with bloodshot eyes. "Handcuff him!"

Behind the window Chitu and Ramu trembled like a coconut tree in a storm. And Padmavati fell into a dead faint.

Just then dafadar Raju Jena and chowkidar Jadu Mallick appeared dragging the Japanese monk. Though the man offered no resistance they were raining blows and kicks on him.

Raghu babu protested. "Do not hurt him. He is a very learned saint. Several times in the prayer meetings of Mahatma Gandhi he has offered evening prayers. This wise man has collected material to write the history of the freedom struggle of India by travelling over the whole country. Do not raise your hand on him. Dibyakishore! This sin will definitely visit you. Why are you doing this? For a promotion or a medal? For that you will go against your dharma, Dibyakishore?"

Someone hit Raghunath's cheek with terrible force. He fell silent. Dafadar Raju Jena bent down to peer at Raghumastré's stunned face. Baring his teeth in a grin, he asked, "Would you like another one, mastré?"

The Buddhist monk Kajyoyoda and Raghumastré were handcuffed and tied with ropes like common criminals before being led away. Among the villagers crowding the bank and watching the spectacle, was an old man in khadi. He said loud enough for everyone to hear, "Brothers and sisters! India will become independent. That auspicious moment is not very far away. There will be the formation of a new government. There will be voting. At that time we will make Raghumastré stand from our electoral constituency. We will make him win with our votes. Then we will see to this arrogant police officer. Raghumastré zindabad! Inquilab zindabad! Bharat mata ki jai!"

The dafadar sprinted to thrash the old congressman. But Dibyakishore ordered, "Hold it! We will take care of him next time."

Four

The congressman's prophecy came true sooner than expected. With the bombing of Hiroshima and Nagasaki, the Second World War came to an end. Within a year, in 1946, a pre-independence interim government was formed at the centre as well as state level. By that time Raghunath Kalama's reputation as a freedom fighter was established. His name figured prominently in the list of ministers for the interim government. The newspapers mentioned that he had been offered the Home Ministry.

Ramu had been promoted to the eighth standard. Chitu's matriculation examination were over and Raghu babu was preparing to send her to college. But Padmavati wanted to get her daughter married at the earliest. Raghu babu would often say, "I meet Dibyakishore quite often. He is very repentant. How could anyone imagine that India would become independent so soon? He, poor Deba, did not know the power of nonviolence as a weapon! His son has already passed BA. Now he is studying for his MA degree. Shall we proceed?"

Padmavati was aghast. "Doesn't that man have an iota of shame?" she asked. "Or is it that jail has turned you satyagrahis into bullocks? Where is your sense of self-respect? Hai! That man had you handcuffed, got you slapped by the dafadar. He must have done much worse inside the jail. Is it Mahatma Gandhi's teaching that one will tolerate disrespect and insult? Are you not ashamed?"

Though Raghunath was hurt by Padmavati's words, he tried to maintain his smile. "Listen Padmavati. It is certain that I will be a minister with the police department under me, and Dibyakishore will be an officer there. However unjust and insulting his behaviour may have been, he has never tried to break his promise to accept Chitu as his daughter-in-law. As a police officer whatever he did was in the call of duty. The Second World War was on. The fear of a Japanese invasion was rife. He was given the responsibility of capturing spies. He performed his duty with sincerity. What is his fault? Now he will work under me. He will have to do his job according to the laws framed by our government. Service is one thing, getting one's children married is another. The Deba of today is not the Deba of the British days. Now he is a free, conscientious citizen of independent India. It is his conscience that tells him to stand by the proposal of getting Chitu married to his son. I do not have any objection. But one thing is clear, Chitu is not going to marry now. First let her stand on her own feet. It is our duty to educate her for that. Other things will come later."

"As you wish," Padmavati said grudgingly and tried to get into the discussion of sending Chitu to Cuttack for her higher education.

"Is that still a problem?" Raghunath smiled, pulling his wife closer to his side. "Remember Paddu, from now on you are no mere housewife. See how much we owe my childhood friend Deba? If he had not arrested and sent me to jail that day, then today I would have remained the same Raghumastré as before. Now you are the wife of Minister Raghunath Kalama! The education of Ramu and Chitu will never again be a problem. You will get a big house in Cuttack. Your house now will be abuzz with servants and cooks. Consider yourself and your children lucky. Would I have known the power of satyagraha, if not for Dibyakishore? Or about the moral and spiritual courage of ordinary people? Hence the saying, If you want immortality first do tapas at Yama's door. It would not have been possible for Nachiketa to find immortality if he had not bothered to meet the God of death himself, at his own house. The man who does not fear death is the best fighter for justice – at all times, then as well as now."

Padmavati was becoming used to the idea of being the wife of a minister. To some extent that dream had also affected their children. Ramu often asked Chitu, "Dei! You'll go to college everyday in father's motor car. How will I go to the school? No bicycle for me, uh-hun! Bapa will have to buy me a motorcycle. Did you see those military motorcycles roaring down the Cuttack-Kujang road during wartime? What noise! Phat! Phat! Phat! Phat! And what speed! I need a big 7hp military motorcycle like those ones. Will bapa buy me one?"

"Who knows? Ask bapa!" Chitu turned her face away.

"Hmmm! Anyway, what business do you have with our house from now on? You're to be Deba mausa's daughter-in-law. I have heard this with my own ears from bapa. Your luck has turned, Dei! Well, tell me what is the name of Deba mausa's son? Do you remember?" The more Chitu scowled, the more Ramu teased her.

A special messenger arrived at Raghu babu's house in Keshanagar. Chitu and Ramu did not find their father inside the house and went to the backyard in search of him. Raghu babu was back to his usual activity. He was working in the tunnel. The metallic sound of the spade could be heard from inside.

"Bapa!" Chitu called after manoeuvring quite a distance into the tunnel. "What are you doing? Somebody has come with a letter from the governor."

"Ask him to wait."

The two teenagers crawled out of the hole again. Soon, Raghunath emerged from the tunnel, covered in dust from head to foot. Ramu nudged his sister and whispered, "What would the governor's messenger think if he were to see bapa now?"

"What?"

"He would think, From now on farmers will become ministers and labourers will become governors! And as for those kings and ministers of earlier times – they will be seen only in costume dramas under the light of petromax lamps."

Without bothering to wash or change, Raghu babu went to meet the messenger – a government officer in suit, boots and tie. With him was a chaprasi in starched white uniform with a red sash embossed with the insignia of the Government House. On his head, standing upright like a cockscomb was a big red turban. The officer handed over a sealed letter.

It was an invitation to the oath taking ceremony.

FIVE

Raghunath Kalama did not take the oath. He never did become a minister. In fact, though he and his family did start out well in time for the oath taking ceremony, Raghunath never reached the gates of Government House.

On that day the roads of Cuttack were swarming with humanity. The crowd was particularly large in the Lal Bagh area. Motor cars, horse driven coaches, hand pulled rickshaws were trying to make it to the premises of the Government House. Outside the walls loudspeakers blared patriotic songs like Vande Mataram, Bande Utkala Janani and Tunga Shikhari Chula. These songs were being sung by school children. Every now and then the music would be drowned by the shouting of slogans.

"Inquilab zindabad." "Victory to Mahatma Gandhi." "Victory to Jawaharlal Nehru." "Victory to Harékrishna Mahatab." "Victory to the tricolour."

Just then, a fresh procession was seen outside the walls. They had their own set of slogans.

"Lies, lies! All lies!" they screamed, in one voice. "Partition politics, Murdabad murdabad." "Gandhi dayee, Gandhi dayee." "Jawaharlal zahar piyo, zahar piyo." "Mahatabi Congress tautari banda karo, banda karo." "Jai hind, Delhi chalo."

"Subash Bose zindabad, zindabad."

"Aamar neta Lenin, Stalin."

"Lai Bagh re lal pataka udiba dine re udiba dine."

The policemen on duty were on the alert. Cuttack's SP, Dibyakishore was insistent that the district magistrate should agree to first tear gas, then lathi charge the crowd and, if needed, allow them to open fire.

The magistrate said, "Just listen to the larger crowd, Dibyakishore. The Opposition is in a minority. Lions versus sheep ... Let the sheep bleat." As they watched, they noticed Raghunath Kalama's carriage being stalled by the crowd. The horse was nervous.

Raghunath got down. At once the crowd surrounded him. Someone said, "Raghu babu! Please do not join this party of liars. Please go back! Go back!" And then from the crowd there emerged a black robed Buddhist monk, piercing the circle of excited people around him. And above the unusual din he heard the words – "Raghunatha you have now reached the most opportune moment of your life. It is here that the wise make their best decisions." And the familiar voice continued:

"O Gyani!

Ichham bhavanam attano naaddasasim anositam
osane tweba byaruddhe diswame arati aha

He had heard that voice several times earlier. It was the Japanese Buddhist monk ... Kajyoyoda! As ever, he had chosen a quote from the Buddha, from the Attananda Sutta: This world completely lacks essence; it trembles in all directions. I longed to find myself a place unscathed – but I cannot see it.

He saw around him the milling crowds, people engaged in quarrel, shouting futile slogans against each other. Yes, there is no end to that quarrel. Yes, he had arrived at last at the turning point in his life!

Raghunath felt an unusual pressure in his chest. He was filled with ecstasy. The next moment he was surrounded by peace and quiet. The noise of the world was no longer audible! He heard the monk say, "Raghunatha, your soul must crave for a last word with your wife and children?"

"No bhikshu!" Raghunatha wiped both his eyes with the end of the spotless white khadi dhoti that he was wearing.

"Then why the tears?"

"These are not tears of sorrow, bhikshu! I had given up all hope of ever seeing you again. I had given up that hope after my childhood friend Dibyakishore had taken you away from me that day. I thought they would have killed you with inhuman torture. Now that we are reunited, let us start the work that we had planned to do."

And so they walked, until they reached a riverbank. The bhikshu asked, "Do you know the name of this river?"

"Kathajodi."

"No. That is the modern name. This branch of the ancient river Anoma was not even in existence two thousand and five hundred years ago."

Raghunath was surprised at his own ignorance, "When did this river originate then? When Bhagwan Tathagatha started his journey towards the north from Kapilavastu, where were the rivers Kathajodi and Kuakhai?"

Raghunatha looked at the dry sands of Kathajodi. In the distance he could see the other branch of the Anoma, Kuakhai. Munda Muhana was the point where the two rivers separated from each other.

Kajyoyoda groped inside his sling bag and brought out a piece of paper. It looked like a miniature copy of an old map. After studying it for sometime he said, "In this map there is no mention of the names of these two branches. Kathajodi, Kuakhai – or any other river that branched off from the original Anoma. These must be names of recent origin. But, lower down the river there is a vast lake that you can mark in this map here. See this blue spot – the reservoir has a very old name – Debadaha or Debahrada or you may call it Debakunda. It is mentioned in Buddhist literature as a water body lying on the border of the kingdom of Debadaha. Sometime later, the flood waters of Anoma crossed its banks and created these two tributaries – Kathajodi and Kuakhai.

"There is no mention of this river in the maps of the Buddhist era. But, there was an ancient river on the borders of Kapilavastu – your Bhubaneswar of modern times. Its name was Rohini. It is said that a king of Magadha named Mahapadma Nanda had conquered Kalinga and, in order to win over his subjects, he dug a canal. When the Anoma flooded, its waters entered this canal and created a new river. Your Kuakhai.

Raghunath's eyes gleamed. It seemed as if his search could see the light of day. And as if reading his mind, Kajyoyoda said, "Raghunatha, it will be a difficult and time consuming task that we will take on. It's true that renunciation and travel and research open our eyes to the truth. These bestow Buddhatva on us, Raghunatha, enlightenment. We've started our journey for the attainment of that Buddhatva. Come! Come! Let's not delay any more. People must be actively searching for you. Walk faster."

And so the two nameless persons, attired in their nondescript, mud-coloured clothes started a long journey. They were travelling towards the history of an old, long-forgotten past, fully conscious of space and time and their role in the present. This was the cause for the unusual attraction between the two of them. From the moment Raghunatha Kalama met the monk in the tunnel, his life had changed. He had discovered a purpose far beyond his imagination. Everything else – family life, freedom struggle, the ministerial post – paled in comparison.

Dibyakishore had always understood the power of Raghu to get into things with singleminded passion. Many a time Dibyakishore had admitted to how Raghu had helped him advance in his career, while talking with friends and family. He would say, "See! What a useful friend Raghu is to me. Both of us got appointed to the police service simultaneously. I joined. He didn't. Had he done so, maybe he would have been in the post of DIG in my place. Who knows! Again by playing host to a Japanese spy, he helped me for a second time. I raided his house. I arrested the Japanese spy and got a promotion and a medal, eventually rising to the rank of superintendent.

And then when Raghunatha was about to get the greatest opportunity of his lifetime, Dibyakishore conspired again. When it became clear that Kalama's role as a satyagrahi was making a public hero of him, Dibyakishore conspired to keep the monk in prison till the time was ripe for his release. Dibyakishore knew very well that the monk had a strong hold over Kalama. Therefore the release was made to coincide with the oath taking ceremony. And Kalama, instead of being the Home Minister, was now untraceable. Dibyakishore had indeed played his cards well.

Six

It was Padmavati who was singularly hurt by the dramatic event which occurred that day in front of the Governor's house. After waiting a long time for Raghunatha, sitting in the horse drawn coach, she heard that her husband had gone away somewhere like a madman, following after a sanyasi.

To her children, she said, "Start searching! This must be due to that Kajyoyoda. I knew this would happen. Your father has never been the same since the day he met that monk. Search for him. Search everywhere …"

But when Chitu and Ramu approached the police for help: File an FIR at the Lal Bagh Police Station, they said. Padmavati balked at this. How could she possibly file a written statement saying that her husband, a respected freedom fighter who was about to become a minister, had suddenly, without any reason, disappeared? What would everyone say? No, it was better to go back to the village with her children and keep quiet.

But even in the village there was no peace. Everyone wanted to know what had happened and why. Rumour and speculation abounded. Raghu babu had been lured away by a monk who had knowledge of tantra-mantra. Raghu babu had got cold feet at the last minute and therefore he had fled. Perhaps it was just as well. Even if he had become a minister what good would that have done? It requires a cunning person to run the country by turning falsehood into truth and truth into falsehood. Earlier, thieves and dacoits were terrified of white skinned officers. But the congressmen of today are already nurturing such thieves and dacoits. In the villages dacoity and robbery went up overnight, the moment they heard the news that India had become independent. Wait, you will see. Let some five years pass. Like others who taste power Raghu babu too would have feathered his nest and made his ancestral house into a palace. He was not Mahatma Gandhi.

Another cause for worry was a rise in thefts in Keshanagar. One night Padmavati heard some whispers. The voice resembled that of dafadar Raju Jena.

"This house is not an ordinary house. There is gold here. Raghumastré took some of it away. But even then a lot of wealth is still there below its foundation."

The next morning Chitu and Ramu saw footprints all over the backyard. They were particularly obvious near the tunnel. One day maybe all this digging and ferreting would bring down the entire house.

In a moment of great insecurity, Padmavati decided that the best course of action would be to move with her children to Cuttack.

She sold some of the farmland, keeping back the ancestral house and a few acres. A tenant farmer took care of the property in her absence. He also agreed to send her part of the produce from the fields. And, in Cuttack, they took a house on rent, a humble two-roomed place in a poor locality, all that Padmavati could afford. But the people in the neighbourhood were kind to her. Everyone had heard of Raghunath Kalama, the freedom fighter who gave up a minister's post to become a sadhu baba. They said, "Maa! You stay in our locality without fear." And Padmavati turned her full attention to Chitu and Ramu. Chitu was still at home after passing her matriculation. Ramu's education had stopped after he'd left the village school. But soon Ramu was in school. When Chitu was filling up forms for her admission into college, Padmavati said, "Maa, select your subjects carefully. I dream of seeing you as a doctor."

"Bou, I can't stand the sight of blood, pus and all that gore ... How can I become a doctor? I will do my BA and LLB. I will become a lawyer."

Padmavati shook her head. "Chii, chii! Your father would never have approved of it. Mahatma Gandhi has said there will be no lawyers in independent India. No lawyers, no police, no army. That is swarajya. And now you say that you want to become a lawyer? You'll wear a black coat? Defend thieves and murderers? No, no ..." However, Chitu took history, economics and tarkashastra, logic, as her subjects for a BA degree.

The first year passed uneventfully. But word did get around the college that Raghunath Kalama's daughter was a student there. The disappearance of her father continued to be a subject of speculation in the media. Every now and then, she would be stopped by a teacher or a student who would express concern and sympathy for her. In those days the State Legislative Assembly sat in a vast hall in the college. And Chitu started attracting attention for another reason. Those were the days when students were politically active, still under the fervour of Cuttack's own Subhash Chandra Bose and Gandhiji. For various good reasons there were constant student protests in the college. And at a time when girls rarely participated in such student movements, Chitu was prominent and vocal. One morning the members found a beautiful girl dressed in khadi barring their way. She was lying across the steps, preventing the ministers from entering the building. Word went around that she was Raghunath Kalama's daughter and the Honourable Speaker, an old congressman, came up to her and said in a kindly voice, "Arré, Maa, why are you lying down here like this? Your father Raghu babu is a respectable man. If he were a minister today, would you block his path? Please get up, Maa. Give us way."

Chitu remained silent. The Speaker tried again. "You know the name of this house, don't you? The Legislative Assembly. It is here that the laws are made. Is it the right place for students to go on strike? Now get up. If you have any demands for us put them in writing. We'll consider it."

This time, Chitrotpala spoke up. "I do not want to obstruct law makers from making laws. If you are doing so according to the law, please step over me and go in."

A young MLA said, "Yes sir, do what she says. The times have changed. Mahatma Gandhi is dead. During Gandhi's time there was justification for this kind of protest against the British government! If you encourage such dharmaghata, farmaghata in independent India, then you will keep standing outside the Assembly Hall all your life. Step over, sir, or call the police!" The policemen were not very far away. Hearing the commotion they rushed to the spot, physically lifted the girl and carried her off as if she were a dead body. Within minutes the college campus became a battlefield. The other student activists started shouting slogans, throwing brickbats at the policemen. A lathi charge was ordered, then tear gas. Many students were injured and rushed to the hospital in police vans. The others were rounded up and taken to the police station. Chitrotpala was the only girl amongst the arrested students. By the time she had spent one day in jail everyone who did not know her earlier now knew that she was not merely her father's daughter, she had a special quality of her own. Its name was fearlessness. And the eyes of whosoever met her at whatsoever place, softened, or was simply lowered.

But soon after this incident, Chitu had a disturbing encounter. She had just stepped out of the girls' common room and was heading for a lecture with a group of friends, when she noticed a tall, fair, slim man. Dressed in shirt and trousers, at first glance he looked like he came from a well-to-do family. But the way he stood, leaning arrogantly against a pillar in the corridor, his eyes fixed on her, made Chitu's blood boil. Her friends cautioned her. "He has a terrible reputation, Chitu. He will sweep you off your feet ... and his father's the local police chief."

Chitu shrugged her shoulders. In the past year she had learned to deal with young men of every ilk. In the college, the bazaar, the neighbourhood. And they had, in turn, learnt to keep out of her way.

Walking straight up to him, she said, "What are you staring at? Do you think you are Lord Jagannath and your great big eyes give you the right to ogle at every passing girl?"

The young man smiled.

"So you want to stare at me, do you? Well then, I'll match you stare for stare. Let's see who looks away first!"

The smile vanished. The young man's eyes widened but there was a flicker of uncertainty in them. The young man lost the staring match. He looked away and muttered something. Chitu said, "Don't much like being paid back in your own coin, do you? Who are you? Which year are you in?"

"Bagdatta."

"What?" Chitrotpala looked him up and down.

"How should I address you – apana or tumi?" The question had an easy familiarity. "Do you know what bagdatta means? My name is Ramakishore. Does it ring a bell?"

After a moment's silence, Chitu said, "Thank you for the introduction." Then, with as much dignity as she could muster, she turned and walked towards the classroom.

There was a time when her heart would dance on hearing the sound of Deba mausa's horse on the bank of Chitrotpala river. Her face and ears would grow warm. She would run away and hide herself in the kitchen. Yet her ears were eager to catch Deba mausa's voice. She had heard this name several times. Ramakishore! It would send a trill of excitement through her. But today all that the name provoked was a burning hatred. And a twinge of fear. As if someone had tried to claim her. *Bagdatta! You are mine. I have rights over you, Chitu.*

SEVEN

B reakfast table arguments between father and son were a regular feature and Nalini was quite used to them. Rama's way of talking would greatly annoy Dibyakishore but he had learned to control himself. Dibyakishore was not an ordinary policeman and he didn't treat his wife or child that way. He was cultured, well read and well spoken. Perhaps this aura of refinement had helped create an image that was popular with the higher ups. Nobody ever complained that he had disregarded a request from a senior officer or minister. His promotions and medals bore testimony to his widening circle of powerful well wishers.

However, Rama was not in the least bit in awe of his father. He seemed to take a certain pleasure in baiting Dibyakishore. That morning as they sat at the breakfast table a police constable doubling as a cook and two other constable peons were busy serving breakfast. And Dibyakishore, by way of conversation, asked, "So how are your studies progressing? Your college is on strike most of the time. I wonder if there are any classes held at all."

"Taking your advice. You've always said that an MA has no value anyway. Finish your BA and prepare for the civil services examination. That's exactly what I'm doing."

"Very good. What are your subjects for the IAS exam?" Dibyakishore asked, applying butter on a fresh toast.

Ramakishore cut a bit of the omelette on his plate, speared it and popped it into his mouth before replying. "History, Political Science."

"Good. They'll fetch you marks. Go ahead my boy. I want to see you soon in the chair of the district collector of Cuttack."

"Daddy, what do you know about marks?" Ramakishore asked in an affectionate, teasing tone. "You've just been very lucky all your life."

Dibyakishore said, "Well, fortune favours the bold."

Nalini sat there, her long and shining black hair just slightly dishevelled, her fair skin shining like the image of a Devi. Her aristocratic demeanour was as usual augmented by her glittering ornaments, especially the heavy stone studded gold chain. The chain had a long history, she always said. She had received it as a wedding gift from her grandmother. And her grandmother had received it from her grandmother who was the daughter of a very rich zamindar. Nalini liked to dwell on the grandmother of her grandmother. "She was the granddaughter of a Maratha Peshwa hero." A long history was etched on it and she traced the necklace to the Maharani of Mukundadeva, the last independent emperor of Orissa.

"But it wasn't boldness that earned you your good fortune, was it?" asked Ramakishore.

"What do you mean?" Dibyakishore looked up from his plate. The question was addressed to his son but he glanced at his wife through the corner of his eye.

Nalini who was eyeing her husband coquettishly gave a start and fretted at her son's spiteful remarks.

"Your fortune is mostly thanks to one person, isn't it? His name is Raghunatha Kalama."

"Nonsense!"

"Daddy, yesterday I saw that gentleman's daughter in the college corridor." Rama added just one word to sum up the encounter. "Firebrand!"

Nalini asked, "What did you say?"

"Firebrand! What would you say of a girl who stopped the Assembly from functioning for as long as fifteen days?"

Dibyakishore was not unaware of Chitrotpala Kalama's satyagraha. But he behaved as though he was hearing the news for the first time. He dabbed his mouth and the long well-shaped nose with a napkin and asked, "What is your interest in that girl? Are you studying for your IAS examination or mixing with riff-raff?"

"Riff-raff?" Ramakishore gave a thin smile. "Throughout my childhood you couldn't stop praising this riff-raff. Was it all a lie, then? Didn't you say that the girl was like Sita in the Ramayana?"

"Sitas are not firebrands, they are agniparikshas – they don't set fire to things, they put themselves to test by fire."

"You don't like firebrands, do you? Was that why you sent Raghunatha Kalama away?"

"I? I sent him away? What do you mean?" Dibyakishore broke into a coarse neighing laugh.

"It's no secret. Why, you've bragged about it yourself! How you arrested an innocent Japanese monk and passed him off as a spy. That got you promotions and medals, didn't it? Again at the last moment with the object of turning Raghunatha Kalama away from his ministership, you released the Japanese monk. These are not your secrets Daddy, these are your achievements, your crown of glory. Listen, you can still atone for what you've done. In fact, I've decided ..." Ramakishore stopped midway. He needed another glass of water to wet his dried up throat.

"What have you decided?" Nalini asked. "Are you bringing that wretched girl into this house?"

"Not I. You two will bring her into this house as your daughter-in-law. It is you who know everything about her and her parents! You take that responsibility. Why should I?" Ramakishore got up and pushed the chair on his way out.

Dibyakishore looked at Nalini. Nalini looked back at Dibyakishore. Just at that moment a constable orderly sidled into the dining room cautiously. He saluted, saying, "The station-in-charge of Keshanagar police station has sent information. Last night there was a big dacoity at the ancestral house of Raghunatha Kalama."

EIGHT

The stench from the open drain hung over the house, thick as a cloud. Ramu sat at the study table, books open, a handkerchief pressed to his nose. Padmavati was trying to get a chulha going in the inner veranda. The smoke rising from the freshly gathered kindling stung her eyes.

Thinking that his mother was weeping over their misfortune, Ramu removed the handkerchief from his face and said, "Don't worry, Bou! Chitu said that Ramakishore spoke to his father a few days ago. That boy is not a bad sort. Deba mausa has agreed to launch a search for bapa."

Just then they heard a motorcycle stop right outside. Padmavati looked out of the window. Chitu was getting off the motorcycle. Ramakishore sat on the front seat, his legs planted firmly on the ground. Padmavati was aware of the friendship that had developed between her daughter and Dibyakishore's son. The young man had been regularly giving Chitu a lift home but so far, he had never come all the way to their doorstep.

Standing at the front door Chitu called out. "Bou! Look who has come! This gentleman is very shy. He is terrified of you. Shall I invite him in?"

Padmavati opened the door. Ramakishore was a replica of his father. Seeing him sitting astride the motorcycle reminded Padmavati of the days when Dibyakisore would come riding along the riverbank to their house. It brought back the scent of the Anoma, the sound of Raghumastra's voice. But only for an instant. The voice was no longer in her life and neither was the river. What remained were the worries and fears in her mind and the terrible miasma rising from the drain in this narrow street in Cuttack.

Chitu said, "Rama, do come in and meet Bou." To her mother she said, "You know, Bou! Rama has got some information about father from the police."

"What did you say?" Padmavati's voice was apprehensive.

"Yes, it is true! The police know everything but unless there is pressure from above they will not divulge anything. You know who Rama is? He is the son of Deba mausa." Chitu introduced the visitor to her mother as if he were a stranger.

They entered the outer room. This room was used both as a sitting room as well as a bedroom for Ramu. His bed was still lying spread out on the cement floor. The narrow room was further congested with his used shirts hanging from hooks on the wall. The rest of the wall was covered with pictures of Hara-Parvati, Lakshmi-Narayan, Sita-Ram and Radha-Krishna that had obviously been cut from calendars. Chitu tidied the room. She rolled up the bedding, put away the clothes and brought in two rickety cane chairs from somewhere. She invited Rama to sit.

To Padmavati, she said, "There is fresh information about bapa. He has been traced to Bihar – what is the name of that place?" Chitu looked at Ramakishore with a smile.

"Kushinara," Ramakishore replied. "Yesterday a Special Branch officer told me this. The Special Branch people of that area saw Raghunatha Kalama in the company of that Buddhist monk, fifteen days ago."

"Then why didn't the police bring him back?"

"How will they bring him in?" Ramakishore asked. "They are not criminals. Can the police arrest and bring in sadhus and sants at will?"

"If that is so then how is it that on that day the police handcuffed my father and Kajyoyoda and dragged them to the police station?" Ramu asked, adding, "The incident happened in front of Deba mausa's eyes. He did not utter a word. The police had beaten up that Japanese monk and my father. At that time I was small. But if it were today ..."

Padmavati said, "Leave it son, it is all in the past."

"You are right Bou," Chitu said in a firm tone.

Chitu was saying, "Bou, you remember that a year ago I met this gentleman in the corridor of the college. A lot of water has flown down the Mahanadi since then. And have you heard the latest? There is a rumour that thieves have taken gold coins and stuff like that from beneath our ancestral house. This gentleman overheard the village dafadar reporting this to his father just this morning."

"What are you saying!" Padmavati sat down, her head slumping into her open palms.

"Please don't worry, Mausi." Ramakishore got up from the chair. He sat on the floor in front of Padmavati. Holding her hand like an elder reassuring a child, he said, "I will find out where Chitu's father is and bring him home. I will do whatever I can to recover the articles stolen from your house. But tell me, what do you think might have been stolen from the house? Was there buried treasure?"

Padmavati decided to trust this young man, even though he was Dibyakishore's son. Despite his appearance and his manner there was a ring of sincerity to his words. "Listen, son," she said. "My husband was no lover of gold and silver, though he spent years excavating into the foundations of his house. I never really knew what he was looking for. But I believe he was searching for some kind of proof. He had a deep knowledge of history. Throughout his life he has delved into things past. When he was a schoolboy, a teacher had said something to him that had led to this obsession with his family's history, he always said."

"What did the school teacher say, Mausi?"

On behalf of her mother, Chitu answered. "The ancient name of Chitrotpala was Anoma. Legend has it that one day in the early hours of dawn Prince Siddhartha Gautama arrived there on his horse Kanthaka. He had left his home the previous night. With him was his charioteer Channa. They came to a vast river. Prince Gautama got down from the horse. What is the name of this river? he asked. Anoma, said Channa. The prince took it as an omen. For some time he kept looking at the far bank with thoughtful eyes. Then he said, One day I too will become as vast as this river, Anoma. He took out his sword – Bapa used to say the name of that sword was Prabalayudha and ... it is believed that even now a portion of this sword is kept in a temple in some forest near Narsinghpurgarh. It is worshipped as the goddess Prabala. Anyway, to get on with the tale, Prince Gautama cut off his hair and handing over the sword and the reins of the horse to Channa, he said, Go tell my father that from today I renounce the world.

There was an ashram on the banks of the Anoma, set up by a sage by the name of Alara Kalama. Gautama entered the ashram and stayed on for several years. Later, he crossed the Anoma and went north ... I have heard all this from my father. Now, the question is what was that priceless treasure that bapa was looking for?"

Ramakishore said, "Surely he must have given some hint?"

Ramu joined in. "Yes, he did ... I have heard him talk about how our village got its name – Keshanagara." Ramu held a lock of his own hair and with the other hand mimed a scissor snipping it off.

Ramakishore leaned forward. "What was that? A lock of hair?"

"Yes!" Ramu laughed and started horsing around.

Chitu grabbed him and gave a resounding slap. Ramu dashed out of the room and Padmavati got up to go placate him.

Alone with Ramakishore, Chitu said, "The thieves were not strangers ... I have heard you father tell mine – Samudi, don't forget to pass on some of the treasure as your daughter's dowry. And bapa would smile. He would say, I'll give everything but there is one thing that I will not pass on. I dream of it quite often, a sage telling me that priceless treasure is buried very deep. Then I see a big stone casket. Inside is a second casket made of copper. Inside that a third casket studded with precious stones. The secret lies in that casket. I don't know for certain what it is but I can make a good guess. Maharishi Alara Kalama was the first guru of Prince Gautama. Later the fame of the disciple far exceeded that of the teacher. Could Alara Kalama have foreseen that it would be so? Is it possible that when the prince cut off his hair, the sage might have saved one lock for posterity? If this is true and I discover that casket, I will never let its contents leave my family. It is proof of more than my lineage. It would be what my father has been searching for all his life. And mine. Proof that Lumbini was not in Nepal but right here!"

Suddenly Ramakishore asked, "You said in the beginning that the thieves were not strangers. Do you suspect my father?"

After a pause Chitu replied, "Rama, don't take it amiss ... I have often wondered why your father came to our house regularly. It was not to see me or my father. Whenever he came he would ask about the tunnel and whether bapa had managed to discover the treasure."

"Are you saying that the promise he made to your father – that he would make you his daughter-in-law was a mere excuse to pry?" Ramakishore sounded quite angry.

"I'm not saying that," Chitu took a deep breath then spoke in a firm voice. "Rama, your father does not just catch thieves. He uses them for his own ends. He knew that there was something buried in the foundations of our house. In the last few months, ever since my father disappeared, that treasure too has vanished. How did that happen? I would like an answer from Deba mausa."

Ramakishore did not wait to listen any further. Leaving the house without a word, he started his motorcycle and drove off.

Padmavati came running. "Why did he leave like that?" she asked. "What did you say to him?"

Chitu's voice was curt. "Nothing."

Nine

Ramakishore was on the Paradip-Cuttack road, driving like a man possessed. The fire that had been ignited by Chitrotpala's words raged in his head. After leaving her house he had simply driven around till he hit the highway. The vehicle was a powerful 7hp motorcycle that had been used by the military in the Second World War. At the end of the war, it had been auctioned. Dibyakishore had bought it for his son as a present for graduating from school with a first class.

He crossed the town of Bidyadharpur. This area was not entirely unknown to Ramakishore. He had visited it in his childhood and remembered an orchard of the sweet kasi koli berries. As a boy he had raided the orchard with his friends. But now the orchard was gone. In its place was a building that looked like a government office. A bit further up the road Ramakishore came to a culvert where a narrow canal branched off from a larger one. At this point a kuccha track led off the highway towards the north. After a while he came to a hillock. Rama's motorcycle rode over it with ease. At the very top the vista expanded so suddenly that he felt breathless.

So this is Chitu's Anoma.

Anoma. Anoma. Anoma. The word reverberated in his head like an incantation. Suddenly he knew why he was here and where this journey would end. Keshanagar. Though he had never been there, he was sure he would reach it eventually. Until then he had seen it in many a dream while listening to that girl about her village and its location somewhere on the bank of the Chitrotpala towards the lower part of Mahanadi. Now he was being guided by those dreams alone. It was those dreams that impelled him to say, over and over again, "Anoma! Keshapura! Alara Kalama!"

In the 1950s, to drive a motorcycle on the bank of the river Mahanadi was like proving your valour in a wrestling competition. But for Ramakishore, the only son of police officer Dibyakishore, it was a life or death challenge. He had come straight out of that thatched house by the side of the stinking municipality drain with the object of putting to test a strong urge derived from a sense of sincere love and admiration but his ego was hurt, too. He continued to argue with Chitu: Stop! I cannot accept your accusations so soon, Chitu, until I see with my own eyes! You cannot cast aspersions on my father's character. Maybe he is cruel and opportunistic. He might have punished and misguided your father time and again. But he is a good police officer. He is not so crass to eye your family wealth on the pretext of making you his daughter-in-law. Daddy and Mummy are not the kind who'd get your house dug up by thieves! Note this Chitrotpala. I swear – I swear by the waters of this Mahanadi – if ever your accusations come true then in the waters of the sacred Anoma's Vedic name, I will atone for the sins of my father. Chitu, I swear.

By nightfall, Ramakishore had reached Keshanagar. He asked for directions to Raghumastré's house. The villagers were reminded of the police officer who would ride in on his horse during the war years, as they gave him directions and stood watching his motorcycle ride along the riverbank and stop in front of the dilapidated house.

The house had been pulled apart. There were huge piles of rubble all over the compound. In the middle was a deep hole that looked like the entrance to a tunnel. This was where the Japanese monk had lain hidden. His father had ordered that arrest. But it was wartime, Ramakishore reasoned. And his father was only doing his duty.

Suddenly Ramakishore felt another presence. He turned around. A tall, dark man was looking down at him. There was something menacing about him. Ramakishore trembled, but keeping his voice steady asked, "Who are you? What are you doing here?"

The face cracked into a smile revealing two rows of betel stained teeth. And then came the counter question, "Who are you? Are you after Raghumastré's buried treasure? Will you come along to the police station or do I have to drag you?"

Affecting boldness, Ramakishore said, "Do you know who I am? My father is DIG Dibyakishore Das. And you want to take me to the police station?"

The effect was instantaneous. The man dived for Ramakishore's feet and begged pardon, introducing himself as dafadar Raju Jena. Thereafter it was not at all difficult to obtain the dafadar's version of events.

"Bada saheb? You mean my father? When did he come here?"

Raju Jena was only too willing to answer all of Ramakishore's questions. After listening to him, Ramakishore asked one last question. "You say there was a stone casket lying out in the open yesterday?"

"Yes, sir. The police have seized that casket. It is in the custody of our station-in-charge, sir."

Ramakishore kick-started his motorcycle. He switched on the headlight and by its light saw a portion of brick wall – with a painting on it. The vivid colours seemed to glow with life. There was an ancient house and part of a horse. The head was missing. A little clearer was the image of a well-built handsome young man in princely attire. He held a sword in one hand and a fistful of long hair in the other. The lower part of the picture had been destroyed.

The sight of that ruined painting saddened Ramakishore. He took a deep breath and turned the motorcycle towards the road. It was almost midnight when he reached home.

TEN

The next morning Ramakishore was up at dawn. Bathed and dressed he went out into the long veranda and paced up and down rehearsing what he would say to his father. He glanced at his watch. Breakfast was still an hour away. Feeling that he could not wait any more he tapped on the door of his parents' bedroom.

Nalini opened it. She was surprised to see Ramakishore. Before she could ask him anything, he said, "Mummy, please wake up daddy. I must speak to him about that priceless archaeological discovery. What has he done with the casket? I want an answer right now."

Dibyakishore appeared in his night suit. "What is the matter, boy?" he asked. "What are you talking about? Are you out of your mind?"

Ramakishore walked past his mother and faced Dibyakishore. He said, "You went to Raghunath Kalama's village for an inquiry. What did you do with the stone casket? What was inside it? Where is it now, Daddy? Please tell me the truth. Otherwise I can't live in this house another minute."

Dibyakishore had dealt with all sorts of men in his life. And now, his back to the wall, the first thing that emerged from his mouth was a vulgar abuse. Turning to his wife, he said, "This is not my son. Who fathered him? I hope you didn't sleep with a constable, or did you?"

His words hit Nalini like a slap on her face. And in front of her son!

She raised her head and hissed like an angry cobra. "All your life you've spent nights in dak bungalows with the wives and daughters of those constables. So you should know."

"Shut up!" Dibyakishore reached for Nalini's throat and before Ramakishore could stop him, he'd snatched the heavy necklace from around her neck and flung it to the floor. "For a wife who needs a new necklace every day, how does it matter whether her husband is of good character or not, honest or not?"

Ramakishore noticed that this necklace was different from the one which had sparkled on his mother's neck yesterday. His mother must have taken it out of her ornament chest last night.

Nalini picked up the necklace and said, "Beware ... This is my mother's necklace. Unlike you my father did not toady to the powerful in order to rise from a lowly SI's rank to that of a DIG. He was a dewan bahadur, a zamindar."

"Dewan bahadur, my foot!" Dibyakishore snatched the necklace away. He sneered, "Is this your father's property then?"

"So it is your father's?" Turning to his son Dibyakishore thrust the necklace at him. "Take this!" he said. "It belongs to Raghunath Kalama. I know you've been going around with that daughter of his."

Ramakishore could not believe his ears. He took the necklace and turned it around. The morning light fell on the stones giving them a rich beauty. It appeared to be a very old necklace. Which century did it belong to? For a few minutes there was pin drop silence in the room. Then it was shattered by Ramakishore.

"What have you done? Why? For this? This means nothing to Raghunath Kalama. Kindly hand over the fruit of Raghunatha's lifelong research. What happened to that jewelled box in which the divine relics were kept? Bhagwan Buddha's ..."

"Oh! The box with hair?" Nalini suddenly became animated.

Ramakishore fell at his mother's feet. In an imploring voice he asked, "Mummy! Is that box with you? Have you kept it? Where is it? Give it to me quickly. Quickly ... Soon ... Immediately ...," the words almost choked the boy.

Without brooking any delay Nalini took out a bunch of keys and opened the safe.

The glitter of the gold within dazzled Ramakishore's eyes. In that instant he knew that none of it was rightfully his mother's. That Chitu had been right. His father was hand in glove with thieves.

Nalini quickly found the jewelled box in her ornament chest. She pressed the box in Ramakishore's hands, saying, "Take it! You went to the village yesterday only to search for this? That thief of a dafadar confiscated this box with the necklace from those dacoits. That wicked fellow told your father that these were the only two things that the dacoits left behind during the chase. God knows where the rest is. Your daddy has taken up the case personally. Now take it! See what is there inside it."

Ramakishore barely listened to her. He carefully examined the casket. It had a coppery sheen and looked very ordinary, like the sort of box married women use for sindoor. He tried the lid. It opened easily. Who would expect the lid of such an archaeological find, buried under the earth for thousands of years, to open so easily? This casket has been handled by many hands. Thieves, dacoits, dafadar, police and, finally, his mother! Yet reverently touching the casket to his head, Ramakishore threw open the lid of the casket.

"Arré! What is this?" Ramakishore exclaimed loudly. Seeing a copper coin inside the casket he shouted, "Was this in the casket? Who put this copper coin here? Where have all the relics gone? Where's ..."

"Careful now!" Dibyakishore said, butting in. "This is not an ordinary coin. It is worth lakhs of rupees. Look at the inscription. This coin was struck to commemorate the coronation of King Ramachandra after he returned from Sri Lanka to Ayodhya ... You ask your mother what she did with those other relics-felics or whatever you call it."

Dibyakishore spoke calmly, trying to muster some dignity after becoming a thief in the eyes of his son. But Rama's shrieking and shouting reached a crescendo, and Nalini finally said, "Chhi, does any one keep a dead person's hair in the house? I threw it away. I kept that coin only because the chowkidar who brought all these things here insisted that it would bring us good luck. Your house will overflow with gold, money, dhana and jana, gopa and lakshmi, he said. I opened the casket and looked in. And there was just this bunch of hair inside it! I felt like vomiting. I threw away the hair and put this copper coin in its place."

Ramakishore couldn't believe his ears. "You threw away the hair? The hair of Bhagwan Buddha?" He raised his hand as if about to strike his mother but Dibyakishore caught it and after a brief struggle overpowered him. He pushed Ramakishore to the floor. Then he sat down and held his head in his hands. Rama lay on the floor, his body heaving. Surely it was not the few blows and slaps. This was the first time Dibyakishore had hit his son.

Dibyakishore helped his son sit up. Ramakishore turned his face away. Dibyakishore knew what was going through his son's mind: He would never be able to look his father in the face. Dibyakishore understood. But it was a long, long while before a strange question rose reluctantly from his throat. "Rama, what will I have to do to atone for this sin?"

Ramakishore looked away. What could he say? The knowledge that Chitu had been right in her accusation did not hurt as much as seeing his father shorn off his dignity.

Meanwhile Nalini was emptying out the contents of the safe onto a turkish towel. She pulled the four corners together in a knot. Then she dropped the bundle before Ramakishore. "Take this. Give it back to its rightful owner."

Seeing the bewildered look in his son's eyes, Dibyakishore said with a harsh laugh, "Yes, it's Raghunath Kalama's property. Return it to his family. The dacoits had recovered all these buried goods from under their house. That dacoit was no other than I myself. They merely carried out my directions. Take them."

Ramakishore recoiled as if stung. Kicking the bundle away, he said, "Compared to what you've thrown away as a dead man's hair, this is nothing!"

ELEVEN

Three years had passed since Raghunath and Kajyoyoda started out from the Kapileswar temple. In Orissa they had passed through Lumbini pargana or modern day Lumbei, Debadaha or Govindpur, Kodanda on the eastern edge of Cuttack. Then they reached the river Chitrotpala and entered the village Keshanagar but Raghunath didn't cast one single glance at his ancestral home. He calmly passed it by. They crossed the river Chitrotpala and went along, following the landmarks in the map Kajyoyoda carried. They followed the ancient routes to the north that Prince Siddharth had taken some 2500 years ago.

Passing through Dharamshala, Anandapur and Kendujhar they reached Champua and crossed into Bihar. They had spent some weeks in Rajgir and Gaya and so had reached Kushinara where Tathagata had attained parinirvana. They spent six months in Kushinara.

Drawing upon his extensive knowledge of the Buddhist scriptures, Kajyoyoda quoted a line in the Pali language from the Mahaparinirvana Sutra, explaining its meaning,

"Tathagata then became eighty years old. That day he had accepted bhiksha from the blacksmith Chunda's house. The bhiksha had been contaminated with some kind of local liquor and pork. And Bhagwan fell ill. Seeing the full moon of the Baisakha rising in the sky he moved away from the river bank into the forest. He called Ananda to his side and shared with him the premonition.

"Ananda asked in a voice filled with anxiety: My lord! What shall we do? Let us go, my lord. We will carry you to some nearby city like Champa, Rajagriha, Sravasti, Saketa, Kosambi or Varanasi.

"Tathagata reassured Ananda and his disciples. He said: This Kushinara is an old and famous sacred place. Out of Lava and Kusha, the famous twin sons of Ramachandra, of Ayodhya, the country named after Maharaja Kusha had Kushinara as its capital.

I have chosen this sacred place for parinirvana.

"After this, Bhagwan entered a sal forest. Ananda prepared a bed for him between two big trees and he lay down on his right side resting his hand on his head. And in the last quarter of that full moon night of Baisakha, Tathagata breathed his last."

Chitram Jambudwipam Manoramam Jivatam Manushyanam. The two men stood on top of a hill overlooking the beautiful Hiranyavati valley. Kushinagara was the last place of Bhagwan Buddha's pilgrimage. He had walked many years and had reached his eighty first year.

Kajyoyoda said, "It was in a sal forest on the banks of the Hiranyavati that Bhagwan attained nirvana. Observing the natural beauty of Jambudwipa, he said to his disciple Ananda, on the last evening of his life, that those who are born in this land are naturally pious. The incomparable natural beauty and the simple lives they lead make them so."

"But where are these people now, bhikshu? The people of today kill a great mahatma like Gandhiji. To use those words to describe the amoral and ignorant society of this country is a joke." Kajyoyoda smiled. He understood the dilemma of his companion. "But, Raghunath, please do not forget Nagasaki and Hiroshima. Your Mahatma attained nirvana with the words Hé Ram! In Japan, the atom bomb vapourized lakhs within the twinkling of an eye. Not even a word of grief could they utter. Your country certainly is more fortunate."

"Bhikshu," Raghunath said, "Bhagwan Buddha said to his disciples that if the principles were consistently observed, Buddha dharma may last a thousand years. But how many years will Gandhi dharma last? Do you think Gandhi dharma has any relevance in this country of mine?"

"The scriptures prescribe that bhikshus and sanyasis should not stay in one place for too long. In a world where change is the only constant, it creates an illusion of permanency that prevents the soul striving for nirvana from continuing its journey." After a pause Kajyoyoda continued, "Raghunath, you are not able to forget your earlier life. Do you want to return to that family life? If you like, we can return. Shall we? As for me, I'm homeless forever. I will keep travelling till the end."

"No," said Raghunath firmly.

TWELVE

Asti Uttarasyam Disi Devatama
Himalayo Namah Nagadhiraja,
Poorbaparodwaya Nidhibagahya,
Sthitah Pruthibyaiba Manadanda

As Raghunath had his first glimpse of the Himalayas, his excitement became intense. The stanza he would recite so often was a Sanskrit poem from a school text. It was a passage from the epic Kumarsambhava, written by Mahakavi Kalidas. Unable to contain his joy, Raghunath said to his companion, "Do you know why I feel so happy? With each step I take, I can feel Shiva's heartbeat in my blood."

"I understand," Kajyoyoda said, "This is your inherited tradition. The people of this land rejected Buddhism because the tradition of Shiva consciousness is so strong. That's just the way it is."

Though Kajyoyoda was just as pleased with the natural beauty, he was looking for the route to Rumindei or modern day Lumbini. And then, they came upon a pillar standing at the edge of a thick forest. "That is the Rumindei pillar. It is here that the stone inscription was found which the historians say represents the proof of Buddha's birthplace. Come. Let us examine it."

In the sixth century BC all this was part of the Sakya kingdom. Shuddhodhana was the king and Kapilavastu the capital. He recalled having read that every year on Akshaya Trittiya, king

Shuddhodhana would go to the fields and sow the first paddy seeds himself. That would mean that paddy was grown in this area all those many centuries ago. He looked around and saw that the forest had been cut down. New human settlements had come up and tractors were clearing the land. Kajyoyoda was looking at Raghunath, smiling, with a question that seemed to take off from Raghu's own thoughts.

"Do you know the meaning of the word Shuddhodhana? It means pure rice. But rice was planted in this area only after India became independent. You won't find Shuddhodhana's paddy fields here, my friend. You have left them far behind near the village of Kapileswar in Orissa!"

And then Kajyoyoda had spoken of the famous German archaeologist, Dr Feuhrer, who had come across the stone inscription proclaiming that four stupas and a stone pillar had been constructed on the orders of Emperor Ashoka in 249 BC. That was the year Ashoka had paid a royal visit to the garden of Lumbini where Sakyamuni was born ...

"Now read the map. What is the name of this place?"

Raghunath leaned over and looked at the map. "Padariya."

He looked at Kajyoyoda with bewildered eyes. The monk explained, "Yes, it was in Padariya, this village, that Dr Feuhrer found that stone inscription in 1896, that is, two thousand, three hundred and eighty five years after the parinirvana of Bhagwan Buddha. This discovery got worldwide publicity. Suddenly everyone knew of Rumindei." Kajyoyoda burst out laughing. "Rumindei is the modern day name of Lumbini. That is how the local people pronounced it."

"It is indeed strange!" Raghunath said. "If Padariya can be Rumindei and so Lumbini, then why not Lumbei? Did you not say that in 1928, another similar stone edict was discovered at the village Kapileswar and is now in the Ashutosh museum at Calcutta?"

Kajyoyoda said, "From the day I set foot in India I have been consumed by this question: Was Tathagata one person or more than one? How can one man take birth at two different places at the same time?" They reached the Ashoka Stambha, the world famous Terai Pillar. Raghunath stared at it. He had limited knowledge of the Ashokan pillars but this one seemed different. He said, in a voice full of doubt, "Ashoka pillars are broad at the base and taper toward the top, don't they? This one is of uniform girth top to bottom. Besides where is the bell shaped top with the four lions?"

"I have wondered about it as well. Ten years ago when I visited this place, I was just as disappointed as you are right now. I could not accept that this was once the garden of Lumbini. I have studied this stone inscription and compared it to a similar one in Kalinga. The inscription says more or less the same thing as this one, except for one additional line that gives the year of origin and the signature of the inscriber. Now my question is which of the stone inscriptions should we accept as prima facie evidence of Bhagwan Buddha's birthplace?"

It was the Japanese monk who finally broke the silence. He patted Raghunath and asked with a smile, "Let us go. I would like a darshan of Kailash."

Raghunath looked up curiously. "Why do you wish to go to Kailash Mansarovar?"

Kajyoyoda looked at him through narrowed eyes. "Why do Hindus?"

Raghunath replied, "It is an old tradition. The path of renunciation brings us to the north."

Kajyoyoda listened with keen attention. But all the while there was a hint of a smile in his eyes. Suddenly he opened them wide and burst out laughing. "Well? Why did Siddhartha Gautama who was born in Padariya village in the Himalayan foothills go south in order to renounce the world? Was Gautama Buddha not born in the Indian tradition? Then why did he break it? Or did he?"

Flashes of his past came back to Raghunath. He saw clearly his ancestral house on the banks of the Chitrotpala. He saw himself digging at the foundations of the house in an effort to trace his lineage. What madness was that? At the end of it, what did he achieve? Raghunath looked sad. He felt as if a big piece of stone nearby was inviting him to sit down for a while.

Raghunath sat down. He saw that Kajyoyoda had suddenly become still. His eyes were closed. After some time Kajyoyoda raised one of his hands in a mudra that Raghunatha had never seen before. He was reminded of a unique, mysterious form. Although he had only seen it in a picture before, he now experienced its living source in his body of flesh and blood. And the monk shining in his Agnyachakra seemed to appear like Paramahansa Ramakrishna, next like the Gautama Buddha, his object of worship and then from all the many forms of Gautama, one picture fixed itself in his mind's eye. Of Prince Gautama mercilessly cutting his hair.

The monk Kajyoyoda tapped Raghunath gently to break his meditative trance.

Raghunath said softly, "Let us go forward to Kailash Mansarovar."

"Vatsa," his co-traveller of many years said. "No, not now. Your time has not yet come Raghunath." As if commanding he said, "Prepare yourself! The sansar is in need of you. They are coming! I could see them coming towards us clearly in my dhyana."

Raghunath was puzzled. "Who are coming?" he asked.

"They – your wife, daughter and then your friend Dibyakishore with his wife and son Ramakishore. Now it's time you forgive and forget," the saint whispered.

"The primary quality of the Agnyachakra is forgiveness. Time has not yet come for you to go to the Himalayas. You will go back again to lead a worldly life. A lot of your duties remain incomplete there. Do not resist the demands of your destiny and those which you have yourself caused to exist."

And as Raghunath waited calmly to take in Kajyoyoda's words, the party had indeed arrived.

Monk Kajyoyoda looked on at the family reunion from a distance. For a moment a passing reflection of his own family life flashed in his mind. A long forgotten event of his life triggered his memory to work. His long dead mother's pale and withered face seemed to be visible for a moment. Kajyoyoda met his mother for the last time before he left Japan for India years back. The news of her death had reached him in India. He had never till now met her in his dreams but at that instant her face suddenly appeared to materialize in front of him!

Chitu prostrated herself at the sanyasi's feet. This was the first time she had seen him since that shocking event of his arrest at their Keshanagar home all those years ago.

Tears rolled down the monk's cheeks. Kajyoyoda's hand touched Chitu's head and he blessed her, "O Anoma's daughter! Soubhagyavati bhava."

ক

KASHI NATH SINGH

WHO'S THE THUG
LOOTING THE CITY?

———◆———

TRANSLATED FROM HINDI BY
PAMPOSH KUMAR AND GEETA DHARMARAJAN
first published in Tadbhav, April 2001, Lucknow

NOMINATED BY SARA RAI

Shringar ka din. It is the day the gods and goddesses of Assi Ghat are bejewelled and bedecked. The pathway is flanked by twin peepal trees. Very old trees. On the stone platform under one sit Hanuman and Shiva, the other ensconces Durga, Bhairavnath and Ratneshwar Mahadev. These modest shrines have been decorated, as also the peepal trees and the shops. Strings of coloured bulbs twinkle all around.

Two stages face each other across the path, all set for the question-answer contest, the famous Biraha Dangal. There's Bullu and Party on one side, on the other Hiralal and Troupe. They are reputed birahiyas of Poorvanchal, singers invited far and wide. Bullu holds the kartal, ready to bring the best off the wooden blocks with small bells at the fringes. Hira is to alternate between the tambourine and the jaw harp – the faar and the chang. Both sides have the harmonium, the dholak and the drums with stretched skin, the nagade. Cymbals, flute and electric guitar are at the ready for the contest of wits.

Every year, the three months of cold weather, actually four or five, are reserved for the gods. There is no lane, street, junction or crossroad where a god or goddess is not being dolled up. And where there's a shringar, there are the performers, the kajali singers and the birahiyas and the qawwals, (people who, in between, earnestly audition for or participate in an orchestra or a cinema show; mostly unsuccessfully.)

These are the parties that will pit themselves through songs set to different ragas, tunes and biraha rhythms against one another with tales lifted from the Mahabharata, Ramayana or Puranas, historical narratives or folklore in the making. These tales are topical, if not, they are twisted into pertinence. So what if it's old, it strikes a personal note and there's the audience, with it.

Here's Hiralal, the one with the chang, in a Gandhi topi, unbleached mill-cloth kurta, dhoti, a small towel across his shoulder. And there's Bullu in a bright kurta, dhoti and smart shawl, holding the kartal. A clash of generations, a certain acrimony. It's not the questions and answers that matter as much as taking the story to its conclusion. Both sides weave their way through a maze of melodies and tunes. The first bout is over. So's half the night. This incident dates back to when the nation was celebrating its fiftieth anniversary as a democracy.

All approaches to the crossroad are jam-packed with the young and the old, babies and children from the neighbourhood and outside. Rikshawallas and tempowallas, thelawallas and daily wage labourers, small-time *shopkeepers in large numbers, college students, as also bench-warmers from Pappu's tea shop loiter around, chewing paan. Perhaps that's why Bullu's selected this tale of present day Assi.*

With dawn, the tale is over. We are back in the twenty first century. And there's a bloodied torso of a man ... Friends, behind this story lies the essence of that biraha tale. The basic pattern and framework is that of the birahiyas, all I have done is add a bit of colour and polish.

An isle amongst isles, Jambudweep. The subjects of Jambudweep are sad. Call them subjects, call them citizens, what does it matter, they are a sad and troubled lot. By what? By Air, Water, Sunlight and Cold. No law or order, no amount of force prevail on them. As if they dance solely to their own pleasures and desires. When they please they bring on gales and storms to uproot villages, trees, buildings and roofs and electricity poles; rivers flood and sweep off entire settlements, standing crops rot. As for the Sun, just don't ask! It desires and instantly there's drought and heaps of skeletons. And the defenseless helpless people? What can they do but watch silently and curse their fate, be silent spectators of atrocity and injustice. How can they tolerate sandstorms, a barren desert when all they long for is water, or swamp when they need sunlight and dryness. Oh, they simply do as they please, this Sun, Moon and Wind.

Panchayat after panchayat was constituted. One, two, three and then a fourth ... Panchayat after panchayat deliberated and pondered. *What* can be done, what *can* be done? Nothing worked.

After a great deal of thought, the public formed yet another panchayat. The members elected a sarpanch. Vrindavan Bihari Lal. Call him sarpanch, call him pardhan or Raja babu, what does it

---

The birahiyas are accomplished folk singers with an amazing talent for the extempore. They spin and twirl the storyline, bend and turn a raga on public demand. The tale may be set to rhyme and rhythm or the birahiya may choose to tell it in plain prose or dialogue. He may poke fun at his opponent or crack jokes at him. Sometimes, one side stops midway for the opponent to complete the story. And the audience, hungry for it all, rewards their favourite birahiya with ten, twenty, hundred rupee notes. If lucky, it's garlands of currency notes. It's a birahiya's duty to announce the amount and thank the

matter. When Raja babu, Bihari bhaiyya, took over, each and every home sang felicitations, lit ghee-filled diyas and cooked a festive dinner. If Bihari bhaiyya is king, then we are kings too. Each and every soul in Jambudweep is sovereign.

The members of the Panchayat, the Panch, said, "Bihari bhaiyya, don't think of this as Assi. Think this the Delhi of Jambudweep.

You know their plight, the masses call.
You are our mother and father, all.
You're wise, your duty you never shirk.
Do act sensibly, you know your work.
What can we say, look and see,
our kind and dear pradhanji.

And Bihari Lal replied: "Don't say a word, you won't go unheard. I've pledged to lead all into the twenty first century."

Sleepless nights followed unquiet days for Bihari Lal. How could he wipe out poverty? The king's woe was the public's woe was Bihari Lal's too: On whose command does Wind blow? On whose order does Rain fall? Who asks Sun to rise and set? These are the real issues. Solve them and all problems are over.

Raja babu aka Bihari Lal
asked the experts one and all.
He quizzed his vazirs and his Think Tank,
asked them to be free and frank.
The Ministers were in complete sync,
the Think Tank too did a quick think:
Who can question, who can do what,
who has control over God?

---

person publicly. Birahiyas are not original creators but fundamentally no less. On occasions, they employ nirguna in their contests, that pulls the rasikas away from the mere grammar of life and the technique of the biraha. So say, one sings a riddle:

Billaiya acts coy, ei sadhu baba, billaiya acts coy.
After devouring Brahma and chewing up Vishnu.
After hurling Shiva against the Himalayas.
Billaiya acts coy, ei sadhu baba, billaiya acts coy.

God! The word was etched on Bihari Lal's heart. One night, he shouted his lungs out, "Catch God! Even if you run roughshod!"

Macebearers scurried.

Spies, police and the courtiers worried.

Where was God? Not here.

Not there.

Where was God? Found?

Not found?

What next? What next?

So then, Chacha Hiralal, what next?

Hiralal's party's on now. Hiralal picks up the chang. He stretches out the alaap. Ah my brothers! If affairs of the state are hard to understand, more so is it to understand the Raja. Had it not been so, on Bihari Lal's throne would be Bullu. Or me Hiralal.

The Raja shouted, the Raja ordered, the Raja discussed and talked. But they who should have obeyed orders and sent out messengers, sent the mafia instead. With an entire arsenal. Go get Him, get Him! Wherever He is, go net Him. But for god's sake, make it legit.

God was in Ayodhya. He had just stepped out of the mandir and was on His way to the masjid when he was surrounded. Abducted. Brought to Mumbai.

Now see the situation spawn. Don't just listen ... see what's on.

A five star hotel in Mumbai. At the back is a swimming pool as

---

And turning to his opponent, asks: Now tell me bhaiyya, what's billaiya?

Or, tell me, they'd challenge, Immersed in the Ganga, the beautiful girl delights,

knowing not that machharia has stolen her jhulaniya.

So what do the fish and nose ring denote, bhaiya for the girl plunged in earthly delights?

The birahiyas' range has expanded today to include current politics, social and cultural issues and the old folk tunes and songs are laced with the latest pop and video music. Bollywood music has ruined the traditional biraha.

wide as a lake. In the middle, a temple. God sits in durbar. It's afternoon. Before Him are four tycoons.

> *One from Delhi and one from Mumbai,*
> *one from Kolkata and one from Chennai.*
> *The swimming pool has on all four borders*
> *keertan groups, distinct and diverse.*
> *Pleased by their dutiful deeds,*
> *their prayer beads,*
> *God's come in person, to give darshan.*
> *Raghupati Raghav Raja Ram.*
> *Pati tapavan Sita Ram.*

"O Lord, what orders do you have for us your devotees?"
God looked as if in everlasting bondage to his devotees, fearful of being eternally mortgaged.

> *"Whither devotion without fear?*
> *Wind, Water, Sun and Cold are but my gear.*
> *These are my curses, some of them boons.*
> *Every creature on earth fears these my tunes.*

"And you people want to take my weapons away?"
"We aren't asking these for free, are we?" said the Seths.
God looked at them dejectedly.

> *"Bhagwan, please!*
> *Don't be agitated or angry, act with acumen.*
> *We're not demanding, we're just human.*
> *Say it or not, we know you've been through a bad day.*
> *But where would you be, if atheists and communists*
> *had had their way.*
> *They'd have all but annihilated you.*
> *Except us, how many are left to inquire about you?*
> *Temples, mosques, churches, all in such a sorry state.*
> *Fear's rampant. How many stop by your gate?*

"And all you do is sit around swatting flies."

God asked, "Did you abduct me just to make me listen to all this?"

The Seths replied, "What are you saying, Prabho? Would we have the audacity to kidnap you? Who else have we but you to cry out our sorrow? If there's something to ask for, whom else do we have in view?"

A tender smile touched God's lips. "Indeed. How better can anyone beseech me?"

> *"Bhagwan, don't lose your cool. Look at it this way, then.*
> *Your population touched thirty six crores, who knows when.*
> *In the meantime, new versions of you have appeared. In billions.*
> *All of these – women folk, brethren, offspring – are your minions.*
> *Your earlier abodes are ramshackled,*
> *they desperately need to be tackled.*
> *That you need new houses, is a discreet matter.*
> *Everyone needs food and drink on a platter.*
> *The only way is through pujan, yagna, havan.*
> *Remember you're entangled in property disputes, even.*

"If you don't bother about all this, who will?"

"So you want to strike a deal?" asked God.

The tycoons laughed. "Bhagwan, what do we know apart from making deals."

> *"Am I a fool to not understand your motives, the temptation*
> *you throw?*
> *I understand the public psyche much better than you know.*
> *The subjects follow whatever the Raja does.*
> *They have faith only in their Raja, not in tycoons and*
> *hoarders. Bas!"*

The tycoons said, "And what if the Raja does what we decree?"

And God said, "Talk to the Raja first, then talk to me."

God stood up to take leave.

"We aren't going to let you go just like this.
You can't leave us feeling so amiss.
If you think you understand the public psyche,
then we too understand the Raja's big play.
We desperately need you, Bhagwanji!
But the Raja needs us as much, you know.
Without us, there is no Raja, ji.
How about a quid pro quo?"

God noticed that the doors to the temple were shut. Armed guards stood outside. Beyond them was the lake. God stood up and almost immediately sat down. Seeing no way out, He got irritated. "This is the limit! I'm fed up of you. Please! Air, water, whatever, you're always after rupees. First pollute it and make money, then clean it up and make money. How long can you carry this on?"

This was followed by such a wrangling between the two sides. The tycoons openly expressed their doubts about God as the Supreme Being.

"We've never seen God with a moustache spread.
Never ever seen God sporting a sacred thread.
Never jittery like you – God's smiles always linger.
No bow? No flute? No sudarshan chakra on your finger ...
How can we accept all this isn't odd?
How can we accept that you indeed are God?"

So brothers and all. Both opponents were sharp and clever. Hard headed. God had seen how smoke from mills and factories on earth had shrouded the sky, how the air as well as the streams and rivers had been polluted. How sirens blared day and night, loudspeakers, radio, transistors and horns screamed away as if to render the outer space deaf, dumb and listless. Nothing was going to remain unpolluted for long. However, there was a good chance that if God struck a deal now, it would be to His

advantage. The day wasn't too far off when nobody would give a
hoot about Him.

On the other hand, for the tycoons it was now or never.

If we were in His place, we might have held out a little longer.

Why rush?
The rates are going to go up, we'll be plush.
Maybe He never saw the day
when what keeps man alive would be sold
in packets, bottles and polybags gay.
Air, Water, Sunshine and Cold
like spice, milk, pulse, flour and rice.
Whoever wants to live would
have to pay the quoted price.
Or face a sad demise.

Each side understood the needs and compulsions of the other.
God was helpless and the tycoons unyielding on the point that,
hard or soft, the deal had to be struck. It was to everyone's
advantage. Who knows how long this earth may last?

After a great deal of haggling, a settlement was arrived at:

Whatever was God's on Earth, was with the Seths.
That's that.
In return, all glory would be His.
The tycoons would nurture
His interests.
And please, no backchat.

The deal was made. After all, what else is there except what is
already on this planet? The Seths were ecstatic!

Bullu beta, tell us what they did.
The Water Seth, the Seth for Sunlight,
the Seth for Cold, the Seth for Air lite.
Tell us about the government's cures,
for the rest of the tale is yours.

Bullu takes centre stage, break ke baad.

As I said earlier, facing each other across the road are the stages. The space between them and on the sides is covered with durries. Sitting on these durries, wrapped in thick bedcovers and blankets is the bidi-smoking, tobacco-chewing audience. However, the real crowd is on the streets and the footpaths. These whole night music and dance shows, along the roads and ghats are a regular feature of Assi. Today's just one such day.

It is a customary practice among the birahiyas that as long as the tale is gathering momentum and the audience is eager, their ears attuned to the telling, there is no banter. When people start getting fidgety, the birahiyas switch over to ridicule.

That night, both birahiyas were steeped in ganja and bhang, marijuana and opium. One wasn't allowed to have bhang again and again, but could take a puff just before one's turn. And then they would cast a spell with their chang or kartal, bringing drops of sweat on the listeners' foreheads even in the height of winter. And the bajaiyyas would get into the swing. The enthralled listeners would shower ten and twenty rupee notes on the players.

Bullu was an expert in copying the latest film tunes. What more could the audience ask for? As he played the kartal, he'd dance, flinging his hands around in abandon. For ten minutes the crowd would be in a frenzy. The musicians would stay wholeheartedly with them. Tidik, tidik dhim ... Dhurrh dhurrh dham dham tidik ... Till at last, Bullu would signal them to silence.

So bhaiyya, join me. May God bless old man Hiralal.

> Who knows what they made of Him, brothers.
> A trader, dealer like many others?
> But it's certain that news didn't reach the papers.
> Instead was a mention
> of Bihari Lal and his men.
> And their brihat Mumbai convention.

But even these worthy newspapers didn't mention the dinner that was organized in the five star hotel at the same time. The party was hosted by the four tycoons. The guest list included a government representative: The finance minister. This vazir of the Khazana delivered a speech. A sensational speech.

That in this very century, some of the world's nations have leaped into the twenty first century.
We are lagging behind.
That we have a lot to accomplish, a long way to go, a lot of this and that to do and by doing this and that,
the next century we must find.
That there was a time when we showed the way to the rest of the world, gifted them with the Light of Knowledge, taught them culture and etiquette,
is all but known.
That it is now time for a repeat performance is our humble request to the world at large. Invest in us.
Help us march to the future throne.
Come on, give us a hand!

So Friends! This speech was for the press. And splashed it was in New York, London, Paris and Tokyo before anyone could figure out what was so great about it. What mattered was that it was a closed door meeting. Between the tycoons and the vazir. And here too there was an argument. Listen.

The first to speak was the Mumbai tycoon. He said:

"On Juhu, Marine Drive and other seashores from wherever the monsoons approach,
I've raised structures so high that not a single cloud can stray in from any direction or encroach.
The entire country can have godowns of seasonal, unseasonal, grey, black, red, white, wet, damp or dry clouds.
And now we can collect, sort out and hoard all kinds of such shrouds.
Depending on the rain a particular region needs, the other clouds could be blown out.

Dark clouds for heavy rainfall, grey for light rains; light, fluffy
clouds for a cool shade, can all be made to sprout.

"We can achieve similar effects through waterways –
rivers, canals, dams, rivulets, tube wells, et cetera.
What we'd like to know from you is this: How can you help us?
Now don't give us a mere chimera."

"These matters shall be considered," the vazir said gravely.
"Please continue."

"This way the clouds won't sweep away village after village. But
that depends on you. Or else the cloud can render dry and kill too."

A turbaned Seth from another city now said:

"We got a raw deal – from Sun.
But we have no regrets, not one.
At last, after a lot of hard work, Sun's no longer our dread.
It is so huge that it cannot be stored in a single blast furnace.
Therefore, we constructed several, each in a different place.
It has been a very expensive exercise,
but, complete control over Day and Night, we no longer agonize.
You are the government, tell us what you wish.
Say Day, it'll be day. Command Night, and total darkness
we'll accomplish.
What is there for us to do here?
If Sun shines, you shine. If it is extinguished, your end too
is near.
The matter is of mutual interest.
We understand it and so do you. God manifest."

He had barely finished when the third Seth began to speak,
about the air and atmosphere, disease and gas leaks. The minister's
mouth turned dry. When he heard the Seth saying that air-prana-
heart-heartbeat-heart attack, he thrust his fingers into his ears
and blurted out,

"I understand quite a bit.
You don't have to explain it.
Our main consideration are the masses,
and all their many causes.
As long as the public is there, so are you.
And we too.

"Therefore, you people would do better to think of their happiness and restrict the argument to that."

"We don't argue, ji. We leave that to our servants and bureaucrats, to you people, as well. We just do our work. Just as you are not your master, neither are we. There are people above us – in Japan, Germany and America. Just say Yes or No. Our shareholders, suppliers and agents across cities and towns are waiting impatiently for your reply." He sought support from the Seth in a suit and tie. "What do you say, Sethji?" adding, as an afterthought.

"Oh yes, this much we can tell you,
the godowns are fully stocked with goods new.
Want to export them, please go ahead,
for no shortage could vex your head."

"I think that the public ..." began the vazir.

"What public, public are you going on about?" the Seth with the contract for Cold burst out. "Is this a press conference? If you must talk of public, go and do it at the Boat Club, in the Ramlila ground or the Red Fort. As it is, in the Lok Sabha you do enough of it. You may have time to spare, we don't. If the terms are acceptable, it's fine, otherwise go and start preparing for midterm elections. It will become clear there who cares more about the public, we or you."

"No, no ... Don't be angry," the Sun Seth intervened. Turning to the minister, he said, "Ji, we understand your intentions. Have faith in us. We aren't all that selfish. We won't put you in a mess and you will hear no censure. Go! Assure your public of your success."

"I'd like a word first," the Seth for Water said. "There's one thing you could do – ensure that the people are prompt and ready. If this continues to be a nation of shirkers, laggards, idlers, gossip mongers and the slovenly, then all progress is over. So is our leap into the next century. No pain, no gain. There are those who hang around indulging in pointless gossip, smoking cigarettes and bidis, chewing tobacco, spitting paan, going haha, hoohoo – how on earth do you expect change? How do you expect progress?"

The minister glanced at his watch and sat down once again. "You're right," he said thoughtfully, "but, what can we do?"

"Tell us what you can't do."

"Even so, what can you do?"

"Huzoor, is there anything we can't do?" the Seth asked. "What are we for? This entire issue is connected with the market.

> "Your job is to look after governance,
> ours to look after the bazaar.
> We do our job, you stick to your sarkar.
> A bazaar's nothing bizarre.
> It's not the roadside stall,
> not the shop around the corner,
> not even the showcase mall.
> The bazaar's what is at your doorway,
> in your portico, your drawing room, bedroom,
> your kitchen, your toilet, in your almira's array.
> Why just that?
> It's right on you, from the hair on your head
> to the nails on your toes.
> Anyone who visits your home
> or sees your clothes
> starts salivating, loses sleep,
> craves for what you have and not they.
> Yearns so much that he simply has to
> have it by the end of the day.

"And till then nothing holds interest for him – neither food, nor water, nor life. So, that's how it is. Go on, you take care of governance. And listen, just tell us which is the hour in a twenty four hours' day-night schedule, that gives you the worst of headaches?"

(Then for sometime, a clash of instruments followed by a light exchange of words, and then, pause ...)

So, Chacha Hiralal.
In a twenty four hour day,
which is the hour that poses, pray,
for government and its vazirs all
the biggest problem – can you recall?

Faar in hand, Hiralal stood up.

So has begun the timely search
for powerful, satanic, dishonest Time.
A convoluted, long drawn research –
Where is it? And why? Whither Time?
Who knows how many governments were shunted
while Time was being painstakingly hunted?

Bihari Lal too formed a commission, the commission formed study groups, the study groups set up inquiry committees. These committees started working from block and ward level to detect the criminal problem hour.

The search went on. In the meantime, the government saw quite clear:

The water outside is dirty, inside the bottle it's pure.
The sunlight outside is pale and weary, inside it's bright and azure.
The air outside is unclean, inside the box it's brand new.
The cold outside is bitter and freezy, inside it is crisp and true.
The waters of the Ganga are poisonous sulphur.
Bottled Pepsi is sweetest Lehar.

The Seths were doing their job well.

The hunt continued. A big country, therefore a difficult search. Billions and trillions were allocated. America and Japan were the new Gangotri and Jamnotri.

Who all were involved, we don't know.
Who worked how hard, we don't know.
Who stole how much money, we don't know.
Where did the billions and trillions vanish,
we just DON'T know.

All that is known is that the entire report was drafted sitting here at Assi ghat, in Ganga Mahal. In a three sixty five page report, with detailed discussions over Morning, Noon and Night, it was concluded that Evening was the real problem hour.

Evening: the toughest, most tiresome, most dangerous hour.
Evenings are quite outside our power.

"Mantriji, we had always known this.
Now, since you've identified this abyss,
with no further delay, we can help you out.
Trust us and please don't doubt."

This is the hour when children get back from schools,
their return means quarrels, kich-kich, everyday.
Headaches, fisticuffs, quarrels, jump and play.
Hulla gulla. Gulli danda. No rules!

There's just one cure – look at it this way, they are not children, they are the future. And there's only one prospect for them – multinationals. Beg them earnestly into thinking that this is their goal, their destination. They have to make it. They have to get it. Before anyone else. Make up your mind right now, What do you want to be? Engineer? Doctor? Outdated. Collector? Fine, but reservation has killed all incentives. Take a shot at it, or two, if you like – but a multinational, now that's something altogether different. Today Hong Kong, tomorrow New York, day after Paris. The difference between a dollar and an Indian rupee. But son, this is not a game of gulli danda, it's a jalebi race. Remember, those competing against you are not in thousands and lakhs, but in millions and zillions. So, run ... With all your might. Just do it!

Shabash!

And bury them under a mountain of homework, so that there's no time for kich-kich.

This is the hour when unmarried girls
hover around doors and window –
dissatisfied, depressed mouth curls.
What to do? Where to go?
Live or die away?
Hello! Hi! Wow! Hey!

My darling daughters, may you live for a million years. If you're fed up of studies and don't want to become a steno, private secretary, receptionist or probation officer; if becoming a doctor, engineer, air hostess is beyond you, despair not. Get in touch with Shahnaz Hussain and open a beauty parlour in your city or locality. Or take a good look at yourself. So what if you were not born in Bombay, Delhi, Bangalore, Hyderabad? Are you less than any Sushmita Sen, Aishwarya Rai or Lara Dutta? There's no dearth of fashion shows, no lack of serials, no scarcity of video albums. There are scores of television channels. Even if not a veejay, everyone is on the lookout for good figures and cute faces. Take a good look at your figure. If there's some inadequacy, the market is stocked choc-a-bloc with SMS solutions. But,

As long as you are a papa-mama loyalist,
these doors, windows are shut on you.
You're very much on our welcome list
Glance this way, we welcome you.

Yes the deal had indeed been struck. The tycoons were busy.

It is the hour when wives – bored and irritated – enter their kitchens to make chai and bemoan their fate. Chai and chulha, bed and brats. What a life! Is there nothing else beyond this? Of course, there is. Just look around. Why are fast foods selling so well? What are restaurants and hotels for? To break the monotony of the kitchen, right? To revolutionize the concept of taste.

Order what you like – for lips, teeth, nose, ears, eyes, eyelashes, brows, forehead, skin, hair. For all these and more, the market is stuffed with goods for pauper and millionaire. Just look around!

This is the hour when old men and women of the household wake up from their afternoon nap and worry about the fact that they have become a burden to their families. Why are we living? This question bothers them, as well as their sons and daughters-in-law. In fact, when we made the deal with God, we didn't quite appreciate the craving for temples and gods among these people. Anyway...

> So, Mantriji, show these old men and women the way to
> the temples.
> The road to peace, quiet, release, and heavenly miracles.
> Baba, shed this desire-misfire,
> stop this hai-hai overtire.
> What giving-taking, lena-dena fables,
> why the world and all its troubles?
> There are scores of places in this city,
> hundreds of thousands of places of piety,
> millions of gods and goddesses,
> each one so distinct and pretty.
> Somewhere a Ramkatha,
> somewhere else a Ramlila,
> somewhere a yagna,
> or a navagrahha parayana.

This means that there is not a single evening when all this is not happening in ten different places in your neighbourhood. Go on, build your own moksha, divine release. You've sinned enough in this life. Left now are those who are in their prime and the middle-aged.

This is the hour when they return home from office – tired, fed up and irritable. They are your real problem. Your headache. They down cups of tea, then are out in the streets with a scowl on their faces. At tea stalls, at the paan shops, meeting, interacting, gossip, adda, debate and counsel. And then starts a wild, never-ending cycle. Processions, speeches. Hartal, dharna, hunger strike, gherao. Speeches and loud slogans. Zindabad, Murdabad. Effigies are burnt and resolutions made.

Who are these people? Identify them.
They are the lot on the crossroads with Time to condemn,
to mock at government, vazirs and you.
A lot that goes hungry. Yet their laughs and jokes will us subdue.

These are the people with time on their hands every evening. They are the ones you have to think about. When after a long day's work, a man returns home tired, what does he look for? A cup of steaming bitter chai, a smiling, dolled-up wife and entertainment. For these very things, he used to visit the kotha once. Now he gets out into the streets. For cinema, for tamasha.

We've made everything available to him at home. Not just one type of tea, but at least fifty different brands. All the cosmetics one might require ... Why go out for films? Here you are ... These are all the local as well as foreign television companies ... VCRs, CDs, video games, music albums. Is there anything else you want?

Mantriji, this is what is called intelligent thinking. No article 144, no riots, no curfews. No one will dream of calling it a house arrest. His house, his prison. Of his own will. If there's anything left after this, subdue them with the cost of living. They'll choke on it and forget all about evening amusements. So this is our anti-virus for the menace hour:

For some the multinationals,
for some its peripherals.
Temples for some,
entertainment for the glum.
And for all the rest,
the high-price arrest!
Jai Vrindavan Bihari Lal!
Let Dharma win.
Let Adharma spin.
Let there be harmony among living beings all
Har har Mahadev.

The dangal was getting heavy. The crowd became restless, they had started shifting about and talking among themselves. Hira's societal analysis had all but uprooted the fun. Then, Bullu stood up and tactfully resorted to mockery:

Look, Hira's gone senile
O babu log
His wits are at an end
O babu log
His mare is getting heated up
O babu log
His lower cloth is slipping
O babu log
His topi is unravelling
O babu log.

So, bhaiyya log. Hiralal saw the Seths' markets, the weather baskets, the inflation caskets. He saw everything but these, he did not see – Assi's sad parody, spring's sweet melody, music's arduous underbelly.

And who knows what else?

Bhaiyya, although nothing much was left of the Jambudweep

evenings, for Assi, the evening meant the hour of the donkey. An hour when those who fly-kick with their hind legs are active. Whether anyone listens or not, they keep braying. So bhaiyya, the government has taken care of everyone's evening. But what does one do with this donkey hour?

> So let the tune gallop and graze.
> The time brings forth the mule, hooves cloven.
> Four years pass in that many days.
> The hour of the donkey? Don't ask even.

So bhaiyya, after seeing all this and listening to it, what did Assi say to the government?

> Kya bolti tu?
> Hum to saiyyan se naina laraibe,
> hamaar koi ka kari hai?
> We will live as we have always done.
> Laugh our heads off, have rollicking fun.
> We'll dance, sing and play.
> Which saala will dare stop us, pray?

The sarkar said, is that so, desi? And one evening, it quietly sent a tempo to Assi.

It was Bullu's turn again. And let me tell you that we've now reached the '80s. Welcome to the two-legged town with two streams, Varuna and Assi that lend their name to the city – Varanasi. No car, no jeep, no scooter. Just rickshas, cycles and your god-given two feet. Vinoba's car. If you wish you can cover the entire world with these two feet.

And then ...

On Assi's very own roads, a tempo!

At the sight of it, Gaya Singh hollered, "Look, just look! Delhi has been thrust upon Benaras."

A tempo on Assi's Delivery Road!
Why is it called Delivery Road?
Take a look at the potholes.
Pregnant women needn't lug far their loads.
All they have to do is sit
in a ricksha long enough and just not quit.
Not too far, just a furlong –
and surely soon will come along
labour and the baby. Like a song!

On this very road, the tempo bumped, jumped, jerked along –
trrrr ... tunnnn ... frrr.

"Ramji bhaiyya, what do you think?"

And Ramji bhaiyya instantly said, "Think? I'm trying to make head or tail of this twenty first century, instead."

This made Ramji Rai so pleased that he pulled out a twenty rupee note and thrust it into Bullu's hand. At once, Bullu sang out loud and clear a song in praise of Ramji bhaiyya.

So, bhaiyya logon. What did the tempo say? It said, Run! Scoot! Speed it! Those legs aren't of much use now, use your feet and you'll be left behind. Look around you if you can! Cars, Rajdhani expresses, helicopters, aeroplanes. You don't have any of that, but at least I'm there.

A ricksha ride is fifty paise, but we'll charge you twenty five paise.

Before Ramji had time to think, understand or speak, his BA-pass MA-pass son had bought a tempo. With a bank loan. On the front, he wrote, Jai Mata Di. On the back was a couplet:

The driver's life is all laughter and play.
If saved from death, Central Jail's his stay.

One day, he told Ramji Rai, "Old man, why do you waste your time in useless khi-khi at the shops? Come, take a ride in the tempo."

"Get lost! Take you and your tempo to your mother's suchandsuch!"

"The old man's gone crazy," the son sighed and zoomed off.

Ramji's temper had barely cooled off when the respectable Kaushik Guru landed up at Pappu's tea stall. He had a hangdog look. From his corner, Ramji said, "Looks like you have been doing quite a bit of practicing last night?"

Kaushik opened the wrapper, took out a tablet and swallowed it with a gulp of water. Then he addressed Rai saheb. "That mother-fucker! My son came to tell me what a great blockhead his father is. Had a job all his life, and now he's hammering the footpath with his chappals. And look at me. No education, no occupation, yet I am a Mahanagari man."

"Mahanagari? You? A bigtown man?"

"Not me, guru, it's that twenty-five paise son of mine," Kaushik said worriedly.

"Arré, your younger son? The fellow who sits on the ghat with the white skinned?"

Kaushik was silent.

"Kaushikji!" Vakil Suresh Chaube said. "I'll tell you one thing, for the business he is involved in, he won't even get a bail. Advise him."

The gathering was silent for a while.

Tanni began, "Everyone is running. But where to? Looks like everyone has a rocket thrust up their backside. But happiness? Contentment? Kaushik, tell me one thing, once human beings too had a tail ... Why did it fall off?"

Kaushik looked at him without speaking.

"We had it because it was needed. When required, lift it up – for a regular job or an irregular one. But when Man was gifted undergarments, the tail gradually disappeared. Likewise, Kaushik, our legs too will disappear. Does anyone want to walk anymore? Who's got the time?"

The tone was light, but the content was philosophical.

While the gurus were on a jihad against speed, there was a new bombshell at the crossroad ...

D id I tell you we have been taken to a month in '84 now? And Hira was belting it out again?

One day, Guru saw a huge hoarding at the crossroad when he was returning from his early morning dip in the river.

> *Guru was returning from a Ganga snaan.*
> *It was the hour for Ramanaam.*
> *The Crown television hoarding had a heroine sleek,*
> *strands of hair across her forehead and cheek.*
> *Shining were her white teeth,*
> *as he stood gaping underneath.*

The day soon came when all street corners, crossroads, streets, mud tracks, and shops as well as all the newspapers were carrying advertisements. This was a new wave, the new obsession. These hoardings, posters, advertisements of local and foreign companies, with attractive faces and persuasive words were irresistible.

> *One saw them, one bought them,*
> *the consumer goods.*
> *New agents, new shops and before them*
> *the mesmerized broods.*

The city was watching television – in shops, at homes, in the neighbour's drawing room. On television, it watched coy, coquettish, curvaceous women, lively, laughing, lascivious girls.

In Assi's Pappu's tea shop, the gurus struggled to read the meaning behind what anyone with eyes saw. This tea shop was the centre for debate and discussion on happenings all across the country and the world – the twofaced and fourfaced nature of governments, the break up of political parties, the crossovers and makeovers, the double standards and the substandards. At this shop on whose tables and benches,

> *Governments were formed and dissolved,*
> *and the mighty deeds and expertise*

of the ministers were evolved.
Where their dishonesty, deceit and sleaze,
the wherefores and the reasons why
were argued till they begged for pity,
with a soft and penitential cry ...

One evening, a television box quietly took its seat. No one got a wind of this. Out of the box emerged Amitabh Bachchan, Rekha, Hema Malini, Dharmendra, Amrish Puri, Kumar Sanu, Alka Yagnik, Anup Jalota, Aasa Ram Bapu, soaps, artists, songs, ghazals, religious discourses, sensex, share markets and uproarious laughter.

For the gurus there was no space to sit or stand in the shop. That was monopolized entirely by the artists emerging from the television screen and the boxed laughter. The gurus appropriated two benches for their use and settled down outside the shop. They knew each other very well – each other's joys and sorrows, the ebb and flow of thoughts – because not just from shops, they had been turned out from their homes too.

In spite of their resistance, the television had entered their homes and that too deviously, by way of loans and installments, exchange of ornaments, cuts in the food budget. Call it family pride, call it conceit, what does it matter, how long can women and children gape at the neighbour's television? Now it's loud in each one's home, and a fixed unblinking gaze it brings on. Ah if this alone can satisfy! But barely did a television enter the house, it brought with it a litany of demands.

> "*Arré, listen.*
> *The dal doesn't cook in the zinc pot,*
> *and the rice is soggy or uncooked a lot.*
> *Why don't you bring home a Prestige?*
> *An inexpensive cooker, it works well.*
> *A refusal could mean a quick farewell.*
> *(Anyway, how can the man who loves his wife refuse Prestige?)*"

"In today's world who uses ash and brick powder, ji?
Washing-powder Nirma will show your vision."
"Are you deaf? Hear our television idol, Lalitaji.
Go get Surf. It's a wise decision."

"What sort of soap is this?
Does anyone use this stuff anymore?
I saw all types in Badri's store –
Hema Malini's and Rekha's soap
is my hope.
Go, return this."

The world was changing much too fast for the gurus. It made their heads spin. At least, the grown ups use their brains ... Children simply demand. First they pester their mother and then their father. The father gives them two tight slaps and directs them to their grandfather. "Go, ask him. He's got plenty of it stashed away."

Among the gurus sitting on the bench outside, Gaya Singh was the first to speak. "Guru, I've deciphered the language of television. Do you know what it says?

This is a campaign against our laughter and joy.
Don't laugh, just look at the man who's having fun.
You can't laugh just anywhere or enjoy.
Laughter has a distinct place. On TV.
It also has production centres – in Kolkata,
Mumbai, Chennai and Delhi.
Whoever wants to laugh may at these centres appear,
laugh and earn his money and make his future clear."

No one reacted to this long lecture. Not one. Kaushik continued to hum.

Ramji Rai asked, "Kaushik, do you only write verses on 15 August, 26 January and about the famous Langda mango? Or do you see and listen to what's happening around you?"

Kaushik turned his gaze upon him.

"I am asking because I read an article recently. It said that America has developed a vaccine. A laughter-repressing drop. Just one drop and the newborn won't laugh for the rest of its life. I've heard that it's been tried out in Japan. The theory is that newborns cry at birth and that is the true nature of man."

"Why don't you say," Virendra Srivastava, chewing paan, added, "that this vaccine is being used right here as well. Haven't you seen the children?"

"Arré, the laugh-drop is not any old drop-wop. It is television," Gaya Singh said.

Kaushik stopped humming. "Blockheads. Arré, we've spent our life laughing and singing. We'll spend the rest of our lives the same way. The saying goes,

"Brinjal says to Potato,
Ei alu, the royal elephant comes, bells clanging.
Alu says, why should I fear?
Fear's for the one who is hanging.

"So, guru, you and I don't have a thing to be scared of. Listen, since last night, this line has been running around my head,

How do I go to my bridal bed, when my dreaded sister-in-law holds the key.

"Great na? But, bhaiyya, I just can't find a line to rhyme it with."

It was Bullu's turn again. He twanged his jaw harp and crooned –

"Here's the rhyme," Gaya Singh said,

"Tomorrow we'll take out a procession – with posters and banner against TV."

Gaya Singh's josh made everyone laugh. Tanni guru stood up and said, "Shabash, doctor! For this let's catch hold of the artists of Reva Kothi."

Though there was no procession, there was a poster exhibition at the crossing. It was titled, Operation Eighties: What does television say?

"Laughter is not to be laughed at.
Laughter's for hearing and watching.
Stay away from it and ... that's that!"

"Stop the laughter, save the nation.
Rid yourself of all frustration!"

"Beware! Laughter is much sought after.
Television's villain's laugh, the hero's laugh.
Man shall endure, but not man's laughter."

The most significant feature of this exhibition was that there was a speech but no one to listen to it. The passers by called it the useless jabbering of idiots. Soon the organizers reviewed the situation: Where was the audience that should have been here at this outstanding exhibition with its thought provoking speeches? They found that some elderly men had gone to the nonstop hari keertan at the ghat, while others had gone to the religious lecture hall, the youth were sweating for competitive exams, the working people, back from office, were watching the television serial, *Yeh Jo Hai Zindagi*. The rest were at the grocery shops, haggling.

Tanni guru presided but he did not speak. He was there and elsewhere too. He saw that things had changed. He had no control over it at home or anywhere. The remote had it all. Within Assi, a new city was growing. And the day was not far when all the gurus would roll up their own bits of Assi and carry it away to the margins, where the city's garbage dump was situated.

Tanni's life was worn out
at the Assi ghat, so devout.
At the footpaths he had hung,
crossing over to Bahri Alang

He had managed with just a towel and a short waist cloth. What soap could be better than sand and mud? He rubbed it on his body and rinsed it off for hours in clean water. Money was filth.

Roasted chana and the Ganga water tasted better than thirty-six different delicacies. And happily he lived along, not sharing, not caring. Neither a borrower nor a lender be was his formula for life. Cheerful was his life, laughter his breath. The highest position, the grandest bungalow, governorhood, a PM's post – it was all the same to him. If you have a problem, sorrow, distress or worry, tell me. If I can help you, I will. Otherwise please don't bother me.

Guru amongst gurus, was Tanni guru. Call him sanyasi, call him fakir, what does it matter? He once had a home, a family, sons, daughters, grandchildren. He kept his eyes and ears open. What was happening where? Who was doing what? But he didn't think it necessary to find out how anyone in his neighbourhood lived. What did they eat and drink? What did they wear? And these youngsters! They barely know how to wash their backsides, and here they were, comparing their status with that of the neighbours'. Just listen to them! And however he said it, they stayed glued to the television or homework.

And how do you blame them? The boys from the other neighbourhoods talk gibberish, harbour dreams of becoming doctor, engineer, officer and god knows what else. And these lots are still cramming their tables. Doctor, engineer, officer ... What will I be? ... No one wants to be a human.

What was sorrow? He had grown old without ever finding out. And these children? They'd look at the world with frightened eyes, anxious and restless.

On 31 December, 1992, the Government detailed out programmes for peace, plenty and prosperity. It announced the good news that it had succeeded in controlling laughter, the biggest obstacle on the path to progress.

Left out of all this, the gurus choked in the discussions held every evening, and IDBI, UTI, ICICI, Off Season Sale, NSC Stocks and Shares – seduction danced at the crossroads. There was no bar on laughter. Laugh as much as you want to. Dance, sing, guffaw, hoot ... But who knows what happened? Bit by bit joviality started to disappear. On these same crossroads, the same streets, the same houses, the same shops. Yet, once they grew gloomy, there was no stopping. They couldn't manage to get together at the same time. Even if they did there was no teasing, abuses or jokes. And yet, no one had put any restraint at all.

So, bhaiyya logon, as Assi grew more crowded, the crossroads grew less crammed. The first to leave was Gaya Singh. Next, Ramvachan Pandey, Kaushik, Kishore. And finally one day, even Tanni guru left.

As Tanni was leaving, his son pleaded,

> "What have we done? What fault, blunder?"
> "Nothing at all. Everything's fine."
> "Is it the television, my car, I wonder?"
> "How do these concern me? I'm not upset."
> "Compared to others we're not dishonest, corrupt, we don't plunder."

"Stop this bakwaas. I'm leaving."

"Arré, at least change your lungi and banian."

Guru glared at him. Glancing at his wife, the son murmured, "The old man's a cussed fellow. Does what he likes. Doesn't listen to anyone."

The wife had been trying to signal to him, Let him go. Don't stop him. Guru had seen this but even that didn't make him smile. The son came with him to the gate.

"Be happy, khush raho beta!" Tanni said, stepping outside.

The son looked towards the garage. "I'll leave you wherever you want to go."

Tanni stopped, he stood there for a while.

"Have you forgotten something?" the son asked. Tanni said, "Beta Kanni, I'm going Nowhere. But I don't know if I'll ever meet you again. So, there's something I want you to explain."

Kanni looked at him with curiosity and surprise. "Son, for long I have been puzzled. What is unhappiness? It isn't just living for yourself, I guess. So is it happiness for us when others are in unhappiness?"

This was a question Kanni had never considered. He looked at his father, perplexed. Has he gone crazy? He knows only one thing right from the beginning:

> There was no way he would get away
> from being called a louse,
> as the one who threw his father
> out of the house.

"Kanni, the day you discover the answer, let me know. I'll come back." And Tanni guru reached the turn from where the gate of his house was no longer visible.

The whole group left their home in likewise manner. Except Ramji. All the gods and goddesses smiled from their allotted places in Ramji Rai's room. For many years, he worshipped them all. He left at crack of dawn to collect a towel full of sacred leaves and flowers – gurhal, genda, bela, chandni and belpatra – from the Sadhubela Ashram to offer to the gods. He also read the namaaz thrice a day. One day his daughter asked,

> "Why do you pray so much?"
> "It's an understanding. You look after me. I'll look after you."
> "An understanding? Who's your crutch?"
> "God, beta, God. I say, you take care of me
> and I'll take care of you. Or else I'll review ..."
> "Should God be so abused, please let Him be."

"Beti, that's the way of the world. Do you notice what happens at Sankatmochan? When they go to the temple casually, they have darshan without offering anything, or sometimes with eight annas worth of flowers or a pav of laddoos. But when they've passed an examination, they go with one and a quarter kilo of laddoos from the best shop and the costliest of rose garlands. What does it mean? You do your job well and you'll be rewarded. That's the way the world operates."

"But you've never said what you really want?"
"What would I want? Who can give me my favourite jaunt?"

"Wah! Wah! Re mauj fakira ki.
How delightful is the bliss of the hermit, ji!
That the Almighty gives all at every level.
Drop your worries and marvel
at the benevolence of the Only God.
When we waited in the womb for His nod,
what expenses did one bother about?
Kinarai is carefree, no doubt!
The Almighty takes care of everything.
Wah! Wah! Re mauj fakira ki."

It was known to everyone at the crossroad that ever since his friend Sulaiman was killed in the riots of '92, Ramji was not quite right in his mind. He worships, but he doesn't know why. If anyone asks him, he recites these lines. All this worried his daughter, who knew when he would leave home, and she would be left behind, alone?

And so, gradually everyone left Assi, each carrying a bit of it with him.

Then, who are these people who resemble them, on this road?
Their clones or perhaps mummies with life bestowed.
This is the Assi crossing, isn't it?
It was ... now, it's Tulsinagar, you twit!
Assi was moved somewhere else lock, stock and barrel
along with the gurus and their talk of peril.

What's here is not a community, it's a museum.
Angrez-angrezins', gymnasium.
If you want to know what Benaras was
once like, go there – but just mind the cars.

There was a hullabaloo in Parliament.
"Why did this happen? Why is it that slowly the entire
basti emptied out?"
Bihari Lal smiled.
Raja babu, Bihari bhaiyya said,

"They are dangerous people,
let's not be vague.
Like a germ in them laughter lurks,
like cholera or plague.
It spreads all over, eats the perks.
And it was beginning to affect
our developmental works."

The opposition looked at each other in surprise, "What disease?"
they asked. "They were just living a life of fun and frolic."

"You call idleness and worthlessness, fun and frolic? Don't you
see that it was because of these people that we had to eliminate
Evening from the Day-Night cycle?"

"If you can't provide them with employment,
If they don't ask your help for their enjoyment,
Don't snatch what you have. Don't,
do things by hook and crook. Won't
hurt anyone's interest,
laugh their way through life's damnedest,
Then why do you act so hard to please?"

"How do you know that they don't hurt anyone's interest?
Gentlemen, you all should thank me that without imposing an

emergency or sanctions like AASUKA, RASUKA or TADA on the entire isle amongst isles, Jambudweep, we have managed to rid ourselves of laughter.

"Do you know that what you call Laughter is what they called Democracy? How can you have two democracies in the same country?

"And do you know what they meant by democracy? Mocking at development programmes, attacking the government. Whatever one does, they are not satisfied. Find fault with every job. Talk about bribes, dishonesty, corruption ... We are not responsible for all this. Anyway, it's not something new. Is it right that we criticize corruption as plunder, and get no work done? Get stuck in the nineteenth century? Look gentlemen, when you use a pot full of water to fill glass bottles, a little is bound to spill. It may also happen that more water spills than fills the bottles. The one who's doing the filling should be prepared for this. Conceive of the big and small programmes as glass bottles."

Without giving the opposition a chance to speak, Bihari Lal ended his rhetoric on a quiet note,

> *"I haven't inherited this post.*
> *Today, it's me as host.*
> *Tomorrow it could well be one of you.*
> *Try and understand, my dost!"*

Hiralal got up – Listen so much have I sung that it's early morning now.

> *Ai, listen to what Hiralal says.*
> *Now how can Japan compete with Assi?*
> *Listen to what Hiralal says.*
> *Every house has fridge, car, TV,*
> *an AC and a CD player.*
> *Mummy, daddy guard the yields.*

Wifey tours Dubai's fields.
Son smokes heroin and charas,
while the daughter sings malhar, alas.
When there's no water, no electricity,
what celebration, what domesticity?
Hey, listen to what Hiralal says.
Which wind of which age blows from the south?
The rogues are up to your doors, bhaiyya
like unknown wolves, with hungry mouth.
Listen to your Hiralal.
Where have the sons of my Assi gone?
Hey, listen to your Hiralal!

* So bhaiyya, what was that name you said? Gaya Singh or Gone Singh? So, this is a reward of rupees fifty from Gaya Singh. I salute him again and again ... What did the poet say? Wah, wah! Long live beta Bullu. The poet said that Assi is gone from Assi. The spot where we stand, sit, chew paan, sip tea and sing is not Assi. It's Tulsinagar. So said the poet.

So come, let's go to Tulsinagar and listen to this new voice.

There were just four or five days to the New Year when a siren screeched through the skies of Tulsinagar. It was that time of day when there was space for not even a sesame seed at the crossroads. The shops and streets were a sea of people. The biggest crowds were at the shops for gifts, cards, presents, sweets and chaat.

Women weren't lagging behind either. They thronged the jewellery stores and the cloth shops. In all this there was an ominous groaning sound.

As if hundreds of cats, on the peepal trees at the crossing, are wailing together.

As if packs of dogs, at the entrances to the city's lanes are
baying together.
As if herds upon herds of foxes in the nagva fields on Assi ghat
are howling together,
their faces turned towards the city.
Never before had Assi heard such an evening ditty.

Fifteen, twenty years have passed since Assi became Tulsinagar. But they who call it Assi are still alive.

So, the siren. Its ominous wail. An unknown, unseen, unheard of, unique fear gripped the entire bazaar and the city. People stared at one another, aghast, and then, seeing others flee, they fled too. Huddling together in lanes, verandas, at windows and railings, they peered out fearfully. Nobody figured out what was going on because this siren sounded completely different from the one heard during an air raid. It was not the season for wars, so it was unexpected.

Shopkeepers pulled down their shutters. Within seconds, vehicles swarmed the streets, announcing curfew. PAC trucks and police jeeps and cars with red beacons glowing. The city magistrate stepped out of one. He looked around – there were

No kites in the sky,
no crows on the electric poles,
no stray bull loitered by.
Except Cold Air, nothing on patrol.
Sun too moved across the Ganga and away.
This was called Evening in an Assi day.

It was for the first time that the city saw the deployment of jawans, police officials and home guards in such large numbers. The magistrate took over the mike and began to speak, "You are given half an hour. Return home as quickly as possible. No one must be seen on the streets, maidan, lanes ... If you notice any suspicious character in the vicinity, call up this number immediately."

Alarmed and frightened, the people stayed at home, watching television and wondering about this suspicious character. Who could he be? An ISI agent? A vicious terrorist? An infamous dacoit? A kidnapper with a reward on his head? A murderer, robber, thief, a Human Bomb?

There were over fifty television channels, airing bhajans, kirtans, ramkatha; astrological discussions on lagna, rashi and griha. One channel showed a documentary on Mathura's raas lila, while another ran a film on Vaishno Devi.

> Television channels were showing a movie,
> or sitcoms with laughter, loud and groovy.
> There were one or two news channels around,
> but what could be newsworthy about a small colony or town?
> One hoped for something on the city channel,
> but there it was the lotus flower on an antakshari panel.
> The news was just about due when electricity failed.
> Don't know if a black out or power cut prevailed.

So, bhaiyya, know this about Tulsinagar – before it's dawn and we learn some more about the suspicious character – learn about the city what it was before the curfew. This city, bereft of its lazy, idle and worthless people, keeps everyone busy, everyone troubled. Nobody knows anyone. Ask, Where does Gone Singh live? And you are asked back, Who's Gone? Why Gone? How Gone? Where Gone? And if he's in a hurry, he won't even hear you. These people have spent their whole lives in this city, yet they know no lane, sector, or house number. A murder in their home? Don't worry, someone will get to know it in four days, when the smell reaches them. And say a thief enters your house. You shout for help and your neighbours left right, up below, will shut their doors tight.

Cars, buses, tempos, scooters, cycles and feet.
Hurrying, scurrying on the street.
Often too often there are accidents,
gang-robbery, snatching, theft, violent incidents.
Murder too, but who's got the time
to besiege the bus, scooter or man in the crime?
Injured in the street, even if you're killed,
give way, don't get trampled,
get out of the way of feet and tyres.

It's preferred that father, mother, son, wife take themselves to the hospital – those are our desires.

Die in peace, don't bother us,
don't upset the household, cause a fuss.
One unwell person means ten well people
attending fetching running – its not that simple.
If you die and move to the funeral line,
for Ram naam satya hai, who has time?
It's one long trek to the ghat gates,
wasting hours in funeral rites.
Who's got the time for such a bash?
Please lie down and turn to ash
at the electric crematorium.

So, bhaiyya, the urban environment may be considered polluted in other parts of the world, in Tulsinagar, there is no such danger. As you know, Air, Sunlight, Cold, Water, Virus, Fungus and every type of infection has been bottled, bagged in polythene, sealed in cartons. Purity guaranteed, no contamination. They are Life. Health. Easily available. At any shop. All one needs is money, the skill to earn it. And this is a skill that every man in Tulsinagar has. Those who don't have it, have left.

So in this very Tulsinagar, dawn arrived. On holidays it arrived late. The citizens slept peacefully all night, reassured by the policemen patrolling the streets, the thak-thak of their boots.

They were awakened by the sound of temple bells, bhajans broadcast over loudspeakers and the announcement that the curfew had been relaxed.

A fog shrouded the Ganga. Only its luminosity indicated that the sun had risen many hours ago. The newspaper arrived, as it did every morning. But it was censored and so no fun. No one understood the reason behind the curfew. Rumour had it that that suspicious character was a really old man, not carrying an AK 47, nor in possession of RDX. So, how was he such a big threat to the city's peace and security? The paper only said, "... bald, toothless, in slippers, dressed in a vest, lungi. He's trying to sneak into the city; may already be in."

Oh yes, there was one more bit of information about him on the television and in the newspapers,

"Appears absorbed in his own world. Contentment shows on his face and he laughs like a child."

There was a reward of a lakh of rupees on his head.

Nobody had an answer to this stupidity of the government.

Day passed. Night fell, and with it all the problems began.

Ever since their birth, the television had provided the only knowledge the city's children had of fun and laughter. They'd never heard anyone laugh at home, the street or in the market. So they were overwhelmingly curious about this news. Astonished and anxious. What if this strange old man enters our house? They would peep out of the doors and windows and bang the doors shut at the slightest sound of boots in the streets. Was there really in their midst a man who could actually laugh. They pestered their parents.

Mummy, what is laughter? Papa, what kind of person laughs? Is it someone who has everything? If so, why doesn't Uncle Khanna laugh? Papa, look! It's written here, "He laughed spontaneously." How does one laugh like that? Papa, in lesson seven, it says, "As soon as he heard this, he guffawed." What does "guffaw" mean? Mummy, is there a coaching centre for laughter? May we join it?

The parents had troubles of their own. They too were up all night puzzling over several questions: After all, why is he happy? Is his neighbour dead? Has his brother been murdered? Has his wife swallowed poison? Was his enemy's house robbed? Did his unmarried daughter set herself on fire? Has he gone mad? There had to be a reason for laughter or happiness. If it was one of these, then what was the need for the curfew?

Then, there were the elderly – no one really bothered about them. Attention to them was drawn by a journalist of *Time* magazine, and that too, after two days of the curfew. That is, on 30 December.

As always, the elderly were annoyed with the younger generation and lamented their fate. For the last two, three days, the ramkatha at the dharam sangh had been stopped. So had the sant pravachan on the ghat. They noticed that other aged people did not die in their homes, they were sent to hospitals to die. What do the dying need? Just love na? Who cared enough even to be a pall bearer, to support the dead on their last journey to Harishchandra Ghat? To buy nine maunds of firewood for the pyre? Forget praying at Gayaji to avoid ostracism, they wouldn't even feed five brahmins!

The *Time* journalist had a chat with three old men.

"Are you happy?" he asked the first one. The old man screeched at the top of his voice. The second old man was a shade better. The journalist asked him to recall when was the last time he had laughed. The old man stared at him for a long moment. Drew a heavy sigh. The third one kept massaging his forehead, then suddenly snapped his fingers and said, "Yes, saheb, I recall now. I did laugh once. Must have been 15 August, 1947."

So, bhaiyya, it was the morning of thirtieth December. The reward had been raised from one lakh to one crore rupees. For any information about the old man. Why? Because there was strong pressure from the public. If this state of affairs continued then there would be no New Years' Eve and no New Year. The rest of the country would move into the twenty first century. Assi would stay behind. Therefore he has to be caught, or the drama ends now. The opposition too was hounding the government. Can't even catch an old man. A worthless government. Must be changed.

The government did not spare any effort, neither did the police, the secret service or the astrologers. The astrologers were in great demand on the twenty four hour television channels. They spoke endlessly on the astrological configuration at that time. How long will it take to catch him? Is his laughter auspicious or inauspicious for the country? What is the astrological status of the country? And how is the sadhe saati phase of Saturn going?

The government had its own worries. There were at least fifty old men in the colony. And they all looked alike. Give them a charkha and they would look like Mahatma Gandhi. But where had the childlike laughter sprung from? And would it last till the police arrived? Can such laughter come at will? The most amusing thing was that the computer generated image being shown on the television looked like Mahatma Gandhi's face.

The residents of the colony felt harassed. It was the news of the century on Star News, with the Press both national and international. "Laughter is gradually becoming extinct. But this news is nothing less than sensational! There is a spot on Jambudweep, where laughter has survived."

To add to the government's dilemma, the BBC correspondent reported, "This kind of laughter is different from the usual laughter where the mouth is opened, the lips widened and the teeth displayed. In this particular case, the eyes, nose, cheeks, ears and the entire body participates, together with the soul. It is said that this has no relation with hunger in the belly."

With this commentary began the rumours: A study group from America had arrived to study pollution of the Ganga. An international gang of smugglers had sneaked into the city. Two different mafia parties had arrived from Mumbai. America it seems had told our government that they wanted a Festival of India at their expense, provided that the old man was brought there. They had everything, except that kind of laughter.

So bhaiyya, though it is not quite clear what happened, by evening the government had called off Operation Assi. Bihari Lal immediately transmitted a message to Jambudweep: "As you know the old man appears to be somewhat bewildered. O my son! The entire nation is proud of you just as we are proud of Ajanta, Ellora, Khajuraho and Konark, Taj Mahal and Kohinoor. Come out without any hesitation. Republic Day is twenty six days away. We shall present you before your countrymen and the world. In a global launch."

So bhaiyya, the curfew was called off, the police was withdrawn. The streets are gleaming, the roads are gleaming, and houses are gleaming all over. The city has spread out its arms in a welcome, the world's eyes are full of adoration. For whom? For the old man. For his childlike laughter. But where is the old man? Who is that old man? When will he come?

I don't know, Bullu bhaiyya might, though.

So my son, Bullu, did the old man come or rebel? Get up! Warm up the assembly. Cast your spell.

> *What the hell can be the spell*
> *with no chillam, ganja, bhang to help me tell.*
> *Bhenj Bam Bhole!*
> *What tale can a birahiya display*
> *when the throat is not warm, the voice is hoarse.*
> *when you sing so loudly, all joy is coarse.*
> *Because our pockets lack money*
> *our voices are not honey.*
> *Bhenj Bam Bhole!*
> *What tale can a birahiya display?*

W ah, wah! Well done ... Just listen to the tabla. The tabla casts such a spell that neither chillam nor ganja, bhang do I need. Wah, wah bhaiyye.

For a long time, Bullu swayed to the rhythm of the tabla.

So bhaiyya, why was the curfew imposed? Why was it withdrawn? Because America said so. Voice of America said so. BBC said so. What did you say? That laughter is a priceless jewel? Nature's miracle. That means you do not have wits of your own. Whatever America and BBC say is right.

But bhaiyya come let us explore, listen, for I have to speak lots more.

Kanni of course knew who the old man was. And why not? His childhood and youth had passed in his company, but Kanni had not recognized his ingenuous, innocent, idyllic laughter.

Daadur basat nikat kamalini
ke janam naa ras pahichaane.
The frog whose life is with a lotus spent,
doesn't notice its fragrant scent.

Kanni had assumed that he'd done the only thing he could do. But his father, had he wanted it, could have too, but he hadn't wanted to hurt anyone. That would have killed his laughter.

Ever since the day he saw the sketch of the face on television, Kanni had been worried. And now with the curfew revoked and the reward raised to one crore, he was truly restless. The echo of the announcement lingered like a worn out record. "Ai, my son! We are proud of you just as we are of the Kohinoor ... noor ... noor."

How old was the old man? What was he made of? Had he paid heed to his father, he would be loitering in the streets or counting days sitting on a gumti. Others had fathers too ... Kanni's theory was – No risk, no gain. Had he not taken risks, neither this bungalow nor the car would be there, nor would his sons be studying in Nainital and Dehradun.

But whatever the grievances that Kanni may have had against his father, there were none against his mother. Tanni left, but the old lady refused to go along. Kanni loved his mother very much. He had constructed a servant's quarter behind his bungalow, beside the garage. A single room with an adjoining toilet. Ma stayed there so that no one would disturb her puja-paath and daily routine. Kanni bought her two strings of prayer beads – one of tulsi, another of rudraksh – with a hundred and nine beads. And if you are bored of all this then there are other things – broom, pipe, bucket, mop. Right in the beginning, Kanni had observed that his mother would have to wait long hours for her meals. Lunch at two pm, dinner at ten. At her age, to be hungry for so long was unbearable. He put aside all his urgent work and arranged for a stove, a gas cylinder, a bag of rice, pulse, flour. Here it is, cook whenever you feel like. Eat and be happy. Only the mother knew – how happy she was.

Ma knew about the curfew. Once at her daily bath at the Ganga, she heard about the search for an old man, a dangerous criminal. No one told her so, but she concluded it wasn't her old man. Yet, she was reminded of him. And her love for him. She began to cry for him. She even asked Kanni but he had no time. Some times happy, sometimes sad, he left early in the morning and returned late at night. The lights in his room would be on all night. Who knows what sort of people came to meet him? Once, she did ask Kanni – about the curfew and the old man. And Kanni asked, "What curfew? Which old man?" He laughed and added,

No, it doesn't ring a bell. But don't worry, Ma. All is well.
It was enough to increase his mother's worry.

At the ghat, she learnt that the curfew was lifted. She returned to her room, haunted by memories of the old man. She had never imagined that he could be so hardhearted. Yes, he did ask her and it was she who had not gone because of her affection for her son. But if it was really his intention never to return, he could have taken her along.

So bhaiyya, this was the state of the old lady. Now hear about the son. Wah, wah dholak! Well done, son. Bhaiyya, listen to the ways of Kalyug.

Half the night had passed and here it was the last day of the year. 31 December. Kanni was pacing his bedroom. Glass in one hand, in the other, the remote. The mobile phone had been switched off, the telephone's receiver was off the hook, and he had instructed his wife that if someone came and asked for him, he was not there. That she didn't know where he was either. His wife, whose name was Lakshmi and whom he called Dolly darling sat in a corner, trying to understand him.

For the first time he was beyond comprehension.

"Are you looking at this remote? Today it runs the world." Kanni's fingers played incessantly with it.

Dolly got up, snatched it from his hands and put it away.

The circumstances had completely changed – the greatest criminal of the city had become an honourable citizen, a national hero. And what if this citizen presents himself to the government? What would happen to the one crore reward?

The city was asking itself this question.

Hahn bhaiyya, listen –

> *Whose name should we mention,*
> *when the whole village is evil, friend.*
> *Whose name can we bring to your attention,*
> *which name can we extend,*
> *when those as close to us as our shadows cause us such*
> *pain?*
> *Friends, what can I say when brothers betray*
> *and trickery runs untamed.*
> *We dream of Rama's ideal, yet we're all made of clay.*
> *Deceit stands unashamed,*
> *and those as close to us as our shadows cause us such pain.*

So bhaiyya, have a glimpse of this tension between Kanni and his wife. "Are you going to drink like this the whole night or will you do something?"

"What should I do, tell me?"

"Arré, am I to tell you what to do? If he surrenders quietly, then all this running about will be of no use."

"What a stupid thing to say. Is it that easy? How can he surrender quietly with the entire police force and the secret service hunting for him?" "So, someone else may well walk away with ten million rupees, yet you don't want it?"

"Yes, you've got it right. I do not want to be condemned for the rest of my life as the son who handed over his father to the police for money."

Dolly stared at him. When the reward was lesser, he had run around, he'd spent sleepless nights. And now? If he did not want the one crore, he could have been more relaxed. Why an entire evening with the bottle? Why the endless whispers into the mobile?

Dolly snatched the glass from Kanni's hands. "I will not let anyone else walk away with the reward. After all he is my father-in-law, my husband's father. How dare anyone else claim it?"

"Well done," Kanni patted her back and started smiling. "What will you do?"

"Do? Just go to him saying, how many years of life do you have in store? All your life you did nothing for us, gave us nothing ... at least now that you are about to die, why don't you do something for us? And it is not as if it's going to be heavy on your pocket. Someone else is going to pay. All you have to do is let us accompany you when you surrender yourself. Take us with you."

Kanni kept smiling. "And where would you get him?"

"Where else? Ghasiyari Tola. That's where he teaches children how to laugh."

"Not to laugh, darling, but to live. He says that laughing is living. But is he there at all? He left that tola long ago to go welcome the twenty first century."

"Where is he now?"

"If you knew that what would you do?" Kanni smiled mysteriously. "Not that I know, but I do know where he will be tomorrow. At least I have an idea."

"Where?"

Kanni did not reply. He looked at the wall clock. The date had changed. 31 December. One am. He started dressing.

"Start preparing to celebrate the New Year," he told Dolly, "on a grand scale."

"Are you going away somewhere?"

"No questions," Kanni said, knotting his tie, "just tell me this – what would be the international market value for something that is worth a crore in Indian currency? And it's not ordinary, it is the Kohinoor."

He started laughing.

"Listen Dolly, if I take away the one crore in rupees as well as in dollars, is there any harm?"

Dolly looked at him in disbelief. "Don't go, you've had too much."

Kanni was tying his shoelaces. "I never get drunk. I wasn't wasting my time locked up in this room all evening. Didn't I tell you? He asked, raising his head, "This remote ..." He put on his overcoat and patted Dolly's cheeks.

"Wish me," he said as if he was off to the war front.

Barely reaching the veranda, he turned back and said in a low voice, "Every 31 December, where does he go? To Bahri Alang, don't you know." Friends, before Kanni leaves for the front, let us take a break, yes a chhota sa break.

Bahri Alang is a tradition so unique to Benaras. They say it is the essence of the city's ancient culture. It is a Banarsi way of mauj and masti, the flavour of life. It is a place with no habitation. The locals call it Nichhaddam, which means stark silence. Desolation. In the Bhojpuri of Assi, it means being wild, eccentric, unaccountable. Some say it is a philosophy of pleasure. Some say it embodies the importance of going to the outer side. Others, that it helps us understand what is fun, what is play, in Assi, the flavour and wisdom of life. Here, there is the freedom to speak anything, or wear anything. The ways of Bahri

Alang include the contentment of exercise and bhang, to have paan and have it dribble and spill beyond the tips of the lips. It is a large tika, kajal, itr. Bahri Alang is the sense of freedom and contentment that comes from an oil massage and a dip in the Ganga. It is that top of the world feeling. After freedom, only the region across the Ganga has been left to Bahri Alang.

To Bahri Alang, only friends follow you, never family.

So babu log, Kanni took leave of his wife and came out. It was pitch dark. And bitterly cold. A strong wind blew. He draped a muffler around his head and neck and rubbed his palms to warm himself and walked into the drizzle and fog and film-like atmosphere. He ran to the car, got in and switched on the headlights. Ahi ré dada! Who was this? Ma ... The mother who said often, "A mother's heart is like a cow's, a son's heart, like a butcher's." Kanni was not a butcher. He got down immediately and helped his mother who was standing by the bonnet. Perhaps she was tired from weeping. Old age had shriveled her into a little bundle. She was shivering uncontrollably.

Kanni put his arms around her to support her. He took her to her bed, made her lie down and covered her with a quilt. Her hands and feet were like ice. He rubbed her palms, rubbed her soles, and just as he put his hand on her forehead, she burst into tears. Laughter is contagious, so is weeping. Kanni was not stone hearted, and he wept too.

It was as if a mother and her son had at last met after ages.

"Ma, close your eyes and go to sleep."

Ma did not reply. After some time she said, "He's quite stubborn, he will not come from the other side. Why do you take the trouble? Just let me go to him."

"But how do I take you to him?"

"You know all the places he is likely to be."

"Yes, Ma, but he is just not there."

"Ask Mithai Lal. Ask Surdas, they might know."

"Surdas must be with him. He is not to be seen."

Ma became silent. Kanni kept massaging her forehead.

"Have you checked Bahri Alang?" she asked finally. "Didn't he go there some times?"

Kanni started laughing, "In icy winter? What are you saying, Ma?"

"What is the harm in checking once more? If you like, I'll come along."

"I'll check there. But how can you go out in this weather?"

It was nearly dawn when Kanni set out on his search.

It was morning but Kanni didn't return. It was noon, Kanni didn't return. The evening was over, but Kanni didn't return.

Dolly had spared no effort for the Happy New Year. Khaneja Electronics took a whole day to decorate the bungalow. After lunch, Jhankar came with the music deck. Speakers were set up in the front of the house. Decorators came from the flower market and wrote half a crescent of "Welcome Happy New Year" on the gate with rose and marigold. Special preparations of fish and chicken were ordered from Hotel India and stored in the fridge. The bungalow was buzzing but Dolly was worried.

She was not worried about Kanni – the car was air conditioned, there were four, five bottles of Bisleri, fruits and stuff, and for exigency, an unlicensed revolver. In a way Kanni had really gone to a war front. On one side, an environment study group. On the other, a gang of smugglers. The mafia and dons on the third and government machinery on the fourth. And Kanni caught in their midst. Alone. However, none of this worried her. She only worried about Kanni losing both the rupees and dollars.

This was the first time when Kanni did not telephone even once during the day. Even the mobile was switched off.

One person who was definitely not worried was his old mother. She was on her feet the whole day. Her son's touch was on her eyelids. He had gone to bring back her old man, and at his instance the bungalow was decorated like a bride. Early or late, the old man would be back that night.

Dolly was bored. She was up on the terrace strolling listlessly, waiting, when she noticed several processions on the road outside. They were beating drums and cymbals, clashing thalis, ringing bells, singing and dancing, running here, there and everywhere. She saw, through the mist and fog across the Ganga, a bridge of boats, strung across the ghat to the sandy bank.

She rushed to the gate and peered out.

The people were cheering a miraculous headless baba. The story went that he used to live near the wetlands and slept in a hut made of sand. The baba's head had the ability to wander around on its own. Whenever the body needed to laugh, the head would on its own return to bond with the body.

She ran back to the drawing room and switched on the television. Surfing through, she stopped at the Siti channel.

On the screen next to something covered with a white sheet was Mithailal. The only witness to that incident was blind Surdas. He was singing nirgun bhajans, which didn't interest Dolly.

Her eyes searched for Kanni in the crowd.

Mithailal receded to the background and a special correspondent appeared, mike in hand.

"The news here is that taking advantage of darkness, fog and mist, somebody has separated the head of the old man from the trunk. The head is missing. A search is on. Borders have been sealed. It is suspected that behind this is a foreign hand."

Dolly's eyes still searched for Kanni.

So friends and brothers! Dawn had crept in, unnoticed but the crowd remained where it was and as it was – ears open to the noise, drowned in pensiveness and stunned. Hiralal and party had packed their musical instruments. Their turn was over. They had no more to sing.

Suddenly, Bullu stopped playing the kartal. He gestured the musicians to stop. Then he called out to Hiralal.

Hiralal took up the chang. He moved forward to stand by Bullu's side, to bring this Biraha Dangal. to an end.

> So brothers and friends,
> what more could we tell you
> or not tell you?
> What more shall we sing,
> or not sing?
> Let's just say, friends,
> the old man was found.
> But he was also not found.

And so we concluded with the nirgun bhajan that Mithailal was singing that day when the head of Kanni went missing:

> "One day all of us will surely go.
> If Ram and Lakshman were immortal ...
> But they'd be with us today, if that were so.
> The mighty, Kumbhkaran and Ravan,
> warriors who let their bravery show.
> Arjun the archer, the generous Karan,
> Bhim, Yudhishthir, all gone with the flow.
> Earth, Air and Sky would all go.
> Sun and Moon would be no more.
> Says Kabir, Will you sing of God,
> only when death is at your door?"

CONTRIBUTORS' NOTES

ASOMIYA

Pradip Acharya has authored six books. His translations from and into Asomiya have appeared in various publications in India and abroad; and his translation of Indira Goswami's novel about Delhi (published by Katha in translation as *Pages Stained with Blood*) has garnered critical acclaim. He is an English professor at Cotton College, Guwahati.

- The Asomiya short story came of age with Syed Abdul Malik's creative documentation of significant moments in community life. Mahem Bosa added a new dimension with his lyric recreation of the rural scene. Saurabh Kumar Chaliha's urbane wit and irony meld with Bhabendranath Saikia's naturalism. The late Seventies and Eighties produced experiments by Debabrata Das and Manoj Kumar Goswami. Present day creativity draws sustenance from Latin American experiments, and Borges is a defining influence. Sibananda Kakoti, Jayanta K Chakravarty, Syamanta Phuken are powerful voices. Syamanta offers cityscapes while Sibananda explores country realities. Mamoni Raisam Goswami exposes the rural women's scene with brutal honesty. Left wing ideology permeates Arupa Patangia's stories of female assertion. Robin Sarma is an academic who writes able satire with a trenchant wit.

- In "The Last Meal on the Water Fresco," Sibananda Kakoti recounts the last day in the life of legendary 15th century Assamese poet, preacher and reformer, Sankardeva, and how death saves him from initiating king Naranarayana to his faith. It is a dramatic monologue in the form of musings that encompass a legendary life, and ranges over poetry, music, faith, friendship, family and affairs of state. It is lucidly told in modern Asomiya with a sprinkling of 15th century lore and idiom.

This section is organized language-wise. It contains the biographical details of the Nominating Editor; the state of the short story in that language and the Editor's reasons for nominating the chosen story/stories. This is followed by the biographical details of the Writer and her/his notes on the story; then the notes on and by the Translator, alphabetically arranged. In languages where there are two stories, the reasons for nomination of both stories come with the Nominating Editor's note, while the Author's and Translator's notes for each story have been placed together for ease of reference, and are alphabetically arranged according to the Author's first name.

- "The Last Meal on the Water Fresco" was first published as "Jalchhabir Sesh Saaj" in *Ajir Asom*, Guwahati, October 2002.

Sibananda Kakoti is the author of three short story collections, one collection of plays, and several articles on post independent Nagaon District of Assam and Vaishnava saint Srimanta Sankardeva. He has won the National Award for Radio Playwright in 1992 for his "Duhsamay Samay." In 1995 he was awarded the Munin Borkatoki Award for a collection of short stories, *Amrityu Amrit*. He is involved with various cultural and social welfare organizations.

- The personality of the 15th century Vaishnavite guru Srimanta Sankardeva always fascinates me more as a human being than a religious saint. His encompassing greatness and versatility enchants me. The story is an imaginative reconstruction of Sankardeva's last day, his successes and failures. Though conceived over a period of five years, I wrote it in just two days.

Parismita Singh is currently with Pratham, a non profit organization working with elementary education. She lives in Delhi and Assam.

- In a sense, attempting a translation of Sri Sibananda Kakoti's "Jalchhabir Sesh Saaj," comes close to an attempt at translating one culture into another. The setting is one that would be familiar to an Assamese reader. But in a translation when one is reaching out to readers unfamiliar with Assamese culture, particular care had to be taken over allusions and word play, and the vocabulary of the Vaishnavite movement, in order to retain the integrity of the narrative. The physical body, the body politic, and the landscape are also integral components of the drama, and this was another relationship that I had to carefully preserve. Another challenge was the complex narrative techniques used by the writer, the idioms and techniques of painting and cinema.

BANGLA

Debes Ray is an eminent fiction writer with more than thirty titles to his credit – of which more than thirteen are novels – and nearly one hundred short stories. He received the Sahitya Akademi Award in 1990.

- Bangla short stories and novelettes have, for almost the last two decades, concentrated on social, political and lifestyle issues. The personal and private relationships between individuals have been overused as themes. The premarital, extramarital and other conjugal relationships are now not popular themes with authors and readers. The problems arising out of the emerging consciousness of women's rights have however not been adequately attended to by writers, not even women writers. But the opening up of the social expanse has alerted writers to changing rural realities. Never before have so many varied areas come to the surface of narratives – short and long. The quality and kind of soil, the difficulties of cultivation, the river systems, are all now themes of Bangla fiction.

- In his story, Jhareswar Chattopadhyay has woven his locale with a delocalized situation. A couple is on their way back from Bangalore, leaving their only child in an engineering college hostel. This is the first time that they will be away from their son. Chattopadhyay has masterfully created a situation where the boundaries of locale collapse before the onslaught of time as history, history as time.
- "Their Only One" was first published as "Old Block New Block" in *Sambad Pratidin*, Kolkata, March 2002.

Jhareswar Chattopadhyay has been writing stories for more than twenty five years. His area of narration is specifically the southern-most part of West Bengal. The earth and water are salty there, fisheries and cultivation being the major occupation. Long trips into the sea, to catch fish, is a local source of livelihood. He won the Bibhuti Bhushan Puraskar in 1973, the Tarasankar Smriti Puraskar in 1996 for the novel *Swajan Bhumi*, the Soapan Puraskar in 1997, the Shiladitya Puraskar in 2003 and the Panchajanya Puraskar in 2004.

Tirna Ray began her career as a journalist, and has been on the editorial staff of leading mainline dailies, including *The Asian Age* and *The Telegraph*. She is currently pursuing her lifelong passion for bhasha literature as a fiction editor at Katha.

- I enjoyed translating the story especially because of the multilayered technique employed by the author. On the one hand, the story talks of a present-day problem where career takes first priority in life. By default, the family becomes an invalid premise vis-a-vis professional success. The demands of modern society dictate that today's parents rationalize the need to mainstream their children, even if they have to spend money or send the child far away from home. The notions of an urban society may have changed, but parents are still vulnerable, deeper emotions are still not bound by theory and reason. Jhareswar coins words with the skilled ease of a master craftsman. His one Bangla word illuminates a hundred emotions, and translating that into English is a thousand times more difficult.

HINDI

Sara Rai is a writer and translator, equally comfortable with English, Hindi and Urdu. She has written an anthology of Hindi short stories, *Ababeel Ki Uraan*. She has coedited a book of regional fiction for Katha called *Imaging the Other*, besides editing and translating *Hindi – Handpicked Fictions*, brought out by Katha. She has also translated two novellas for children, and has several published articles, reviews and stories to her credit. She was the Charles Wallace Fellow at the University of East Anglia for 2003 and participated in the Japan-India Writers' Caravan in 2002 and 2003.

- Despite the general atmosphere of cynicism and the belief that in Hindi, the short story has reached a dead end, thousands of stories continue to be written and published every month. While the merit of some of the stories may be questionable, what is certain is that a great deal of energy is still visible in this field. The Hindi short story has traversed a long distance since Premchand, with women writers actively contributing to the genre, and poets like Vinod Kumar Shukla writing beautiful prose. At the moment, several generations of writers are active on the scene. There has also been a transition from descriptive and realistic writing to a form of magic realism.

- Kashi Nath Singh's "Kaun Thagwa Nagariya Lootal Ho" is a long story written in the stylized folk mode of the 'biraha.' Taking images from real life, dealing with real people on the street and by adopting their colloquial speech, Kashi Nath Singh has created a story that begins to seem like a metaphor for India as we see it today.

- Neelakshi Singh sets "Ek Tha Bujhvan" in rural Bihar. It is a story that is crisply written and beautifully imagined and, bringing in real life scientists and their research to talk about a story based in poverty and non-literacy is a masterly stroke. The tale is of Bujhvan, the mason, who has built most of the houses in the village. He is now old and dependent on his son and daughter-in-law for his needs. However, frail old Bujhvan is gifted with a phenomenal memory which has recorded seven decades of births and deaths. The villagers, prosperous and poor alike, rely on him to keep their past alive. The test comes when Bujhvan is called upon by the Thakur's sons to initiate the partition of their house.

- "Once Upon a Bujhvan" was first published as "Ek Tha Bujhvan" in *Tadbhav*, Lucknow, October, 2001.
- "Who's the Thug Looting the City?" was first published as "Kaun Thagwa Nagaria Lootal Ho" in *Tadbhav*, Lucknow, April 2001.

Kashi Nath Singh, a recognized Hindi fiction writer, has several short story collections, novels and a play to his credit. These have been translated into several foreign and Indian languages. In 2001, he was honoured by the Government of Madhya Pradesh with the Sharad Joshi Samman. He retired as professor and head of the Hindi department at Benaras Hindu University, Varanasi.

- The story "Kaun Thagwa Nagaria Lootal Ho" came to mind when I saw, in a traditional city, the common man's attraction towards multinational products that affected human relations. The story showcases the influence of globalization, liberalization and multinational culture on family life in an urban society.

Pamposh Kumar finds good literature, especially stories and poetry, a source of dialogue with life and its demands. He works as scientist in the Department of Science and Technology, Ministry of Science and Technology, New Delhi.

- The original story, a satire, "Kaun Thagwa Nagaria Lootal Ho" has been narrated in a disciplined yet free-wheeling manner. Flexibility in the use of tenses stresses the strangeness of the changing socio-political and cultural norms and their impact on the heritage of Assi (now Tulsinagar) in Benaras. The old custodians of tradition are made to take a backseat while the next generation is caught in the lifeless web of eroded values. The overall flow of the story was subject to the dictates of satire and the author uses colloquialisms and special songs or verses to paint a compelling portrait.

Neelakshi Singh's stories have been published in a number of magazines including *Hans, India Today* (Sahitya Varshiki) and *Kathadesh*. Her other interests include Bharatnatyam and acting. She is the recipient of the Ramakant-Smriti Award for the year 2002. She works as a probationary officer with the State Bank of India.

- It sometimes happens, that some silent shadows and misty memories of our childhood identify themselves with the present and mix so well that it becomes almost impossible to segregate them. Bujhvan, the central character of "Ek Tha Bujhvan," with his kudal and karni, has lurked in my memory since childhood. The main idea conveyed through this story is that in this age when every new invention announces the end of old chapters, the person without a past is the only one who will survive. The story draws attention to the cries of a generation, who have with them a chain of memories of their past. At this juncture, we need to stop and think that while tuning for this race, how far we have moved from our past. Who will pay the price? The next generation?

Rachna Sethi is interested in postcolonial and translation studies. She has an MPhil in English from the University of Delhi and teaches at Zakir Husain College, Delhi.

■   The simplicity of the story, "Ek Tha Bujhvan," has an immediate appeal. Through her depiction of the households of Bujhvan and Thakur, the writer shows the changing face of Indian social, family and value systems. The story touches on various topics like the attitude of the younger generation towards the old, shifts in value systems and the changing face of rural life. And most importantly, the writer stresses on the role of memory – relationships, incidents – it acts as a linkage and a bond. Some words, more commonly used in the rural areas, might prove problematic for an urban reader.

KONKANI

Vidya Pai was a journalist till she stumbled into the field of translation with the Konkani award that she won at the first Katha Translation Contest organized by Katha with the support of the British Council, in 1993. She was awarded the Humanscape Translation Award in 1996 for translating Mahabaleshwar Sail's Konkani story "Havthan" into English. She has translated Pundalik Naik's novel, *Acchev* and Mahabaleshwar Sail's novel *Kali Ganga*.

■   On the surface, Meena Kakodkar's story is a simple story of an elderly man forced to cope with day to day life after the sudden death of his wife. The 'kakol' or offering of food to the departed soul, which Hindus believe appears in the form of a crow before shedding all earthly ties and ascending to heaven, forms the crux of the story, bringing to the reader the poignancy attached to the loss of a partner in one's old age and the breaking up of the family which provided an emotional cushion in times of sorrow and of joy. The story deals with emotions but the author exercises great control never letting it descend to the level of sentimentality. Though set in Goa, the sentiments expressed are universal and this helps the story stand the test of translation.

- "Expectations" was first published as "Sheen" in *Jaag*, Margao, October 2003.

Meena Kakodkar has authored two collections of short stories and a full-length play for children. Her work has been well received and she is the recipient of a number of literary awards, including the Sahitya Akademi Award, 1991; and the Katha Award for Creative Writing, 1993; the Goa Government Yashodamini Award, 2002. She is actively involved in promoting performing arts and culture and as a social activist is a trustee of the Goa Animal Welfare Trust. She retired recently from the Goa state government.

- Sometimes I subconsciously notice things which lie dormant in my mind. When one of these becomes active, it blossoms in the shape of a story. With "Sheen," it was quite different. It was the pain and loneliness in the eyes of an old man which made me restless, until I translated that pain into words. I do not write to convey anything. My intention is not to give any message as such. Any subject which touches my heart makes me write.

MALAYALAM

Sujatha Devi has several poems, articles and short stories, in Malayalam, to her credit. She is the recipient of the Kerala Sahitya Akademi Award for her travelogue, *In Search of the Rhythm of the Forests*. She is a retired lecturer in English.

- The literary scene in Malayalam boasts names like M T Vasudevan Nair, O V Vijayan, T Padmanabhan, Paul Zacharia and Kakkanadam. However, a number of newer writers are also making their presence felt. Approaches and trends in the field of short fiction, tried and lauded in the West, are being tested here as well. However, the Malayalam writer has added a local flavour to it. In the past decade feminism has been a popular theme and new writers hold aloft its banner. Such is also the case with subaltern and minority voices with political, gender and identity related issues figuring as thematic subjects. The short story scene is alive and challenging with moderation of emotion, brevity of speech and focusing of attention on subtle nuances. The artistry is remarkable, pleasing and different.

- The story "Pakaram Oraal" by Ashita is about Yashodamma's life and her eternal wait for the son who walked out on her when he was sixteen. She tries to fill the void with a Bhaagavata discourse – a Saptaaham – every year in her house but is still in deep anguish. Swami Thanmayan, whom the old preceptor had sent in his place, and who resembles Yashodamma's son, leads her out of the bonds of attachment. She is deprived of the most precious possession of sorrow. The story is one of the rare examples of women writers transcending the limits of the female world without losing the feminine touch.

- "The Substitute" was first published as "Pakaram Oraal" in *Bhashaposhini*, Kottayam, March 2002.

Ashita is a writer with short stories, translations and novellas to her credit. She has scripted and produced a number of feature films and documentaries. She has won several awards including the Katha Award for Creative Writing for Malayalam, twice. Her other interests include music, psychology, philosophy, yoga, meditation and reading.

- While reading Bhaagavata to a cancer patient, I discovered Yashoda in every woman I met, in varying degrees, and a Krishna in every child. The very same situation is repeatedly enacted with minute variations in this story. Every mother loses her child – sometimes in death, sometimes in marriage and in a thousand other ways still undiscovered. The main idea behind the story, "Pakaram Oraal," is that true love eventually bestows knowledge in the spiritual or in the mundane sense. And knowledge gained sets one free from grief experienced from losing a loved one. Love with awareness is freedom to the one who loves and to the one who is loved.

Indira Menon has done doctoral and post-doctoral work on Modern British and European Theatre. She is a reader in English at the Kamala Nehru College, University of Delhi.

- The story "Pakaram Oraal" is based on the universal theme of family relationships, loneliness and compulsions. The strength of the story is that it is non-judgemental. Religion as a prop is discarded when the protagonist comes to terms with her situation. Translating cultural and religious terms always poses a challenge. The problem also arose in translating the names of trees and animals, which have an added meaning in the source language. The effect was, however, lost in translation.

MARATHI

Shirin S Valavade's stories, both humorous and serious, try to bring out the psychological dimensions of human behaviour and take their themes mainly from medical issues and nature. She has received a number of awards for her stories, including the first prize from *Apoorva*. Translated into Hindi, her stories have been published in *Zena* also. Valavade currently writes a monthly news column for the Marathi journal, *Vipulshree*, as well as stories and articles for *Pratibimba*, another Marathi monthly. She is a doctor by profession.

- Early Marathi short stories were focused on the problems of the Maharashtrian middle class. Narration was simple and straightforward. Issues were presented as black and white, and the tone was severely moralistic. After the First World War, new writers like Phadke and Khandekar appeared on the scene, their stories, mostly idealistic romances, with an emphasis on patriotism. The 1930s saw a proliferation of writers with Marxist leanings. Other genres were developed – humour, satire (C V Joshi and P K Atre), women's issues (Vibhavari Shirurkar), problems of the oppressed sections of society (S M Mate).

  The Marathi story came into its own after the Second World War, and since independence. Writers such as Gadgil, Gokhale, Bhave and Madgulkar were vanguards of the new Marathi short story. From the 1970s the Marathi short story widened and deepened. G A Kulkarni's stories haunt the reader with their Brechtian sweep, emphasizing the role of destiny in human affairs. Writers like Bhau Padhye depicted the vulnerable underbelly of society. Women wrote with a vengeance about women's liberation, long after their western sisters had moved away.

  At present the Marathi short story defies categorization. In addition to social and family themes a new genre has been added, that of the political short story. In recent years the problems encountered by Marathi nonresidents abroad, as well of the old parents left behind, are attracting the attention of short story writers. Women centred stories are on the increase, with a stress on freedom – social, political as well as sexual.

- "Jungle" is the story of a woman who has an accidental extramarital experience with a stranger. Using the metaphor of the jungle and the waterfall, Madhuri Mohan Shanbhag tells a powerful tale of a woman caught between her natural surroundings and the wilderness within.

- "Jungle" was first published as "Jungle" in *Vipulshree*, Pune, Diwali Issue, 2002.

Madhuri Mohan Shanbhag's favourite themes are women and fiction. She is the author of many books ranging from novels, collections of short stories and inspirational biographies to translation works in English. She has also been a regular columnist for a number of leading Marathi periodicals, contributing short stories, literary reviews and features on women issues and travel. Her articles on various subjects continue to appear in Marathi journals and newspaper supplements. She has received numerous awards for her work, including honours from the Maharashtra Sahitya Parishad. Shanbag has been teaching Physics at the Govind Ram Seksaria Science Degree College in Belgaum since 1977.

- The seeds of "Jungle" were sown with a comment by a noted psychiatrist from Belgaum: Many women are not aware of their sexuality all their lives. This gave rise to a thought which remained in my mind for a long time: How would a woman who is blissfully unaware of her sexuality behave if she, even accidentally, came in touch with it? As a woman bound by culture, tradition and other constraints, she will carry the burden of this experience all her life. When I visited the lush jungle near the Belgaum-Goa border, the correlation was complete and I wrote the story in one sitting.

  I know women do feel incomplete even after years of married life. Often they can not pinpoint exactly what nags, but the dissatisfying element lingers, like a loose hanging thread. Basically, a writer wants to fix her fleeting thoughts on paper. The effects of her work, I think, will be best known by her readers.

Parnal Chirmuley completed her PhD from the Center for German Studies, Jawaharlal Nehru University in 2003. She is currently working as an editor at the Oxford University Press, New Delhi.

- The story successfully represents what can be considered a serious sociological concern. One specific problem was trying to translate the pronoun, apunko, which did not lend itself easily to translation.

MEITEILON

I R Babu Singh was a translator, editor and essayist. His translations include the plays of Shakespeare and Aristotle and Rabindranath Tagore's poems and short stories. He died most unexpectedly in 2003. We at Katha deeply grieve the loss of a dear friend.

- The short story in Manipur at present is flourishing. Almost all writings in the language are short stories, and the writers have won many awards. Another notable feature is the publication of stories in daily newspapers. The story has a bright future in this language.
- "Kuthi Louba" by Khoiren Meetei is about blind faith. Skilfully depicted characters and situations capture the ethos of human beings caught within an antiquated system.
- "Mangi Pau" by Kengba Yengkhom is about a mysterious and bizarre incident where a man is caught in the web of a ghostly world, which he does not understand initially. The story is beautifully told with details of worldly life and a kind of "suspension of disbelief."
- "Retrieving the Horoscope" was first published as "Kuthi Louba" in *Naharolgi Thoudang* Imphal, December 2002.
- "Dream Tale" was first published as "Mangi Pau" in *Chumthang*, Imphal, January 2002.

Kengba Yengkhom has several novels, short stories and poetry collections to his credit. He is deeply interested in social development activities such as village road construction and nurturing young talent through sports and education. He teaches Hindi in a school.

- The story, "Mangi Pau," originated from the study and interpretation of dreams. I believe that we see a vision of our lives, past and future, in our dreams. The dream narrative can be an engrossing subject. So it has been my desire to write stories based on dreams that give the readers a good read.

Pravabati Chingangbam enjoys translating and likes to view it as a means to convey one's culture to other people. She has a PhD in Theoretical Physics from Jamia Millia Islamia, New Delhi where she taught Physics for two years. Presently she is a post-doctoral fellow at the Harish-Chandra Research Institute, Allahabad.

- The story, "Mangi Pau," has a simple, straightforward style of narration. But it is loaded with hidden meaning, tantalizingly near yet firmly out of reach. It is well executed and has a global appeal rather than a culture specific one. However, it does give one a hint of rural Manipuri life because of its geographical setting. The hardest part was to translate the word "ngasaigido" which means "at an earlier time" and encompasses what transpired between Oja Madhu and the handyman at an earlier time. This is when Oja Madhu was about to board the bus and had put his luggage on the roof of the bus. This is a common feature of the Manipuri language – a whole sequence of events can be encoded in a single word. But translating the crispness into English while maintaining the rhythm of the dialogue was not easy.

Khoiren Meetei is the pen name of Khoisnam Dhiren Meetei. He is a regular columnist with *Naharolgi Thoudang*, a Manipuri language daily based in Imphal.

■ A simple, humorous story, "Kuthi Louba" satirizes the over-importance that people give to superstitions and the horoscope. The story is about a man who is straightforward in his approach but is uneducated and ignorant, and hence, vulnerable. It stresses on the importance of education.

Thingnam Anjulika translates from Meiteilon to English. She has translated two plays by Sahitya Akademi Awardee Arambam Somorendra, *Leipaklei* and *The Unrecognized Soldier*, besides a few short stories. A journalist, she has been a researcher with the NCERT, New Delhi, and the Centre De Sciences Humaines, Ministry of France, New Delhi, she has also served as an assistant editor at Katha.

■ "Kuthi Louba" is a simple story that not only explores the unemployment problem in Manipur in a humorous vein, but also satirizes the importance people give to superstitions and the horoscope. One major problem while translating were the long-winded sentences that were often used where meaning gets tangled up, unless broken down into smaller sentences. A specific problem with this story was the use of English in the original text.

ORIYA

Pratibha Ray is undoubtedly one of the most gifted and accomplished amongst the contemporary short story writers and novelists in Orissa. She has an impressive corpus of eighteen novels, several short story collections, one travelogue, nine books for children and ten for neo-literates. She has received numerous awards and honours, including the Orissa Sahitya Akademi Award (1985) for her novel *Shilapadma*, the Sarala Award for her novel *Yajnaseni*, the Katha Award for Creative Fiction for the story "Shapya" (1994) and the Biswv Award (1995) for her contribution to Oriya literature. She is also the first woman to receive the Moorti Devi Award of the Bharatiya Jnanpith (1991) for her path-breaking work, *Yajnaseni*. Her works have been translated into almost all major Indian languages. For her PhD in Education, she has lived with and studied the lives of the Bondas, one of the most primitive tribes of Orissa. She has been teaching in various government colleges of the state for the last twenty years. Pratibha Ray is a member of the Central Board of Film Certification and a translator of choice literary works into Oriya.

- In Oriya literature postmodernist impressions are visible more in short fiction than in other genres. Recent fiction has been multidimensional and challenges conventional concepts of fiction and tradition. Though written in the realist mode, it provides a newer vision of reality. Conscious artistic experimentation in short fiction, with fine narrative art, modern technique and the use of myth to express the complexities of reality has given the Oriya short story the strength to cross the boundaries of regionalism to universality. Some women writers are brilliant and have proved their excellence beyond doubt.

- "Anoma's Daughter" was first published as "Anomara Kanya" in *Kadambini*, Cuttack, July 2002.

Santanu Kumar Acharya is an academician and an accomplished writer. His published works include fifteen novels and an equal number of short story collections, ten story collections for children and substantial feature writings based on real life experiences with the tribal societies of Orissa. His works are prescribed as textbooks at the post graduate level. He has received the Sahitya Akademi Prize, and the Konarka Prize for his short story collection, *Chalanti Thakura* (1993), and the Orissa Sahitya Akademi Prize for his novel, *Nara Kinnara* (1970). Twice he has received the National Award for Children's Literature from the Ministry of Education, Government of India (1962 and 1963). A senior administrator in the Education Department, Government of Orissa, in 1992 he retired as the registrar of Utkal University, Orissa.

- "Anomara Kanya," a novella, is an instance where rare archaeology turns into a romance and the history of a nation is captured into a family saga. Decades were spent to gather relevant historical data to prove that the real birth place of Lord Buddha could not but be the same place where the ancient Kalinga war was fought in the third century BC, that is, the present capital of Orissa – Bhubaneswar. This was proved, in 1928, when an inscription bearing the information was unearthed. Yet the novel is not a scholarly thesis. I write it as a romance between a pair of lovers betrothed to each other by their parents before Independence. A precious historical relic – a lock of the sacred hair – is the key to the mystery of Gautama Buddha's real place of birth. This forms the crux and substance of "Anomara Kanya."

Bibhas C Mohanty is an IPS officer and was an English lecturer before he joined the services.

- A good story with a rather cinematic ending. The strong point in the story is the author's mastery over the language and his historical research. Overall it is a value addition to the treasure of Oriya literature. The challenge lay in coping with the author's command over Oriya, Sanskrit as also the Buddhist and yogic languages to match his flights of emotion-charged description of situation and events, the characters and their feelings and experiences.

TAMIL

Venkat Swaminathan has an avid interest in the Tamil cultural and literary scene, films, theatre, literature, music and culture – an interest he has sustained over four decades. Seven collections of his critical articles have been published. He has published a film script of John Abraham's Tamil film *Agraharathil Kazhudai* and has also contributed to the visualization and script for Yamini Krishnamoorthi's TV serial *Nrityanjali,* on the history and dance associated with great temples in India. He is in charge of the Tamil section of the revised edition of the *Encyclopaedia of Indian Literature,* being published by the Sahitya Akademi.

- The story "The Harmonium" is about an unemployed man who wants to learn music. Chezhian has a very lucid and engaging style. Irony seems to be the undercurrent in all his writings. For a newcomer, his writings show great sobriety, maturity and confidence.

- "The Harmonium" was first published as "Harmonium" in *Kanaiazhi*, Chennai, September 2002.

Chezhian is a writer, professional photographer, cinematographer and director. He has a few short stories, and poetry, to his credit. His short story, "Tholaivil Theriyum Vanam," won the Kanaiazhi Vasagar Vattam Award in 2002. He is interested in western music classical theory and has passed the Grade V examination from Trinity College, London.

- The story is a biographical account. It refers to the time when I was trying hard to learn music, and due to financial constraints buying a harmonium was difficult. These experiences prompted me to write the story. The idea was to write about music and its abstract expressions, its mythology and the undisturbed silence of a musical instrument.

Ramiah Kumar's interests include Tamil literature, Carnatic music and spiritualism. He was one of the winners in the Katha South Asian Translation Contest for Tamil. He has served as an engineer in several reputed organizations.

- The story, "The Harmonium," is about hope, despair and involvement all heightened by flights of fantasy. The author's attention to details of music theory are dispersed through the narrative – but these build the story without distracting attention. This story had some of the usual idiomatic translation problems. The story uses the technical terms of Carnatic music very extensively. In the translation, many words could not be brought in from the Tamil, but I have tried to provide contextually meaningful details.

TELUGU

Amarendra Dasari is a writer, translator and literary enthusiast and has two travelogues and a short story collection to his credit besides a number of articles, book reviews and literary essays published in various Telugu magazines. He is presently working for Bharat Electronics Limited and is stationed at Bangalore.

- The Telugu short story is passing through an interesting phase. It has always been reflective of society. Transition of the politico-social scenario from a pseudo-socialistic pattern to a capitalistic pattern has affected the middle and lower classes. In addition, issues such as subregional imbalances, rising Dalit consciousness, exploitation of women and tribals are coming to the forefront. All these developments, during the last couple of years, have been well reflected in the wide spectrum of short stories that have originated from young writers of different subregions and backgrounds.

- I liked K Srikanth Reddy's story for its imaginative flights of plausible fantasy, for its strong portrayal of desire, expectations, commitment and perseverance, as also for its ability to leave the ending open.
- "The Silent Song" was first published as "Nissabdapu Paatu" in *Andhra Jyothi*, Hyderabad, November 2002.

K Srikanth Reddy has published two volumes of poems, *Konni Samayaalu* (A Few Times, 2000) and *Ithara* (The Other, 2002), in Telugu. Apart from poetry, he has published a few stories in various Telugu literary magazines. He has a keen interest in existential philosophy, philosophy of language, music, cultural anthropology and translation. He is a lecturer of English in Hyderabad.

- For me a story always begins, as Italo Calvino – an Italian journalist, short story writer and novelist – says, with an image. Or rather, the whole story appears in an image in an instant. Later, this instant is extended into a full-length narrative. The time taken to convert this instant into possible narrative may vary from days to months. Even the present story "Nissabdapu Paatu" is no exception. The image of a man who wants to travel in a paper boat perhaps goes back to my childhood, especially to the long rainy magical afternoons when, while playing with other friends, I wished to travel in one of those paper boats in the rain.

J Bhagyalakshmi has published several short stories, poems, features and essays on literary criticism in leading magazines and newspapers in English and Telugu. She has won several awards for poetry, essay, and creative writing, including the Rafi Ahmad Kidwai Prize, the Potti Sriramulu Telugu University Award for short story and the Jyeshta Literary award for *Maromajili*, a collection of short stories. A freelance journalist, media consultant and guest faculty of mass communication institutions, she is an.Indian Information Service officer. She is the chief editor of the magazine, *Yojana*.

■ The theme of the story, "Nissabdapu Paatu," is unusual. It is not about day-to-day hardships. It is the struggle and relentless strife of a man to make his dream come true. Not losing hope, working against all odds towards one's dream project, is brilliantly and naturally portrayed in the story.

■

Geeta Dharmarajan has been a writer and professional editor for the last 24 years. She loves writing stories and fantasies for children and has 18 children's books, more than a dozen edited volumes, and over 400 published pieces to her credit. She was an assistant editor of *Target*, a magazine for children, where she was fortunate to be groomed by Rosalind Wilson. Editor of the *Katha Prize Stories* series and *Tamasha!*, the children's magazine, she has also served as assistant editor of *The Pennsylvania Gazette*, the magazine of the University of Pennsylvania. Geeta started Katha in 1988 and has been its principal team leader since then, the driving force behind both its publishing and educational initiatives.

The Award Winning Journals of 2003-2004

Ajir Asom (Asomiya)
The Sentinel House of Publication,
G S Road, Guwahati 781 005

Ed: Pankaj Thakur

Sambad Pratidin (Bangla)
20 Prafulla Sarkar Street, Kolkata 700 029

Ed: Swapan Sadhan Basu

Tadbhav (Hindi)
18/271, Indira Nagar, Lucknow 226 016

Ed: Akhilesh

Jaag (Konkani)
201-B – Saldel Apartment, Rua-de-Saudades
Pajifond, Margao 403 601

Ed: Ravindra Kelekar

Bhashaposhini (Malayalam)
Manorama, Kottayam 686 001

Ed: K C Narayanan

The Naharolgi Thoudang (Manipuri)
Keishampat Airport Road, Imphal 795 001

Ed: Khoirom Loyalakpa

Vipulshree (Marathi)
Shrivasta Prakashan, 67 Vipul,
Karvenagar, Shallesh Society, Pune 411 052

Ed: Madhuri Vaidya

Kadambini (Oriya)
Duplex-20, Sailash Vihar,
Bhubaneswar 751 021

Ed: Itirani Samanta

Kanayazhi (Tamil)
11, Nana Street, Thiyagaraya Nagar,
Chennai 600 017

Ed: T Kasturi Rangan

Andhra Jyothi (Telugu)
Road No 3, Banjara Hills, Hyderabad, 500 001

Ed: K Ramachandra Murthy

A SELECT LIST OF REGIONAL MAGAZINES

ASOMIYA

Ajir Asom, Omega Publishers, G S Rd, Ulubari, Guwahati 7
Anvesha, Konwarpur, Sibsagar 785667
Asam Bani, Tribune Bldg, G N Bordoloi Rd, Guwahati 3
Budhbar, Shahid Sukleshwar Konwar Path, Guwahati 21
Goriyoshi, Assam Tribune Building, Silpukhri, Guwahati 3
Prakash, Publication Board of Assam, Bamunimaidan, Guwahati 24
Prantik, Navagiri Rd, Chandmari, PO Silpukhuri, Guwahati 3
Pratidhwani, Bani Mandir, Panbazaar, Guwahati 1
Sadin, Sadin Karyalaya, Maniram Dewan Path, Chandmari, Guwahati 3
Sreemoyee, Agradut Bhawan, Dispur, Guwahati 6
Sutradhar, Manjeera House, Motilal Nehru Path, Panbazaar, Guwahati 1

BANGLA

Aajkaal, 96 Raja Ram Mohan Roy Sarani, Kolkata 9
Amrita Lok, Binalay, Dak Bungalow Rd, PO Midnapore 721101
Ananda Bazar Patrika, 6 Prafulla Sarkar St, Kolkata 1
Anustup, P 55 B, C I T Rd, Kolkata 10
Bartaman, 76 A Acharya Bose Rd, Kolkata15
Baromas, 63/C Mahanirban Road, Kolkata 29
Bartika, 18 A Ballygunge Station Rd, Kolkata 19
Basumati, 166 Bepin Behari Ganguli St, Kolkata 12
Chaturanga, 54 Ganesh Chandra Avenue, Kolkata 13
Rabibarer Pratidin, 20 Prafulla Sarkar Street, Kolkata 700029 (Ed: Swapan Sadhan Basu)
Desh, 6 Prafulla Sarkar Street, Kolkata 700001
Galpapatra, C E 137 Salt Lake, Kolkata 64
Galpa Sarani, Debuvuti Bhavan, Birbhum, West Bengal 731101
Ganashakti, 31 Alimuddin St, Kolkata 16
Hawa, 49 Brahmapur, Bansdroni, Kolkata 70
Kuthar, Canara Bank, 25 Princep St,Kolkata 72
Madhuparni, Sitbali Complex, Balurghat, South Binajpur 733101
Manorama, 281 Muthiganj, Allahabad 3
Nandan, 31 Alimuddin St,Kolkata 16
Parichaya, 30/6 Chautala Rd, Kolkata 17
Pratidin, 14 Radhanath Choudhuri Rd, Kolkata 15
Pratikshana, 7 Jawaharlal Nehru Rd,Kolkata 13
Proma, 5 West Range, Kolkata 17
Raktakarabee, 10/2 Ramnath Majumdar St, Kolkata 9
Yogasutra, TG 2/29 Teghoria, Kolkata 59
Yuba Manas, 32/1 B B D Bag (South), Kolkata 1

DOGRI

Sheeraza, J & K Academy of Art, Culture & Languages, Canal Road, 181 Paharian Street, Jammu Tawi, Jammu-180001

GUJARATI

Abhiyan, Shakti House, Ashok Road, Kandiwali East, Mumbai 1
Buddhiprakash, Gujarat Vidya Sabha, Ashram Road, Ahmedabad 9
Dasmo Dayako, Sardar Patel University, Vallabh Vidyanagar 388120
Etad, 233 Rajlaxmi, Old Padra Road, Vadodara 15
Gadyaparva, 12-A Chetan Apartments, Rajwadi Road, Ghatkopur, Mumbai 400077
Kankavati, 24 River Bank Society, Adajan Water Tank, Surat 9
Khevana, 9 Mukund, Manorama Complex, Himatlal Park, Ahmedabad 15
Navchetan, Narayanagar, Sarkhej Road, Ahmedabad
Navneet Samarpana, Bharatiya Vidya Bhavan, K M Road, Mumbai 7
Parab, Govardhan Bhavan, Ashram Road, Ahmedabad 9
Shabdashrushti, Gujarat Sahitya Akademi, Sector II, Gandhinagar
Sanskriti, Sandesh Bldg, Gheekanta, Ahmedabad 9
Uddesh, 2 Achalayatan Society, Navarangpura, Ahmedabad 9
Vi, 6 Vishwamitra, Bakrol Rd, Vallabh Vidyanagar 388 120

HINDI

Dastavej, Vishwanath Tiwari, Dethia Hatha, Gorakhpur
India Today, F 14/15 Connaught Place, New Delhi 1
Indraprastha Bharati, Samudaya Bhavan, Padam Nagar, Delhi
Kathya Roop, 224 Tularam Bagh, Allahabad 6
Pal-Pratipal, 372 Sector 17, Panchkula, Haryana
Pahal, 101 Ramnagar Adhartal, Jabalpur, M P
Pratipaksh, 6/105 Kaushalya Park, Hauz Khas, New Delhi 16
Sakshatkar, Sanskriti Bhavan, Vaan Ganga Chauraha, Bhopal
Samaas, 2/38 Ansari Road, Daryaganj, Delhi 2
Samkaleen Bharatiya Sahitya, Sahitya Akademi, Rabindra Bhavan, New Delhi 1
Vartaman Sahitya, 109 Ricchpalpuri, PB 13, Ghaziabad 1

KANNADA

Karmaveera, Samyukta Karnataka Press, 2 Field Marshal Road, Bangalore 560025
Mayura, 16 M G Rd, PB 331, Bangalore 1
Prajavani, 66 M G Rd, Bangalore 1
Rujuvathu, Kavi Kavya Trust, Heggodu, Sagar 577 417
Samvada, Samvada Prakashana, Malladihalli 577 531
Shubra, Shubra Srinivas, No 824, 7th Main, ISRO Layout, Bangalore 78

Tushara, Press Corner, Manipal 19
Udayavani, Manipal Printers and Publishers, Manipal 19

KONKANI

Chitrangi, Apurbai Prakashan, Volvoi Ponda, Goa
Jaag, Near BPS Club, Margao, Goa 403601
Kullagar, PO Box 109, Margao Goa 1
Rashtramat, Margao, Goa 1
Sunaparant, BPS Club, Margao, Goa 1

MAITHILI

Antikaa, 2/36 Ansari Road, Daryaganj, New Delhi 2
Vaidehi, Samiti Talbagh, Darbhanga
Mithila Chetna, 1/C Kakeshwar Lane, Post Bali Howrah 1
Janaki, Similtil, Damodarpur Road, Dhanbad
Pravasi, Mithila Sanskritik Sangam, Kendranchal, Allahabad
Pallak, Shri Mahal Pul Chowk, Lalitpur, Nepal

MALAYALAM

D C Books, D C Books, Kottayam, Kerala
Desabhimani Weekly, PB 1130, Kozhikode 32
India Today, (Malayalam), 98A Radhakrishnan Salai, Chennai 4
Kala Kaumudi, Kaumudi Buildings, Pettah, Thiruvananthapuram 24
Katha, Kaumudi Bldg, Pettah, Thiruvananthapuram 24
Kerala Kaumudi, PB 77, Thiruvananthapuram 24
Kumkumam, Lakshminanda, Kollam
Malayala Manorama, Malayala Manorama Building, PB No 26 Kottayam, Kerala 679001
Madhyam, Silver Hills, Kozhikode 12
Manorajyam, Manorajyam Press, T B Junction, Kottayam
Mathrubhumi Weekly, Cherooty Road, Kozhikode 1

MARATHI

Abhiruchi, 69 Pandurang Wadi, Goregaon East, Mumbai 36
Anushtubh, Anandashram, Near D'Souza Maidan, Manmad 423 104
Asmitadarsha, 37 Laxmi Co Chawani, Aurangabad
Dhanurdhari, Ramakrishna Printing Press, 31 Tribhuvan Road, Mumbai 4
Dipavali, 316 Prasad Chambers, Girgaon, Mumbai 4
Grihalaxmi, 21 D D Sathe Road, Girgaon Mumbai 4
Huns, 4 Bhardwaj Apts, Near Krishna Hospital, Paud Road, Kothrud, Pune 29
Jatra, 2117 Sadashiv Peth, Vijayanagar Cly, Pune 30

Kathasagar, Akashdeep, Milan Subway Marg, Santa Cruz East, Mumbai 55
Kavitarati, Vijay Police Vashat, Wadibhikar Rasta, Dhule
Lokaprabha, Express Tower, Ist Floor, Nariman Point, Mumbai
Lokarajya, New Admn Bldg, 17th Floor, Opp Secretariat, Mumbai 2
Loksatta, Express Towers, Nariman Point, Mumbai
Miloon Saryajani, 33/225 Erandwan Prabhat Road Lane 4, Pune 4
Vipulshree, Shreevasta Prakashan, 67 Shailesh Society, Karve Nagar, Pune 52

MANIPURI

Ritu, The Cultural Forum, Manipur, B T Road, Imphal
Sāhitya, Manipur Sahitya Parishad, Paona Bazar, Imphal
Wakhal, Naharol Sahitya Premee Samiti, Keishmapat Madhu Bhawan,
Aheibam Leirak, Imphal 795001

ORIYA

Anisha Sahitya Patra, Chandikhol Chhak, PO Sunguda 754 024
Jiban Ranga, Stoney Road, Cuttack 2
Nabalipi, Vidyapuri, Balu Bazar, Cuttack 2
Pratibeshi, 236 Acharya J C Bose Road, Nizam Palace (17th flr), Kolkata 20
Sahakar, Balkrishna Marg, Cuttack 1
Samay, Badambadi, Ananta Aloka, Sankarpur, Cuttack 12

PUNJABI

Kahani Punjab, Kuccha Punjab, College Road, Barnala, Punjab 148 101
Lakeer, 593 Mota Singh Nagar, Jalandhar, Punjab 144001
Nagmani, K 25, Hauz Khas, New Delhi 16
Preet Lari, Preet Nagar, Punjab
Samdarshi, Punjabi Academy, New Delhi
Samkali Sahithya, Punjab Sahit Sabha, 10 Rouse Avenue, New Delhi

RAJASTHANI

Binjaro, Pilani, Rajasthan
Manale, Jalori Gate, Jodhpur
Mansi, Ambu Sharma, Kolkata.
Rajasthali, Rajasthani Bhasha Parishad, Shri Dungarpur, Bikaner

SINDHI

Sipoon, 13B/3 Jethi Bahen Society, Mori Road, Mahim, Bombay 16

TAMIL

Arumbu, 22 A Tailors Road, Chennai 10
Dinamani Kadir, Anna Salai, Chennai 2
Kalachuvadu, 669 K P Road Nagercoil Tamilnadu 629001

Kalki, 84/1-6 Race Course Road, Guindy, Chennai 2
Kal Kudhirai, 6/162 Indira Nagar, Kovilpatti 2
Kanavu, MIG 189 Phase II, TNHB, Thiruppatur 635602
Kanayazhi, 18 BBC Home, 18, Chievalier Shivaji Road, T Nagar, Chennai 600017
Kappiar, Kaliyakkavilai, K K District, Tamil Nadu 629153
Kavithaasaran, 31 T K S Nagar, Chennai 19
Pudia Paarvai, Tamil Arasi Maligai, 84 T T K Road, Chennai
Puthiya Nambikai, 13 Vanniyar II Street, Chennai 93
Sathangai, 53/2 Pandian St, Kavimani Nagar, Nagercoil 629002
Semmalar, 6/16 Bypass Road, Madurai 18
Unnatham, Alathur PO, Kavindapady 638455

TELUGU

Aahwanam, Gandhi Nagar, Vijayawada 3
Andhra Patrika, 1-2-528 Lower Tank Bund Road, Domalguda, Hyderabad 29
Andhra Prabha, Express Centre, Domalguda, Hyderabad 29
Chatura, *Eenadu* Publications, Somajiguda, Hyderabad 4
Choopu, 204, Neeladri, Seven Hill Apartments, Nizampet Road, Hydernagar
Kukatpalli, Hyderabad 500072
India Today (Telugu), 98-A Radhakrishnan Salai, Mylapore, Chennai 4
Jyothi, 1-8-519/11 Chikadapally, PB 1824, Hyderabad 20
Mayuri, 5-8-55/A Nampally, Station Road, Hyderabad 1
Maabhoomi, 36 S D Road Hyderabad
Rachana, PB 33, Visakhapatanam 1
Srijana, 203 Laxmi Apts, Malakpet, Hyderabad 36
Swati, Prakashan Rd, Governorpet, Vijayawada
Vipula, *Eenadu* Compound, Somajiguda, Hyderabad 4

URDU

Aajkal, Publication Division, Patiala House, New Delhi 1
Asri Adab, D 7 Model Town, Delhi 9
Gulban, 9 Shah Alam Society, 12 Chandola Lok, Davilipada, Ahmedabad 28
Kitab Numa, Maktaba Jamia, New Delhi 25
Naya Daur, PB 146, Lucknow
Shabkhoon, 313 Rani Mandi, Allahabad
Shair, Maktaba Qasruladab, PB 4526, Mumbai 8
Soughat, 84 III Main, Defence Colony, Indiranagar, Bangalore 38
Tanazur, C117 A G Colony, Yousufguda Post, Hyderabad 45
Zehn-e-Jadeed, 7, Cosmo Apartments, Street 12, Zakir Nagar, New Delhi 110025

NB: This is by no means an exhaustive list of all the contemporary journals, periodicals, newspapers (the magazine sections), little magazines and anthologies which give space to the short story. But, for the most part, these names represent the range of publications consulted by the Nominating Editors in their respective languages. However, since the compilation of a more detailed list of publications is one of Katha Vilasam's objectives, the editor would welcome any additional information on the subject, particularly with respect to languages not covered in this list.

ABOUT KATHA

KATHA, set up in 1988 and formally registered on September 8, 1989, is a nonprofit organization that works in the literacy to literature continuum, in the areas of education, publishing and community development. We strive to help break down gender, cultural and social stereotypes, encourage and foster human potential, applaud quality literature and translations in and between the various Indian languages.

Our main objective is to enhance the joys of reading for children and adults, for experienced readers as well as for those who are just beginning to read. Known as a premier publishing house, based in Delhi, Katha focuses on quality English translations from twenty-one Indian languages or bhashas. Katha has been at the leading edge of translation praxis for the last more than 15 years.

Our other main focus area is education – from preschool to higher education, in formal and nonformal streams. Kathashala, with its specially designed curriculum and close community involvement has won international recognition over the last few years. Our attempt is to stimulate an interest in lifelong learning that will help the child grow into a confident, self-reliant, responsible and responsive adult. Katha works with women through various initiatives that help build family incomes leading to community revitalization and economic resurgence.

The two main wings of Katha are –

KATHA VILASAM, the Story Research and Resource Centre. This was set up to foster and applaud good Indian literature and take these to a wider audience through quality translations and related activities including workshops, discusions, collq"iua and literary festivals. The **Katha Awards** for fiction, translation and editing have established themselves as national recognitions. This rigorous and eclectic search for excellence finds, fosters and applauds quality writing in the bhashas.

KALPAVRIKSHAM, the Centre for Sustainable Learning. This was set up to foster quality education that is relevant and fun for children from nonliterate families, and to promote community revitalization and economic resurgence work. Kathashala was set up in 1990 with five children.

Today, we work with nearly 5,000 children who live on the fringes of poverty and come from nonliterate families – in Delhi and in Changlang District of Arunachal Pradesh. Katha's special story pedagogy has been the fulcrum on which Katha's education initiatives have been developed.

WHAT PEOPLE SAY ABOUT US

"... an extraordinary non-profit company called Katha ... has begun to salvage the lost classics of modern India, translating them into English with flair and publishing them in beautiful editions."

– The Independent, U.K.

"Katha is doing an incredibly heroic work. By making available in English translation the best of Indian short fiction. Katha is presenting the "real" India to English readers across the world ... Katha is a celebration of the diversity of the Indian experience."

– The Indian Express

"... the first independent publishing house to insist that translators are as important as writers."

– The Business Standard

"Katha has been able to incorporate tremendous variety in tone, structure, and themes ranging from the absolutely contemporary to the timeless."

– The Hindustan Times

NEW RELEASES

FICTIONS

STORIES: INTIZAR HUSAIN

Spine-chilling! That's Intizar Husain for you. One of the finest living writers in Urdu escorts you along the sinuous bylanes of Hindustan and the glitzy Pakistani shops in Anarkali Bazaar, along runaway clouds and forbidden domains. An uncertain but promising journey, a mind-blowing experience.

Katha Asia Library/Novel
September 2004
5.5" X 8" Pb c. 232 pages
81-87649-87-9
Price: Rs 250

Katha Hindi Library/Novel
May 2004
5.5" X 8" Pb c. 222 pages
81-87649-29-1
Price: Rs 250

OVER TO YOU, KADAMBARI

Alka Saraogi, Sahitya Akademi winner, weaves a brilliant novel for you. Ruby Gupta has lived all her life within the confines of silence and built a wall around her to soak up all the fire inside.

Yet, Kadambari manages to connect with her precious Nani. They talk words and grasp silences; they live life and die fleeting deaths. Till, a stranger comes into Rubydi's life.

NON-FICTIONS

STORYTELLERS AT WORK

Stimulating talks and essays by Luce Irigaray, Krzysztof Zanussi, Dilip Chitre, Ganesh N Devy, Orhan Pamuk ... Writers, translators, philosophers, storytellers, filmmakers and economists wield the power of story to offer a glimpse into their art and craft, thoughts and ideas.

Katha Non Fiction/Essays
July 2004
6" X 9" Pb c. 222 pages
81-889020-01-3
Price: Rs 200

NETS OF AWARENESS

Frances W Pritchett recalls her first experience of the ghazal as "love at first sight," contrary to the disdainful approach of modern Urdu critics. In *Nets of Awareness* Pritchett joins literary criticism and history to explain how the ghazal, for centuries the pride and joy of Indo-Muslim culture, was abruptly dethroned within its own milieu and by its own theorists.

Katha Asia Library/Critique
November 2004
6" X 9" Pb c. 238 pages
81-87649-65-8
Price: Rs 250

CHILDREN

WALK THE RAINFOREST WITH NIWUPAH

Join Niwupah the Hornbill on a special tour to a special place, where the sights we see and the sounds we hear, the scents we smell and the creatures we meet, are like nothing we've ever imagined! A beautiful book written specially for children by two practising wildlife specialists, Aparajita Datta and Nima Manjrekar. And illustrated by Maya Ramaswamy with the exacting eye for detail of a wildlife enthusiast.

THE MAGICAL WEB BRIDGE

A dreamer and a doer. Creative. Sensitive. Imaginative. That's the baya! Fabulously illustrated by Sonali Biswas, this story by Geeta Dharmarajan, an award-winning writer for children, captures the spirit and joy of friendship and team work. A must read for bedtime, laptime or ... any time!

THE SONG OF A SCARECROW

What happens when the scarecrow decides to leave his field one day? An imaginative book, delightfully illustrated, it helps the child to see that freedom and responsibility always go together. This book won the Chitra Katha Award 2002 and received an honourable mention at the Biennial of Illustrations Bratislava 2003.

These Katha Books for Children, Size: 8" X 10", Price: Rs 95 (PB) Rs 120 (HB)

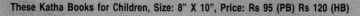

BE A FRIEND OF KATHA!

If you feel strongly about Indian literature, you belong with us! KathaNet, an invaluable network of story and translation activists, is the mainstay of all our translation related activities.

Katha has limited financial resources; it is the unqualified enthusiasm and the indispensable support of nearly 5000 dedicated people out there which makes our work possible.

We are constantly on the lookout for people who can spare the time to find stories for us, and to translate them. Katha has been able to access mainly the literature of the major Indian languages. Our efforts to locate resource people who could make the lesser known literatures available to us have not yielded satisfactory results. We are specially eager to find Friends who could introduce us to Bhojpuri, Dogri, Kashmiri, Maithili, Manipuri, Nepali, Rajasthani and Sindhi fiction. And to oral and tribal literature.

BE A FRIEND OF KATHA! Do write to us with details about yourself, your language skills, the ways in which you can help us as a writer, translator or editor. In case you have any material that you already have please do let us know, so we can together forge an active partnership for the greater benefit for language development and survival in India.

As a friend of Katha, we would like to offer you a discount of 30% on all our publications.

For details, please write to us at kathavilasam@katha.org. Or call us at 2652 4350, 2652 4511.

Help shape my future!

Doctor, engineer, policewoman, computer specialist ...

what will I be?

What happens when 1300 children, a determined Katha team of teachers and activists, and a whole community come together? Yes ... Sheer magic! You'll find this excitement in the air when you enter our school, a brick low-cost building.

We, the children and women of Govindpuri, a large slum cluster of more than 1,50,000 people, have come a long way in more than fourteen years with Katha. But there are excitements ahead. Small but sure steps towards self-confidence, self-reliance touched by the power of self-esteem. Many of us are working today to support our families in ways we could never have dreamt of! Many of us have finished our BAs and BComs from Delhi's colleges. We once didn't even dare to dream ... today dreams coming true, we talk of what Katha's goal of an uncommon education for a common good can help us all achieve. We are fun-loving dreamers-doers at Katha. And we'd like you to join us in our fight against poverty.

Be our special friend! Sponsor quality education at Katha. Giving has never been so easy, or with so much impact. It costs you just Rs 250/ month to provide basic quality education to one of us. That's Rs 3,000/yr. Include computer education for a child with just Rs 1,800/yr more!

Please send your cheque/DD in favour of Katha Resources to Educate a Child (REACH) Fund to **Katha, A3, Sarvodaya Enclave, Sri Aurobindo Marg, New Delhi 110017**. For more details visit us at **www.katha.org**. Or write to us at **networking@katha.org**.

Donations to Katha Reach Fund qualify for 100% tax exemption under 35 AC of the IT Act. Registered under FCRA, Katha can receive donations in foreign currencies.